ABOUT THE AU'

CW00713021

Dale Trigg was born in Dewsbury, West ....
1984 and has since lived in his beloved hometown of Morley, reluctantly,
in the borough of Leeds. Attending Catholic schools throughout his
education Dale took an unhealthy curiosity to Catholicism and other
religions sparking a search for answers to the un-answered questions
posed by religion and its influence on the world.

He carried on this interest as he went to College studying Media
Studies, Film Studies and English Literature at A-Level where he found a
fascinating side to the media that he could put toward what he originally
wanted to be in life, a journalist or a film director. Now he is glad he isn't
a journalist but still wishes for the directing job...

Now working for a well respected manufacturing company in West
Yorkshire he spends most of his free time with his partner Fiona and
behind his computer screen researching and pondering new ideas for
books and thesis'.

When he does have free time, he spends most of it following his
beloved Gunners, watching and playing tennis and defending Tim
Henman to his friends. Listening to Bad Religion, Iron Maiden and
anything remotely lyrical, playing on his Playstation or drinking with his
Dad in the Queens Pub in Morley putting the world to rights.

THE CALIVARI TALE

Dale Trigg

Published 2009 by arima publishing

www.arimapublishing.com

ISBN 978 1 84549 398 1

© Dale Trigg 2009

All rights reserved

This book is copyright. Subject to statutory exception and to provisions of relevant collective licensing agreements, no part of this publication may be reproduced, stored in a retrieval system, or transmitted in any form or by any means, without the prior written permission of the author.

Printed and bound in the United Kingdom

Typeset in Garamond 11/14

This book is sold subject to the conditions that it shall not, by way of trade or otherwise, be lent, re-sold, hired out, or otherwise circulated without the publisher's prior consent in any form of binding or cover other than that which it is published and without a similar condition including this condition being imposed on the subsequent purchaser.

In this work of fiction, the characters, places and events are either the product of the author's imagination or they are used entirely fictitiously. Any resemblance to actual persons, living or dead, is purely coincidental.

Swirl is an imprint of arima publishing.

arima publishing
ASK House, Northgate Avenue
Bury St Edmunds, Suffolk IP32 6BB
t: (+44) 01284 700321
www.arimapublishing.com

With thanks to Fi, my soul mate and love of my life.

With thanks to my Mum and my Dad, to Jayne, Thomas, Kim, Sarah, Emily and David.

With thanks to my family, my ever youthful Nan and all my cousins scattered around the country.

With thanks to some of the best mates in the world, to Scott, to Ashley, to Steve, to Dan, to Danny.

With thanks to everyone in Unit 4.

With thanks to the inspirational music that lifted me when times were low including Bad Religion and Iron Maiden.

With warm thanks to the Queen's Pub in Morley.

And finally thank you ... to all us Morleians.

NOTE: - For consideration of the text, Aramaic is deemed an untranslatable language. I am well aware that in real life, it is a well understood speech.

CHAPTER 1
WAR ETHICS

I studied the look on my Professors face. It was the kind of harsh face that came from age and withered with the experience of a thousand battlefields. It took a lot to get a face like that, and when he had perfected the look of 'I'm waiting for an answer' as well, the two together where a scary combination. "I don't know"

"You don't know?" said the Professor with an unwavering tone, "You do not know why the United States of America undertook this course of action?"

"No Sir" I said with a real sense of disappointment

"What if I were to say there was no right or wrong answer, because we do not know the right of wrong answer? What if I told you we use a process of elimination for half the answers on this syllabus and on this test? This test is about your powers of deduction, of finding evidence to back up your claims. Now tell me, young man, if you were to hazard a guess, what would you say the cause was?"

After the long speech I was paraplegic with fear. The tone of his voice had sent a pale blue shiver down my spine; it had all the hallmarks of being shot in the back. "Oil, sir?" I managed disdainfully.

"Oil!" shouted the Professor finally removing his hands from the edges of my desk and looking around the rest of the auditorium. I was starting to believe I was the only one there, that this was not the class of 'War Ethics' and that I was the only one with the answers. It was like a short interrogation, except without the physical beatings, however the mental attacks were far more severe.

The professor raised his book, it was a file lined with red tape and hid all the answers and arguments that the entire class craved. "Yes, there is an argument for oil. Iraq has a fine rich source of the black gold and is well known to barter throughout the world with whoever pays the most money but I beg the question, why? Since the first Gulf War we have had little problem with Iraq that we haven't been able to handle without the need of war. And if it was for oil, why would they not hit a weaker target? Baku in Azerbaijan? Even Egypt? There were many more easy targets"

"But Iraq had Saddam?"

"Who said that?"

The Professors eyes scanned the room. His eyes staring through his rectangle glasses, one of the female students from the back row gingerly raised her arm, pencil in hand. "Why did Saddam make a difference?" asked the Professor

Suddenly the opus had shifted. Now it wasn't me on the receiving end of a grilling interrogation it was excellent to watch the Professor at work. "Saddam was the keystone to the whole mess" said the female student, "He was trying to build an Empire based around fear, trying to control the masses with the threat of being gassed! He was in layman's terms, a bad man!"

"And on that debate lowering end let us finish this discussion as it is time for you all to leave. Thank you for your time today ladies and gentlemen, I hope we have all learned something. For your project at home I want you all to prepare a debate for me. Why didn't the United States not de-throne Saddam Hussein after the first Gulf War? I expect a strong debate; remember there are no wrong or right answers if you can prove what you are saying. And be thorough, I don't want any lame arguments that are to be shot down within moments"

He turned and class was over, it was now that someone from class was called back to discuss something in their previous works by the Professor, to tell them where they went wrong, to make them feel stupid it sometimes felt. "Banner!"

I turned. I felt my stomach drop when he shouted my name and the sense of relief from the rest of the class rolled over me like a strong perfume. He sat on the edge of his long desk that sat in front of the huge blackboard that required a small cherry picker to reach the top. "Banner, why the lack of enthusiasm today?"

"I'm sorry sir"

"I know how accomplished you are in your other fields. Full Marks on your agility, over 70% on your firearms training exam, you even passed a masters course on the bleep test so why do you choose to not be as accomplished in War Ethic? To know War or to know a war zone in its most basic terms is some of the most useful information a soldier can have. Without these basic skills, even a poor soldier can be the best"

I just stood and looked. It seemed like a well rehearsed speech but so did everything that came out of the professor's mouth, he had a stunning way with words that had you transfixed from the moment he spoke to the exact moment he stopped. "Sir, the causes of war just does not interest me! I study movement; I train my eyesight every night to see in the dark as best I can. I keep my body in a mantra style sleep so that it can react to everything I am hit with! I am more a machine than human, ethic just gets in the way!"

The professor just looked at me like he had done earlier at my desk. It was a study for him; he seemed to want to fathom me out but was having very little luck. I was not a complex creature, I just wanted to fight, I was always in trouble as a kid, always scrapping in the streets, always fighting the foreigners at school; it was part of my breeding. "You do not believe in ethics do you?" he said out of the blue

"Honestly sir." I said pausing, "I do have a problem with ethics"

"And what is that problem? Ethics are based on morals and everyone has morals to which they adhere to" he said shifting uneasily on the desk

"I don't sir. To achieve my objective I will do anything and everything in my power. I would kill my own mother to complete my goal. The unit does not need moral soldier's sir"

"But morality is what makes us human Banner, to see the difference between good and evil. To question whether what you are doing is right or wrong"

"I am paid to keep my morals hidden away sir. If I let my own beliefs get in the way of my life I might not ever be able to achieve anything"

"Then I pity you young man. For you will never become a great soldier, not now, and not with this bullish and childish attitude towards your life and the missions"

As the night weaned itself on the remnants of another day's sun, the blinding moonlight speared through my blinds across my chest. There was nothing quite as satisfying as smoking a Cuban cigar while listening to Bob Marley, next to you another beautiful woman with whom you had just spent the most exhausting and pleasurable past hour with. I began to focus on everything in my room; the blurry LED time display on my stereo soon became a clear picture. I fixed my sight on the poster on the far wall, it quickly shifted into perfect alignment and the scantily clad figure curved into shape. Training my eyes had become a nightly obsession; I felt as if I didn't train them, they would lose their ability and that the one time I needed them they would let me down.

The girl groaned beside me. I couldn't remember her name, she was just another one who had taken my fancy that night, and it didn't matter on shape or size or looks, my tastes changed like the weather. It was then that morality thrust itself in front of my mind. Was what I was doing now moral? Meh, who cares! I am young, only twenty two; I am enjoying my life and keeping my body in a peak condition. I am top of all my classes bar one, how can I possibly fail? I am on the road to undertake my dream job, becoming an Operative with MI: 5.

As I put the final drags of my cigar into the ashtray I remembered the debate I had to put together for War Ethics in a couple of days. It wasn't really late, the clock read 23:57 and according to my trained eyes the standby button was glowing on the laptop sat on the floor. I pulled the sheets away from me along with the arm of the girl next to me, and sat down on my leather recliner chair, the centrepiece of my room. The internet browser was already up and several pop-up windows advertising Viagra and other sex toys and pornographic websites had joined the page devoted to the musical talents of Bob Marley that I was reading before I went out.

I closed the page and brought up a new browser with a search engine on. Typing in Saddam Hussein brought up too many stories about his death, about conspiracies on his hanging, how it didn't happen, how it was all an elaborate ruse to fool the American government. One story even linked him with Osama Bin Laden and the Taliban claiming he and Bin Laden were the same person, the internet was full of nonsense.

It wasn't until several pages on that stories with what looked like truth were beginning to take shape. It was then that a small window popped up at the bottom of the screen... with my name on it.

'Banner, someone is watching you, we can help'.

What the hell was this? I crossed it off, but another message came up again.

'Don't be foolish Banner, we want to help you'

Adrenaline shot through my veins as I crossed the window off again. I could feel a burning sensation in my stomach as the window rose again from the bottom of the screen with a menacing pace.

'Watch out'

I felt my shoulder twinge as someone grabbed it, within a second I had spun my right fist around and square into the jaw of my assailant who collapsed to the floor knocked out. I stood over them, slowly coming to the realisation that the woman who I had slept with was concuss on the floor.

"Where have you been Banner? Rumours are frequent but so often untrue; I'd like to know from your own tongue"

"I was arrested last night sir. I punched a girl straight in the face"

"So you are right you have no morals"

"It wasn't like that sir. I thought someone was about to attack me, my computer was flashing weird messages to me like someone is watching me and then they told me to watch out just as she grabbed my shoulder, as if they knew it was coming!"

He looked at me almost on a slant. The Professor was not one to be judgemental, he knew that things happened for a reason and he knew that I had no morals and therefore would not lie about the situation I was in. However, this was a different look; he seemed to want to tell me something and was holding back. It was just about the only thing I learnt in my year of psychology. "Have you ever heard of something called the SES Banner?"

As he said it, each individual letter hammered onto my head. He said it with so much weight, it was impossible to ignore, it was something important. "No Professor"

"Then it is not important. You will only know them if they want you to know them"

"Sir, what is it? Who are they?"

"I am not allowed to say. Forget I said anything, I fear I may now lose my role as it is. If I am not here tomorrow, let me say it has been an honour to lecture you. Please Banner for the sake of yourself, do *not* listen to the last thing I said"

True to his word, the Professor was not here the next day. I couldn't help but ponder this SES that the Professor spoke of. The academy said that the professor had taken a leave of absence due to a family bereavement but I knew better, *he* knew it was going to happen. I would say there was something fishy going on, but I had no proof of anything to go to anyone with, what do you know, I learnt something from him after all.

Two Years Later...

"Agent Banner. Agent Carter. Come in please"

Me and Carter got up and went into the office. "Please take a seat"

We both sat down in front of a large oak desk that threatened to swallow the whole room. A large rubber plant sat in the corner, watching us through the glass of Whisky that the boss had just poured in front of us. The London skyline behind was sifting with fog through the dismal drear that was supposed to be morning. The whole room felt dank, as if the fog had taken hold of the building and squeezed. "As you know..." started the boss.

'The Boss' was really called Mark Granger and was the head of this department. He had come from a long line of departmental heads that had run in his family and he had kept the tradition well. However, his father had recently disowned him at the knowledge of Mark actually being a homosexual. His dad was a pure breaded homophobe who signed numerous contracts agreeing not to allow homosexuals into the division, no matter what position or rank. This was also a man who had tried to ignore racial equality for the past twenty years as well. Thankfully Mark knew that the times had changed, and kept the company as equal as possible.

"... MI: 5 is not a group that defies its own rules. We have benchmarks that are set and stuck to for a reason. However on this occasion we are being advised to bend our own rules"

He turned to look at me, I felt like I was back in the academy. I had graduated eighteen months ago now and was still awaiting my first assignment. I couldn't ignore the fact the money I was being paid simply to keep myself in shape wasn't good, but the yearning for action, to be a hero, it was too strong to keep back. I wanted this to be a mission, to take up arms, to walk into a hotel with a gun in my holster and not have to worry about the metal detectors. I wanted to feel alive!

"The two of you are being sent in"

I couldn't help but scream a mental 'YEAH!'. "In the next 48 hours you are being flown to our contact in Luxor"

"Luxor sir?" asked Carter

"You are being sent to Egypt agent Carter" said the boss with a sense of dismay. It seemed as if Agent Carter had not learned geography.

I had only just met Carter now in the corridor waiting for this meeting but one thing had already struck me about her.

She was slow.

It wasn't meant in a bad way. Nobody who can graduate from the academy and become an MI: 5 operative can be dumb, and there is no way someone being sent on a mission in their first year can be classed as not important to the organisation, but she seemed off the ball and almost eccentric. There was a buzz about her body, she was not thin or even muscley, but bulky and out of shape and yet she seemed to be able to do anything she wanted, there was no limitation for her size. Maybe I was being too judgemental on big women, but I can only go on the experience I have had, and big woman are not normally very flexible, but they try really hard.

"Yes, Luxor. Home of Karnak Temple and Luxor Temple respectively. There have been rumblings lately, and that is the only way we can describe it. Recently, one of the mosques has been relocated due to some underground work being carried out by the Egyptian government. Bad enough you may think, not only have the Muslim community in Egypt rebelled but their has also been a little trouble by some extreme Muslim members"

"As I understand sir, Egyptian Muslims are calm people?" said Carter

"*All* Muslims are a calm people. They are no different to you or I, perhaps their belief is stronger than our own. Anyway, this is just a background event to what is happening underneath"

I leaned over with intrigue; Mark could sense it in me, the eagerness to want to do this mission. He also knew that with anticipation and excitement came rashness, I was trying my hardest to suppress the feelings but they would not go away. "I need both of you in this surveillance assignment"

My excitement died down. Surveillance, the most boring kind of work, the kind that was considered a holiday to the majority of experienced agents working in the ranks. "Carter, you will set up in the Four Seasons Hotel Cairo at Nile Plaza. You Banner, are to be on the same Nile cruise ship as your mark, the African Queen"

He took a giant swig of whisky as soon as he finished. "We do not normally send rookies outside of the EU on their first assignment. But we have reason to believe that the mark will know of every agent we have working on an international stage. That is why we must break protocol by sending the pair of you in. You have both been recommended to me by your respective academies as the best in your fields. Do not let yourselves or your country down. Your target will be hostile if provoked and is deadly in many different situations"

"Forgive me for saying Sir but how do we know all this?"

The Boss put his feet up on the desk after lounging back into his chair, his feet blocking the dim sun from hitting my face, "Because we trained him"

Carter and I both took a second to recover from the bombshell that had been dropped on our heads. It was like a thump in the face, but from Ricky Hatton on steroids. "So you're sending us to follow a former member of MI: 5?"

"That is correct Carter"

"Why is he not with MI: 5 anymore Sir?"

"He left. Due to lack of morals but also a lack for rules. He broke them and many more protocols and was deemed surplus to requirements. The final straw came when he shot dead one of his own team for disobeying orders that he gave that were against the orders of *his* superior"

"Sounds like a bit of a lunatic Sir"

"He is," said Mark with a cringe in his voice, "He also knows every agent that works outside of the EU, and therefore you are the best chance we have of decent surveillance on him"

Suddenly this assignment was not as much a holiday as a trip to hell. The Boss reached into his desk and dropped a heavy file onto the ground with a thud. Dust blew to one side in a maelstrom of unclean furniture. "Darren Mayweather, aka 'The Butcher' was brought to MI: 5 by my father in 1983 from the RAF where he showed a fantastic ability to not just fly but to participate in ground assaults too.

He passed several courses with the highest honours including advanced driving, heavy firearms, hand to hand combat and swimming. He is still only the second man in the history of MI: 5 to have been able to sneak up on one of our Challenger tanks and actually disable it without detection.

He was born in Taunton 1956, where he was raised in a military Barracks with his father Captain Mayfield of the Royal Dragoons and his mother Claire Serita. This man is an expert Agents; I don't think I need to tell you that"

"What is he going to do though sir?" I asked full of inquisitiveness.

"We do not know. If we knew we would put safeguards in place like we normally do in these situations, but there is no reason for his being there. We just don't like it when one of our rogue agents rears his head again after years of inactivity"

"Will we be armed sir?" asked Carter with what seemed like a slight edge of fear.

"Yes you will. Be careful, he will be too and so are the Egyptian Police, the last thing we want is for there to be a full fire fight at one of the most treasured temples that the Egyptians have. Relations are already at crumbling point after refusing the Rosetta Stone back into Egypt. We cannot afford any more unpleasantries"

There was a brief silence for more than a second and it took The Boss even less time to pounce on it. "No Questions? Good, be sure to see medical before leaving. Malaria, Hepatitis and god knows what else are waiting for you there. Enjoy yourselves. And remember the rules. Only fire when fired upon and you are issued with six bullets, if you bring back less than that we want to know when and where they were fired, if you can't account for them we can't cover it up. Be wary and resilient at all times. And one last thing..."

We both stood up as he said it, it seemed to be a good time to leave. "...Good Luck Agents"

The Medical Bay was just what you would have expected from anywhere. As soon as you walked through the factory floor-esque training academy it was the smell of hospitals. It was a difficult smell to explain, but disinfectant was rampant and the pale look of Agent Carter seemed to sum up the whole experience. She sat on the chair next to me, cracking her fingers in what seemed to be nerves. Nerves were an Agents worst fear; nerves targeted you when you needed to be strong and steady. Nerves were an enemy you needed to conquer before you could fire a sniper rifle to a top grade level. Why was she suffering so much?

"I don't like needles ok?" she said, "I can see you looking, judging me for it!"

"I wasn't judgein..."

"Yes you were" she snapped in between, "You combat graduates are all the same, you all think you have no fear until you get on the battlefield and *bam*, fear kicks you right in the balls!"

I decided to keep quiet for a minute. I really should start realising that I am not at the academy anymore; I am not the best in a bunch of wannabes. Everyone here has made it, there are no wannabes here, and we are all as good as a level set by MI: 5 and can probably read each other as well as I believe I can. "I'm sorry, I just really hate needles. They one of the few things I don't like"

"Any reason?"

"I had a bad experience with one in school. One of the nurses missed my vein so many times it just felt like she was stabbing me in the arm over and over. There was no apology and it left my arm the size of a tree trunk"

"I'm sorry"

"And then all the kids did was rip the piss out of me for it. Digging me in the arm, then laughing when it bruised even worse"

I thought back to childhood and thought that it was something I would do. Kids can be the cruellest being on the planet without knowing. They had no reservation of pointing out abnormalities, they didn't know about feelings and the whole concepts of manners were foreign to them until teenage years. "Banner, Carter. Come in please."

The noise over the tannoy was louder than anything in the training facility. It was like someone was shouting in your ear from a couple of millimetres away. We looked at each other, got up, knocked on the door and walked in to the overpowering stench of alcohol based disinfectants and more. There were smells traceable maybe as urine, as if the last person in here had pissed themselves at the very sight of the yeti that was passing as the doctor. His hair tied back, his beard fashioned into a point in front of a ferocious moustache that did as much for his face as a slash with a knife. One of his eyes seemed lightly askew, it looked like he was looking to the side of me but I quickly realised he was looking dead into my pupils. "Luxor for the both of you?" he said with a squeaky voice, one I had never expected.

We nodded in unison. "Two for Egypt Claire" he said

Behind the pale blue curtain at the back of the white room was the nurse. I could tell from Carters expression she didn't know she was there either. The whole of MI: 5 seemed to want to impress, almost as if it was trying too hard. Six vaccines were placed in a tray in front of us, three each. "One for Hepatitis C, one for Malaria and one to cure that horrible local curse known as Pharaohs Revenge"

"Pharaohs Revenge?" asked Carter

"Also known as Egyptian Shits. An airborne virus that is impossible to wipe out, due to the difference in the air in Egypt to our own, it effects foreigners from most other countries"

I could see Carter staring at the needles. "Shall we begin," the doctor said looking at Carter, "You can go first"

The evil bastard, I grabbed his wrist as he reached for her vaccines and said, "I'll go first,"

I winked at her; she tried to raise a faint smile through the ill look of petrifaction. "There is nothing to worry about" I said in as reassuringly a way I could. I couldn't understand what I was doing, this wasn't the sort of person I was. Why did I care if she needed help, she would just get in my way, and I wouldn't be surprised if she was the one who got herself killed. Why did I care? Yet when I looked into her eyes it was hard not to try and help, there was a panic, like seeing your headlights caught in an animals eyes through the windscreen as your about to hit it. The three needles went in, one at a time, pumping god knows what drugs into my body. There was a leaflet with all the... ingredients, shall we say... that they used and a list of side effects but it was useless when they just jab them into you without a care.

She sat there, timid and scared as the needles went in. It was all over fast and the nerves that had shredded her earlier were floundering by the second. "There you go, Egypt awaits now" I said

"That's easy for you to say" she said, "I'm not all that great with flying either"

CHAPTER 2
KARNAK TEMPLE

Two Days Later...

It was November, and Egypt was still hot. When I got off the plane, an Egyptian man working for the tour group I was in told me he had seen rain. Shocked at this I asked him when, and he told me it must have been four years ago! Luxor Airport was a military airport, filled with armed soldiers and very little else. The relatively small group of English tourists were mainly all in their later years and I felt out of place next to the octogenarians. I hadn't brought a lot of clothing or equipment for the assignment. Mainly because I didn't know what I was supposed to bring. The Boss had instructed me to bring several bugs from the office because I was going to be placed directly above Mayweather on the ship, Carter would hear everything on her receivers at the hotel.

They speedily took me through passport control in what was considered an Egyptian straight line, this literally meant all get together in a ball and the first person to the passport booth wins. It was there that I felt I was making myself slightly suspicious putting work as my purpose of visit on the visa I had to fill in.

The farce that was collecting your bags got underway next as the carriage span round flinging everyone's bag except mine onto the turntable. It finally appeared emerging last and battered as if it had gone ten rounds with Ricky Hatton. If the suitcase could talk, I'm sure it would be screaming at me now.

I quickly made my way to the end of the airport and found a solitary man holding my name card up with the words, Blue Sky Travel. I gave him a polite cough and he instantly woke up, "Mister Banner?" he questioned in a heavy Egyptian accent

"That's me"

"This way please"

Outside the stuffy air knocked me back. The heat was everywhere; the air had trapped the heat inside itself and was blowing it around freely making the atmosphere a furnace.

Egyptian kids swarmed at me, all grabbing my suitcase by the handle, desperate for me to let go so that I would give them a tip. I was not going to let go of this case, it would not be a good start to the assignment if I lost my suitcase. The man chauffeured me to his car which sat completely foreign to the rest; it was clean for one thing. It was a brand new black BMW with darkened windows and a swanky set of alloys. "Please, I have been asked to bring you to your boat, and bring you back from the boat when your vacation is complete"

"Excellent"

"Cheers big ears"

That was the problem with foreigners learning English through English people. We use it as an excuse to have a joke with people, not realising they take insults on as real polite terms and then innocently use them back on us. I'm sure many an Egyptian has had a stern telling off that way.

As I got on the boat I looked around trying not to give myself away, which was as helpful as if I had a giant glowing beacon on my head. Remaining inconspicuous was about as easy as eating soup with a fork, remaining in the background was an art, one that I hadn't truly mastered. My group was the first on board, gazing in wonder at the grandeur and palatial columns that lined the lobby with winding staircases arching around a central lift to the upper echelons of the boat.

It was beautiful!

The fake marble floor didn't spoil the granite effect walls that were symmetrically split every ninety degrees by corridors and busts of the Greek God Poseidon above the doorways. It was a stunning effect, marred in no way by everything being phoney. This was in part because everything was solid, whereas in Britain, everything fake is made of plaster or fibreglass or even MDF, the Egyptians did fake very well.

Everything was efficient with our rep for our travel agents being in the lobby, enjoying a red drink that I found to be Hibiscus Tea, not something I was intending to drink when I was well aware it was the number two cause of Pharaohs Revenge. We were handed our keys upon surrendering our passports to the reception, and briefly pointed in the direction of our rooms and as soon as I walked into mine I flaked out. The heat was insatiable, and it was made worse by the fact my room was as small as a toilet cubicle. A bed, a fitted wardrobe and, oh, a toilet cubicle actually bigger than the rest of my room. It wasn't that these ships had small rooms normally, but it was just reassuring to know that the MI: 5 were pretty stingy when it came to sending its agents further afield than Birmingham.

The Victorian colours were beginning to make my head spin, the dark green and reds were all a mesh and it took me till I removed my work file from my suitcase to once again focus in a straight line.

The picture looking back at me was that of my mark. A man as shrew looking as his reputation, a shaven head and neat goatee beard made him look like a stereotypical BNP supporter. No distinguishing features were a good thing, not for me, but for him. Joining the MI: 5 normally means you have to fit into categories of normality, stay under 5'10. Be a medium build. No visible scars or tattoos and certainly no ridiculous hairstyles, in fact, this man was as normal and boring looking as they come and would probably work in the reverse of normality when most people nowadays are kinda weird looking.

I took the bugs out of my MP3 wallet, and pulled a small square of carpet to one side near the edge of my bed. They were the size of a small watch battery and were programmed to turn on when you say its activation word.

"Floppy" I said and the little red light pinged on. Someone in MI: 5 thought they had a sense of humour, obviously.

I put in the bug and started talking to myself about how wonderful it was to be in a country so hot you couldn't breathe because your lungs felt on fire. With that, my mobile rang and Carter was on the other end. "I agree!" she said, "I'm sweating my tits off up here!"

Cute. "You hear me loud and clear?"

"Every footstep and whimper. If you stay quiet we should be able to hear everything from our target. So don't be up to any hanky panky in there!"

"Why? Would you get jealous?"

The line went dead. I wondered if I had struck a nerve or if she was just disgusted by the whole idea, whatever the cause I knew we had a direct line to the cabin below. I didn't bother unpacking, I already looked like a typical English tourist in my bright yellow shirt and khaki shorts without needing to change. I thought it would be best to sit in the lobby and wait for the rest of the tourists to pour in alongside my man.

It wasn't long until the next group arrived. I had found myself chatting with my travel agent rep while waiting for the next group to arrive and was finding it quite difficult to shake her off. She was a nice looking girl, she had a smooth face but one that seemed to highlight if she had had a bad nights sleep or not. She also had this heir of being up herself, the kind you used to get from the Royal Family back in the Victorian days. I couldn't deny she was pretty, but being the same size as Carter and not being embarrassed about showing it was quite unappealing. Sporting navy blue shorts swinging and tightening every bit of cellulite was cute on a woman who felt ashamed and bashful of it; a woman who is proud of it just needs help.

With the next group arriving she sighed and left me to sit on my own, which was as relieving for me as it was reluctant for her. She introduced herself with a spring in her step and when she said "I'm Heather!" I nearly expected her to follow it with, "And I wanna shag that man over there!"

Perhaps I was being full of myself, perhaps not, all I knew was I didn't want to be near her when mating season kicked in. It was then that my mark walked through the plain glass doorway from the dock and stood obediently next to the rep with what I could only assume was his hand luggage slung across his shoulder.

He was as normal as could be.

Short black hair and clean shaven, (both unlike the photo I had) and grinning with the giddiness of a schoolboy at the grandeur of the boat along with the other guests. He seemed to have fitted in very well with the guests already, laughing and joking with a few of them as if he had known them for years. This man reeked of being a pro. He couldn't help it to a man who had been through the same training, you could see why he was seen as the best. It wasn't long before he looked at me, noticing me as he scanned his surroundings like I did as I walked in. At that point I got up, straightened my shirt, and said "See you later Heather"

She turned to me and smiled before turning back to her group. I walked past Mayweather; he kept his eyes fixed on me and just his stare made me nervous. I started to sweat, and within that split second he turned and said, "Hey" in a fixed unnerving voice, filled with years of encounters with foreign agents and diplomats. "What's the food like on this boat?"

I couldn't tell what was happening. Nobody was watching us, I felt like I had been pulled to one side by the professor in War Ethics. I froze, they teach you not to freeze, and they teach you how to stay calm, to focus and think about what they've said! I'm freaking out!

"Erm.... I've not had any food yet, I only got here today"

"Oh, sorry to bother you. Why are you here?"

"Just to see the sights, I loved Egyptian history when I was young"

He looked at me again, a stare of pure fixation, he knew. "I'm sure we will see a lot of each other then this week"

I turned when he did and headed for my cabin. He knows, he knows! I stormed back to my room dialling in Carters number as I barged through the door and slammed it behind me. The line clicked and I shouted "He fucking knows!"

"What? Who does what?"

"Mayweather, he fucking knows we are on to him!"

"How do you know?"

"He said we would see a lot of each other, and the way he looked at me! He knows for sure!"

"Maybe he was just being friendly!"

"No! He knows, tell Mark we need to abort. I've fucked it all up already!"

"No! There is no way I am failing my first mission because you *think* he knows you're an agent. Maybe it's a hunch, he doesn't know for sure! How can he? Go to dinner tonight, get on the same table and make sure you talk to him! Put him on the back foot, get his back up! I know you can do it, I knew from the first time I met you that you were good at this job. Now go fucking do it!"

I was shocked. "I think I'll need to read into some Egyptian history"

"Why?" she said still seething with anger

"Because I told him I was here to see the sights and that I enjoyed Egyptian history"

"Then you better get some books and start reading"

As Carters voice flicked off, I looked in the welcome package that must have been sat on the bed since I got here but I hadn't noticed. Tomorrow we visited Karnak Temple; I had a strong gut feeling something was going to happen there, I wish I knew what it was. I just hoped I could get through dinner first.

There was a knock at the door three hours later, groggily getting to my feet I opened to a man dressed smartly holding a thick folder which he handed to me and said in cracked English, "It is from Luxor Hotel sir, fast courier"

"Thank you" I said taking it as he walked off.

I trudged back to sit on my bed while opening the folder that contained a book on Luxor and Karnak temple with a message on a little yellow post-it note saying, 'Start revising, good luck. Carter'

From my room I worked my way down three flights of curved stairs to the bottom deck where the dining room was. There was a minimalist dress code that asked women not to wear skin-tight tops and hot pants so chafing it showed camel toe, and for men to wear trousers and not prance around in shorts. Most of the men however, flaunted this, deciding instead to wear a whole host of Hawaiian gear with palm trees of colours so vast and varied it made my eyes go funny.

I was asked to sit down at a certain table, number seventeen, and was the first to arrive. I was then asked for a drink. It must be said, for an Egyptian cruise ship the selection of drinks was rather incredible. Six to seven pages of different cocktails ranging from local to international drinks with good old English Bitter on the menu. Boringly though, I had a Cola.

The Dining Room was as grand as the rest of the boat, all capturing that feel of class with as little funds as possible. A large buffet bar sat at the back of the room with four chefs, all Egyptian and all wearing tall white hats, waiting to serve. It was a grandiloquent setting, calm and collected, and above all else, beautiful. I took a plate up and had the creamy Potato Sauce which was essentially Mash Potato and some vegetables, it wasn't much but it was just to make an effort, to try and be as inconspicuous as I could until the target arrived.

And then he did. Walking through the double doors with a cocky swagger, drink in hand and a cigarette placed behind his ear. He was wearing shorts, already against the dress code and a thin 'indie' tie above a pink t-shirt with the words 'young and beautiful' on it. This was inconspicuous at its best, make yourself so obvious that you can't help but be noticed.

The waiter showed him to my table and instantly my blood began to pump. I could feel the adrenaline rush hit me with a force, sweat began to materialise on my forehead and already I could feel him looking at me. He had a glint in his eyes as if he was trying to woo me; it was the kind of fox chasing its prey look that had my stomach boiling with fear.

"Oh, good afternoon my friend. Ready for the early wake up in the morning! Six AM, bloody early eh?"

"Yeah, but I'm looking forward to it, Karnak temple is something I have wanted to see for years" I said feeling my stomach burn. It was making me feel ill, this was pressure like I had never experienced before, and they don't train you for this.

"So you are a student of Egyptology you say? I studied it a fair bit myself, what area have you looked at?"

Thank God Carter sent me that book and now slap yourself for not reading it! Idiot Banner! I plucked a name from first year history. "Mostly Rameses II, he had an interesting view of life to say the least"

"Yes I quite agree. Odd fellow, I myself study Ankhunatom, the man who decided that gods as they where, were not suitable for him and his family"

"Yes I have read of him" I said remembering the name but not the stories. Why didn't I say I loved the mythology of it? Why did I say I knew about one of the Kings, the most difficult subject of all! "He was linked to the god Atom was he not?"

"Indeed. Anywho my dear friend, I will be back shortly, bellies rumbling as they say" he said patting his stomach.

There was something odd about everything he did. It was all fake but it was fake in a typically English way. Nobody in England is like that anymore, the 'old sport' quips and tongue that nobody from anywhere in England I knew spoke anymore. He came back minutes later, and I soon realised that nobody but me and him were on the table. "Looks like were bosom buddies for the tour my friend" he said picking up his knife and fork. "Come join me for a drink tonight on deck. To celebrate two students seeing Egypt and its many wonders for the first time" he said tearing apart a piece of soft chicken between his fork and mouth

"I don't know, we have an early start" I said desperately trying to find a way out

"No no, I insist, it doesn't seem the other Englishmen are going to join us. I am sure we will get on like a house on fire"

"I'm sure we will"

After the dinner that made me ill with worry I sat on my bed in the divine state of anxiousness. I was in layman's terms, shitting myself. He was a more than worthy adversary and the fear of being ousted was without a doubt one of the most thrilling feelings I have ever felt. I had started to calm down with the adrenaline beginning to fade but the night still lingered with agony knowing that the meeting tonight could be my last.

If he knew, or even had a suspicion, I was out.

My mobile rang. "How did it go?"

"Bad. He 'insisted' I had a drink with him tonight"

"When tonight?"

"About ten minutes"

"Does he know about you?"

"I don't know... He just seems like an eccentric Englishman abroad"

She went silent down the line for a minute but I could hear her rummaging through what sounded like papers. "Don't give him any alias' will you?"

"What? Why?"

"He is going to know every single alias you give him that MI: 5 own isn't he. Tell him something completely out of the ordinary"

"Like what?"

"Like....." she said obviously looking through files and books, "...... Edward Meak"

"Edward Meak?"

"An Ex-boyfriend. Good luck"

When I walked on to the top deck I could smell the deep scent of cigar smoke mixed with the smell of cooked meat coming from the hotel across from the boat on the mainland. I always had a soft spot for cigars, the way they looked as well as the way they tasted and made you feel. They had a class about them, from the guise of Churchill to the old adverts, something about them screamed charm.

Mayweather was stood, cigar in mouth, bottle in hand staring at the night sky ahead. The stars were as clear as diamonds against a black background, twinkling like they had never twinkled before, as if there lives depended on it. "Ah old bean. I got you a beer ready!"

I took it but had no intention of drinking it. It was like avoiding date rape, never under any circumstances do you accept drinks from strangers or potential murderers. He turned through the shadows as the aroma of tobacco blew across my face; there was darkness in his eyes. "So old boy. What is your name? I was meaning to ask you at dinner but you seemed flustered and hurried off?"

I couldn't tell if that was a hint at him knowing something or if that was his talk. He seemed to be able to use old time talk as a way of heading his incredibly intrusive and confident nature. "I'm Edward, and you are?"

"Phillip Croaker" he said politely, "From Cheltenham"

My mind quickly ran through the MI: 5 alias list and there near the end was the name Phillip Croaker, I smiled but as I did I could see him looking at me. The darkness in his eyes was transfixed on my expression, he was scanning me for the slightest little wince of movement, and he knew that I was MI: 5, I was so easy to read. "Cheltenham?" I said trying to sound somewhat interested and impressed, "I'm from Portsmouth. The south coast"

"Ah, many a Saturday have I spent on the south coast. Supporting Southampton at the Old Dell, those were the days"

He took a concentrated drag on the cigar and stubbed it out. I looked down the bottle neck of my beer and contemplated drinking it, I knew I shouldn't, it was the oldest trick in the book. "What's wrong old sport? It's not as if it's poisoned"

It was definitely poisoned. "I'm not a lager drinker. More of a Whisky man"

"A man after my own taste. I shall order some"

He rang a small bell that he must have brought himself and it didn't take long for a young Egyptian waiter to come running. "A bottle of your finest Whisky young fellow and two glasses please"

I decided to take the offensive for the first time. "So what do you do Phillip?"

"Call me Phil, please. I work in the Ship Industry. Always have done, from my times down the dockyard on the Mersey, to working down the south, down your way, Portsmouth in fact. I have in my life spent a long time working on 6 inch steel beams precariously walking above a 100ft gorge drop.... those were the days. What about you my friend?"

The young waiter placed a bottle on the table next to us, we sat ourselves down as the waiter poured out two glasses very carefully, then bowed before quietly sliding into the darkness. When Mayweather looked at me I could feel the torrent of study flow, he was like a psychiatrist or a kinisiologist, he looked at everything you did and studied how you moved and worked. He could tell that inside I was squirming.

"I work in Paint" I said trying to find as boring a job as I could. "I work with pigments and raw materials and create water based paints and masonry paint to a pre-determined formula. It's about as exciting as watching it dry"

"Doesn't sound it old boy. The world needs paint. Tell me, what is the most common formula today? Is it that E19 stuff that was so thick and sludgy, or that new stuff, that ED8? I lose track of things like that"

He knew something about everything! There was no way I could ever have guessed he knew something about paint! "Probably the ED8"

"Thought so" he said and then downed the Whisky in one shot.

I reached over and took hold of the Whisky glass, clutching it knowing full well that the Whisky would flaw so many of my skills and abilities. I took a sip and put it down, "It's a strange tasting Whisky"

"I thought so too. That's why I just threw it down so it didn't touch the sides my friend. You should try it!"

He wanted me pissed. He was good, he knew just how to do things to put people in a situation that they didn't have a choice but to just do what he wanted them to. "I can't down drinks. Makes me feel ill as soon as I do it"

"Fair enough old bean. Anyway, early start in the morning. Perhaps we should go to bed. I will keep the bottle of Whisky in my room. Any time you fancy a drink, feel free"

"I will"

"Good night Edward" he said and walked off reaching into his pocket. I flinched momentarily until he produced a lighter and a cigar.

That did not go well. I pulled my phone out as soon as I saw his shadow fade away down the stairs and rang Carter. "He's going back to his room. I won't go back yet and disturb the sound" I said, "See if he rings anybody or mentions me!"

"I will. Stay put. I'll ring you when the coast is clear"

The vibration woke me. The night was still here, and the glasses we had drunk from were still on the table. I answered the phone, "He hasn't been back to his room yet"

"What?"

"Mayweather has not been back to his room, I think he is skulking about"

"How long ago did he leave?"

"About fifteen minutes ago. Were you asleep?"

"Yeah, I'm shattered!"

"Get following him!"

I jumped up, shaking off the sleep and headed down the spiral staircase to the bar floor. The amount of room on this cruise was phenomenal! A pool table sat ahead of me with a library adjacent to that before a long corridor made its way to the wide open bar area with plenty of seats and enough alcohol to keep several alcoholics going for a few years.

I didn't know where to start. He had fifteen minutes on me! I decided that the best thing for me to do was check that he wasn't actually in bed; I ran down to his cabin and knocked on the door. I knocked a few more times before coming to the conclusion that no one could have slept through that and left alone. It was then my phone rang, "There is someone knocking on the door! Sounds like there trying to wake the dead!"

"That's me... Just making sure he isn't in bed"

"Get after him!"

As I turned at the barking order I noticed the tiniest glimmer of light creeping out from the side of the 'DO NOT ENTER' door that was at the side of me. It was a hatch door, and it hadn't been shut. It was screaming at me, delirious with intrigue I pushed through to a gigantic raw wind from the outside. I was astern of the boat, lit up by a bright blue haze from the fly zappers scattered everywhere near the food that was stored here. I didn't fancy eating here again!

I heard voices and dipped down beneath a crate of fish that had been left out in the open packed with ice. The raw smell carrying on the wind wound up my nostrils as my heart began to kick faster and faster. The adrenaline rush was phenomenal as the men past me. They weren't armed, and I'm fairly sure they wouldn't say anything if they saw me, but the thrill was indescribable. Being back at the barracks trying this in training was comfortable and enclosed; this was ferocious and open like a fresh wound, raw to the tribulations of the world.

The men past. I jumped out from behind the crate and saw Mayweather at the end, leaning over the railings with the mobile in his hands. I fished about in my pockets, praying I would find one of those bugs from the bedroom but I couldn't. Damn it! They tell you to come prepared, I'd rushed into this, I didn't know what I was doing, I was in way over my head against an ex-agent so much more experienced than me. I got back behind the crate of fish, leering round the corner as Mayweather turned around the bow of the boat.

I moved on, keeping lower than the railings. I imagined myself getting caught, thinking what the people who caught me would think. This is a civilian boat; there are no men with big guns on here, any security measures and cameras, just some cleaners and chefs, why was the adrenaline rushing, why should I be so secretive. I reached the end of the walkway and backed onto the wall, narrowly missing a porthole at the side of me.

I peered round the corner to see Mayweather stood with his mobile in his hand talking in German. Thinking as quickly as I could I reached for my mobile and turned on the voice recorder on it and held the microphone end toward him.

I didn't know if it would work but it was worth a try.

I kept checking around the corner hoping beyond hope that he wouldn't turn to me at the exact time I was looking. It was the next time I looked out that I actually noticed where he was. It was the bow of the boat, and at its tip (And by what Mayweather was standing by) was a large satellite dish, I gathered to receive the stations in the rooms. Even worse was what was stood on the tip of the bow.

An armed Egyptian guard.

I kept the phone directly at Mayweather. I just hoped beyond hope that I was recording and not just pointing a phone at someone. I looked around, he'd gone!

Shit! We're was he? I looked around panicking. Behind, in front, I even dared an extended look into the darkness in which Mayweather had hidden himself, daring him to catch me. I heard a clatter, then voices and suddenly I could hear the Nile gently resting, the night creatures calling. Everything was bombarding the senses! An overloading sense of noise was bustling over the already noisy Nile wind. I looked behind me, the port side of the boat glowing blue. Tiny flashes of electric fizzed and burned as the flies kept darting to their deaths. I was beginning to feel faint, I looked around, shaking my head and felt myself beginning to stumble. I kept my head up, brushing past the chine of the boat bursting into the lastage before sidling to the hatch door and pulling it open with the last ounces of strength I had. The warm glow of orange light calmed my head as Poseidon stared at me from the ceiling. Groggy and down I fumbled my way to my room like a weekend drunk and pushed through my door and collapsed on the bed. With nothing left, I found the file on my phone, the sound bite I hoped had worked and sent it to Carter...

Hearing the phone go off was of no importance to me right now. I knew what it was and I didn't like it in the slightest. It was the wake up call to go to Karnak Temple and as much as I knew I needed to go, my body was not in an entirely great state of being. It was on fire! My calves burned as I placed my feet and stood up for the first time and my hamstrings were crying to me not to move but I stood firm and looked at my mobile.

'1 Message Received'

I gingerly opened the message: 'Why did you send me a file of interference? Carter'

A shiver ran down my spine. The phone had not picked up *anything*. I rang Carter. "How did it not get anything?"

"I don't know, what happened?"

"I followed him out onto the bow and tried to record him talking in German to someone on the phone! It didn't pick anything up though, (It might have been the interference from the satellite dish I later thought) shit!"

"Don't worry about it. You tried, where did he go?"

"I don't know, he just disappeared"

"Well don't lose him at Karnak. That's when whatever is going to happen is going to happen"

"No pressure then"

As the giant stone obelisks welcomed us to Karnak, the thought was still swimming through my head of what I had to do and how I was going to do it. I had befriended my target which is always a good idea unless it is a woman, getting too close to a woman can weaken your resolve (supposedly anyway) as you can fall in love. All this was taught to us thoroughly, it was a harsh lesson in the art of being an agent but it had to be done I suppose.

The sun was strong, even for 8am, and there was not a cloud in the sky. Temperatures had risen above 34C this morning alone, and with the midday sun promising even more, it was quite obvious that most of these octogenarians were going to get hit by the heat…*hard!*

As we all disembarked the coach, Mayweather stood next to me clutching what looked like a camera bag, holding it like a baby, wrapping it in all the protection he possibly could. The sun radiated off his mirrored glasses, he was a sense of style all to himself with his three quarter shorts and tank top, unfortunately this just gave away how incredibly built the man was.

I could murder a cigar, I rolled my lighter around in my pocket, I just wish I had brought some cigars, the tension was starting to hurt, and only the strong clarifying taste of a cigar would quench it.

"Now if you will all just follow me gent'ʒ and ladie'ʒ as I want to tell'ʒ you about everything I can so you have free time later'ʒ"

The tour guide ahead of us began verbally dragging us through the ruins. Karnak temple was a feat of ancient engineering, tall and filled with grandeur. Two giant obelisks stood at the front, either side of two Egyptian kings, in perfect symmetry to one another. The old sandstone was as smooth now as the day it was built as the suns rays bounced off burning your skin wherever you moved.

"Now this gent'z and ladie'z iz a statue of Rameses the second…" said the tour guide as Mayweather nudged me and said, "It's your guy"

"… notice the cartouche. We can make out the name'z of each king but there name written in hieroglyph on each cartouche, now what does this mean? I will show you now…"

As we passed through into the precinct of Amen-Re we were greeted by a giant hypostyle of blossoming pillars. *"…Now thiz iz one of the most exciting and unbelievable momentz of the tour… notice the tall pillarz, all built single handily… all built with perfect precision and all shaped…"* he cupped his hands in explanation, *"… like a tulip. Notice how it openz at the top. Like a flower…"*

There was something typically Egyptian about the tour guide. It was hard to stereotype the Egyptians without putting them all in Fezzes and robes but he was wearing stonewashed jeans with a bright yellow T-shirt but remained somehow Egyptian. Maybe it was the skin tone, the fact even he had a tan line on his face from where he had tanned around his sunglasses, I don't know.

Then I noticed something, or as the situation was, I *didn't*. Something was missing.

The bag! – Where!

A bright orange and red flame erupted into a cloud of dusty sandstone. Time seemed to lose track of reality as the sands of a thousands years collided into a giant airborne maelstrom of blazing rubble, grains of sand and shreds of timber.

Time returned and Mayweather burst forward, padding his pockets in search of something. I made chase, pushing past the hoards of panicking foreigners, tour guide clip boards thrown in the air as the armed guards huddled together with no sense of contingency plan. I fought against the grain of people, struggling to keep sight of Mayweather as he slipped through the crowds like a snake through the sands of the desert.

The air swiftly became thick and smoggy, a raw wind rifled through the ruins throwing up mini-whirlwinds of dust and sand around. There was a large crack, as wide as a human in the far wall leading through to an antechamber, but not through to the other side but into darkness. I pulled my shirt across my mouth and stood with arm on the sandstone, propping myself up against the wind that had whipped around the temple, staring into the black.

Was there the faintest glint of green? I couldn't tell. The dust was mottling my eyes; the noise had died down behind me as I took a tentative step onto the soft floor of the blackness. I brought out my lighter and clicked it into life; the walls came alive, flourishing with colour. It reminded me of the inside of Abu Simbel where the statues "sing" because of the wind in the crevices, the reds, blues, greens and whites all bringing to life the detailed hieroglyphs.

There was a green, I could make it out now against the walls. The sound of the trickling water above me made my bladder squirm, and the feel of hundreds of tiny stalagmites under the sand made my feet tingle.

There was a shining green strip light on the floor. As I held it above my head, the reflective grain in the sand illuminated a single pair of footprints heading down in the depths.

It was hard to breathe, the air trying its best to stay thick clogs of heat, rather than be pleasantly inhaled. The weight of thousands of years of history crushed me as I stalked the passage. It was beginning to get smaller, above me were hundreds of tiny hand painted white stars on a blue background before a huge wing outlined in gold was spread across and around a small doorway. And above the jamb sat in the middle, directly above the door was a white throne, unmanned and as bright and clear as the day it was painted.

Another green strip light sat on the floor in the next room. A great wave of heat struck me across the chest as I passed the threshold; it was now I wished I had studied those Egyptian books far more seriously. I tried to contact Carter but all I got was fuzz, there was no way a signal was going to get in here.

The room was empty, and trying to stand I hit my head as I pushed my palms against either side of the wall. There was the tiniest hint of footprint on the floor that led to a black rectangle that was a passage to the next area. This was an anteroom. Hesitantly I stuck a foot into the dark; the black was so solid I imagined myself kicking a solid piece of obsidian. Sweat was now starting to form along my forehead and arms and my mouth was parched from the sandy dust, I'd do anything for a drink right now.

Even with my lighter the next room was black. The ground underneath had shifted; it felt solid and almost purposeful, like a platform. Then suddenly, and without warning, two licks of flame burst from in front of me, running in a bend torches erupted into life sending dust flying into floating embers above the flames. Light took over the dark. Pillars rose and emerged through the black and showed me just how close I was to falling into what looked like an abyss. The room, no, this wasn't a room, it was a hall, came to life.

The trail of fire flash-boiled at its end, sat like a flickering figure in a white marble throne. At the centre of everything was Mayweather, torch in hand, staring at the walls. That was, until you realised, that the walls were not walls but shelves, row upon row, book upon book, scroll upon scroll, straining in the light that they had not seen for thousands of years. This was the throne of the gods!

Or was it god? Something didn't add up, a cross curved at its points was sculptured into every pillar. I'm sure I had seen these before...

"I know you're there"

I dived behind a pillar. He can't know, the sound of the fire trail hid my entry, how did he know? Or was he guessing? Was he trying to catch me out? Questions buzzed through my head like a pneumatic drill through jelly. What was that? A soft, silent thudding echoed in the hall.

"You really are good aren't you?"

It was a third ma... woman! Thin and tall with a straight posture walking with the sort of arrogance you only get from a woman thinking she is dominating a male world.

She also looked quite pretty.

"So this is it?" she said, her voice was a hacksaw personified, roughly treated but serrated and deadly.

"Yes" said Mayweather, "I've put the scrolls we needed into a case. I'll sneak out through the night; the boat won't leave without me"

Mayweather sounded different, it could just be the harmonics but the echo was loud and fairly accurate, I didn't really know if the way he spoke to me was real or not. "You are not what we expected. We didn't think you would use such a direct approach. Blowing through a wall is a dangerous stunt"

"What did you expect? Me to dig my way in?"

"Do you know how important this place is?" The woman said with anger on the edge of every word. "An underground temple, built in

642AD? Holding some of the most rare and important documents in history?"

"I got the scrolls" said Mayweather ignoring the history lesson, "I'll keep them until I meet Alpha and get my money"

I pulled out my mobile and created a draft text and saved the words, 'Underground Temple', 'Alpha' and '642AD'. There must be something in the history books about this place. Something like this can't just exist; it would be like hiding the pyramids in London, it just would not happen. I looked up from my phone to nobody, damn he was good. Before he made his way up, I dashed back into the antechamber and ran, not looking back for the light ahead.

CHAPTER 3
THE HAUNTING OF DEMONS

My boat was last in the chain. It was strange but in Egypt they docked their boats side by side, linked together so to get to your boat you would have to pass through several receptions.

The foyer stirred as I walked in, "We thought we had lost you friend?"

"I, er, got caught up in the commotion"

I made my way to my room but heard something interesting on the way, apparently we were fully boarded and ready to sail, which meant that Mayweather had somehow beaten me back. I didn't dare to think why or how. Instead I made contact with Carter, who screamed back, "Where the bloody hell have you been? You were supposed to report nearly two hours ago!"

"Calm down" I said opening the door to my room and sitting on the bed "Mayweather blew a hole in Karnak"

"I've seen it on the news. I knew you would have something to do with it. Did you follow him?"

"Yeah it led to some old forgotten library, there were thousands of scrolls and books and things. Mayweather has taken some, and he is back on the boat but I don't think he is the problem"

"What do you mean?"

"He met a woman there" I said walking to the en-suite and turning the shower on, "And mentioned Alpha, and he needed payment. Mayweather was waiting to get paid; I think he is just a hired goon"

I was thankful for the quiet as I took my shirt off, the shower was only lukewarm but I wasn't expecting much. Outside the window the orange sun was resigning for the night casting palm tree shadows across the white tiles of the bathroom. "I'm gunna need to report all this, I'll see if anybody at HQ knows this stuff. Are you ok? Do you need anything?"

"Just this shower. Good night"

Night crept up fast. There wasn't much of a moon but the stars more than made up for it. The boat was waiting for the others to detach as they all set off in a race for the upcoming dam. I was quite content, a bottle of 'Luxor Beer' (5.5% lager! Ouch!) And a cigar while watching the calm Nile was more than enough for me. The banks were so green spreading on for miles, then it turned to desert, as stunningly sudden as the difference between black and white.

Far to my left, it looked like a farmer (I assume) was trying to drown a cow, although closer inspection revealed he was cleaning the cow, I know I wouldn't go near water with that bloke next to me. Twenty feet away, a small boy was drinking the same water; the HSE would have a field day. It was then, that the whole day came into focus, like a punch to the head or a kick in the balls. It was instantaneous. I'd chased an ex-agent through a wall of dust to a hidden library that nobody had set their eyes on in thousands of years.

Somehow I had avoided that woman. There was no other entrance, and then it dawned. I bet she saw me! She just played out the mini-theatre for my benefit, it was a show, and she wanted me to see! No. No, that can't be right, why would they let me know? There was no sense. I wouldn't mind knowing what was in those scrolls though; it must be something of historic value, nothing like weaponry, not a scroll that old. It had to be information. Wait... how could that woman get in? There was only one set of footprints in the sand, but I didn't look on the way back, maybe there was another entrance after all.

My phone rang as I was in my own world.

"Jesus Christ!" I said jumping in fear, my cigar dropping into the Nile. I answered the phone. "You gave me a God damn heart attack"

"Mayweather has left" said Carter

"What?"

"Did you not hear me? Mayweather has left his room; I think you should look for those scrolls"

"What if he comes back?"

"He will have gone for tea. It's the right time"

"Are you sure?" I took a huge swig of Luxor Beer and stared mournfully at my cigar-less left hand. "It's now or never – Go!"

I put down the beer bottle and ran for the stairs and down to Mayweather's corridor. For the first time training finally came of some use. I jarred the key card lock on Mayweather's door and pushed. It was tougher than training and in training there was never a Greek god staring at you from the coving. What did intrigue me was the oddness of a Greek deity being on an Egyptian boat, but I digress.

I put my shoulder into the door and it swung open sending me to the floor under my own momentum. The room was the same as mine, the blinds were shut and deep shadows lurked in the corners. There was a briefcase at the side of the bed. I laid it flat on the covers and opened it pointing away, the satisfying twang of a spring loaded knife shot out.

Behind the trick knife were several tightly bound scrolls, as I took them out, the weight of history made them feel like solid granite. They were soft to the touch, but soft in a leather kind of way, it was definitely animal skin but of which I don't know.

Unfurling them did nothing to reveal there identity or purpose, there was a possibility it was Latin or some form of writing but I wasn't sure, the only thing that was certain was the two images in the centre. Small and unassuming, with a face of pure compassion and love was the archetypal Jesus Christ, and beside him a second image, a pure white throne. Such iconography was foreign to me.

I took out my phone and took quick pictures and sent them straight to Carter. I haphazardly rolled up the scrolls, put them in the case, pushed back the knife, shut the case and walked out with it feeling the adrenaline begin to pump.

I'd done it! Even the door clinked, locked and the whole situation returned to a depressing bore. I took a deep breath, walking through reception the suitcase felt like a boulder tied to my wrist. I slammed my door behind me and dropped against it with a gratifying thud. I breathed out heavily. "I got the case" I said ringing Carter.

"Excellent!" said Carter with so much enthusiasm it nearly took my ears apart, "What's inside, this could be our big break. What is it?"

"I sent you the pictures a few minutes ago, they shouldn't be long, they have some strange writing or symbols, looks like Latin but I am not sure"

"I'm just printing the pics of now" said Carter, the sound of printers just audible above the sound of Egyptian life in the background. "Hmm" she muttered, "Someone will need to take a look at this. Must be religious, the Jesus is a big giveaway"

It was difficult to listen because my eyes were starting to drift. "Have you seen the news?" she asked, "The Egyptian government are closing off Karnak and refusing foreign diplomats and scholars entry due to an amazing discovery. Must be your library"

"I'd love to talk but you don't know how tired I am"

"Oh" stunned a little, "Well we can talk later, hey maybe we should meet up after all this?"

I was already stripped and ready for bed staring into the strangely deep, darker than usual, shadows and ready for sleep.

At this very moment I took the time to not focus on what was dead ahead but to look at everything else. It was dark, but in the gloom I could make out the paintings on the walls, the shape of the settee and the TV. I could hear *everything*, the cathode ray resting, the bed springs unwinding, even the ground outside settling. I didn't know why but panic had not caught up yet, and I was enjoying this sense of freedom. Maybe this happens because when in dangerous occasions, your brain wants to remember everything; just in case it's the last thing it sees.

Because it was now that agitation and fear rifled through my body. Looking into the eyes of Mayweather, and feeling the gun he held in his hand halfway down my throat.

Shit! There was no other word for it. Shit! Shit! Shit!

"Hello old chum" then he titled his head in thought, "In fact, fuck that 'old chum' lark. Let's have this out eh? Set the cat amongst the pigeons. The carrot from the stick, you're from MI: 5, one of the new recruits because your posture is so straight I could use you as a ruler. This is your first mission, which means *they* know *I* know all agents outside of the EU. They probably caught me at border control in Cairo, damn visas! That's how they knew I was here and no doubt you have bugged my room. Do that a few hours ago eh?

I'm certain they told you how much of a bastard I am, tell you I shot old Vimesy cos he disobeyed orders, did they call me 'Butcher'? I bet they did. I was always too good for them, the bastards! I was nearly in the SES! Yeah – I thought it was rumour or myth too, but its not! It's real! The demons contact you on computers or face to face, but their so mysterious you don't know it! Ha! MI: 5, their shit! Their nothing! The SES demons have been running the world since Queen Vic; oh I've done my research! They have one guy, a legend! McCloud, thought to have died in some war but he is alive, very much so strong and..." he coughed, "But first..." he finally took a breath; it all seemed to come out in one sentence as if he was convincing himself "...I am going to take my suitcase, I'm sure you have looked inside, find anything exciting? I can't make heads nor tails of it myself. I've been told its Aramaic. Whatever that is..." one thing that stopped me from panicking was the reassurance that even if Carter was not listening intently, it would be recorded.

"...All I know is, when I hand it to that bloke Alpha, I am gunna be five million pounds up"

He pulled the gun from my mouth slowly, scraping the slide across my front teeth. My jaw ached and my mouth was dry, I could taste the gun metal. "Where is my case?"

I pointed it out. He picked it up, checked it, then put the knife back and locked it again. "Enjoy Egypt my friend. I plan to"

He pretended to tip a non-existent hat and walked out the door. I bolted for the phone…

"Stop!"

I ceased moving, frozen by the word. Where had it come from? "Wait right there, don't move"

The voice sounded familiar and then the deep shadows didn't seem as deep as they peeled apart and the black figure reached down underneath the table pulling something small out and crushing it in between his fingers. "He's bugged you. He made a lot of bold claims there, he wants to be sure"

"Who the fuck are you?" I said but I almost felt I already knew.

It wasn't just consternation now; something else was soaring through my veins. Worry! I had been watched all the time; those shadows were so deep because someone was in them. "Turn the light on, I won't hurt you"

Five thousand miles, two years and all the qualifications in the world did not prepare me for *this*. "Professor!"

I couldn't believe my bloodshot eyes. "How?"

"That's not a question I can answer yet. All I will say is that you're in way over your head"

His face was like a roadmap of wrinkles, the two years I hadn't seen him had really taken there toll. Although he had tried to teach me morality and how having an opinion was important, even in the military, I had still taken to him as my mentor. The things he taught me are actually benefiting me, the rest I'm messing up due to stress.

"I know that! I was in way over my head before I got here, can you tell me what's going on?"

"Not yet. You've seen something far more important and powerful than anything you can possibly comprehend. Just keep your head down Banner; this is far beyond anything you can grasp"

"Did you get all that!" I screamed down the phone

"What? All I heard was static. I can't understand it, nothing was malfunctioning, it just wasn't picking up"

"Shit! Shit! Shit!" I took an enormous breath and screamed, "Ex-Agent bastard!"

"He was there? In the room with you?"

"Yeah with a gun down my throat"

"What did he say?"

I told her everything. She seemed confused by the SES, as if she had never heard of them before. Nothing really added up, all we knew was someone had paid Mayweather to get and deliver these scrolls so whatever the scrolls said, was worth five million to someone. "Have we heard anything about this Alpha guy?" I asked

"Hang on" she said distantly, "I'm getting another call"

The line went dead. I pulled apart the blinds staring at the Nile and beyond past the palm trees to the desert caves cloaked in the morning dark. I prodded the shadow in the corner, just to make sure. The phone rang; "I'm sending you a package" started Carter, "Should be with you by the morning"

"What's in it?"

"A gun"

"What for?"

"You have an assassination order for Mayweather"

6AM. There was a knock at the door; I'd been too hyper to sleep, "Package sir"

I signed for it, shut the door, put the package on the bed and stared at it.

The day had flown by. The strong sun had rose and set and the night had taken hold again. Egypt didn't have as much sun as people thought, what sun it did have however was strong and would bake any person of pale complexion to a nice crisp. Because of this, it's difficult to explain why it was so cold on a night.

The gun had come with a holster which I strapped on underneath my jacket which was in use for the first time this holiday. I was waiting on the sun deck, all the other tourists went inside as the cool wind felt ten degrees lower than it actually was, but not Mayweather. He sat, in the same place, every night with the same Whisky we had had that first night.

Watching the dreamlike hues swirl along the banks, seeing camel treks through the desert, and even spotting the mini-whirlwinds of sand on the starry horizon. Mayweather saw me. I stood above; behind a railing overlooking the whole sundeck, below was the blue of the dipping pool. Hardly a necessity on a Nile Cruise I always thought. He stood up grasping his bottle of Whisky, and made his way up the stairs and stood with his back to the railings next to me.

I took one step back, pulled out the gun and aimed at his head. There was no one on deck, no screams, no frenzy, just a sea of tranquillity. It made it far more difficult, Mayweather looked composed as if used to having a gun pointed at his forehead, "Ha, you!" said Mayweather

I felt a hand rest on my shoulder and a whisper, "Keep going"

It was the professor.

"So what after this? You kill me, I will no doubt fall, and blood will fill the pool, very Hollywood, and then what? Have you really thought this through?"

He kept looking at the professor, as if expecting something, I felt for a moment as if I was in the middle of two friends seeing each other for the first time in years. My nerves didn't shred, I didn't feel as if I was going to collapse any second, for the first time I actually felt like I was doing well in my job.

"The world will be a safer place without you"

"Really?" said Mayweather "I haven't killed anyone have I? I just took a couple of souvenirs nobody remembered and will sell 'em. If I was an archaeologist I'd be a hero. Greatest discovery since Tutankhamen, a modern day Howard Carter..."

He believed it too, he believed it so much it was difficult not to believe it myself. There was so much conviction in his words.

I pushed the gun to his forehead and saw his eyes squint to focus on the barrel. Was it fear now? No. He actually smiled, through the face of death he grinned, an unimaginable grin of purpose that he had done nothing wrong and somehow everything will be okay. I followed his eyes from the barrel to my eyes, then past me. His pupils widened, his face fell, instead of that grin, there it was, at last. Fear.

"The demon...!"

He *screamed* it, turned, jumped down to the pool below with a lightning pirouette before I could even think. I didn't risk a blind shot, what could make a calm man turn so fast? "Was that you Professor?"

The Professor flew forward head first into the railing.

"No... it was me!"

I span round as if on a pivot, swung my gun round at chest height and before I could do anything my mystery assailant had pulled the slide clean from my pistol. It all happened within a second. I threw a fist, it was as if I was in slow motion and my assailant was in fast forward. He knew what I was going to do before *I* did. He held my fist with his hand and threw it downward. "I'm not gunna hurt you kid"

I hurled another brick like fist but he swatted it from the air like a fly. "Stop trying to fight me and listen kid. I need you to trust and come with me; you're not safe right now!"

"I know! I'm facing you!" I screamed, I thought about attempting another hit but the way he had blocked everything I had done so far was enough to put me off.

"Who the hell are you?" I said; my sense of pride shattered under the weight of his skills. The professor groaned, the swelling over one eye already starting to show.

"No time –"

He pulled me forward with so much force I felt I had left my intestines behind me; this man was like a bear! A bullet flew past, where my head had been yet within microseconds my saviour had pulled out a silenced pistol and returned fire. He yanked me with him, toward the bow, "Are we jumping?" I asked him

"Are you kidding kid!" he shouted back, "I'd get leprosy jumping in there!"

There was a hatch on the floor, built to be a fire exit. It bugged me that I hadn't noticed it before. The following was like a blur, weaving in and out of the steel ventricles of the boat. Finally we came to air, albeit stagnant warm air and the man quickly stuffed me into what, in the dark, looked like an old beat up Land Rover. The engine started with a splutter, "Where are you taking me?"

"We've got a plane to catch, in Cairo, you know too much, if you go back to MI: 5 now they will kill you. Your only choice is to disappear completely, and do what you should have done two years ago"

It clicked together like a jigsaw. Parts of the puzzle in front of me sat still and faded together like the lights of the cars zipping by us in a trail of white on black. My computer two years ago, Mayweather's demonic ramblings and now this guy. The most highly trained individual I had ever seen.

"You're the SES"

"Who told you about *them*?"

"My professor, the guy you just hit"

"Don't worry bout him, he was gunna kill you anyway!"

"What!" stricken with abhor, "He wouldn't, what possible reas—"

"You know too much kid. About the scrolls, as soon as you killed Mayweather, your professor was gunna kill you. The MI: 5 top brass won't let an amateur like you know anything like this; you've served your purpose"

A realisation thumped me hard, "We gotta get Carter before we go!"

"No way kid"

"But she is in this with me! If you're saying there going to kill me, that means they will kill her, doesn't it?"

"Has she seen the scrolls?"

"I sent her copies of em!"

"Shit!" he said padding his pockets before bringing out a phone. "Come on, fucking pick up... Bingham! The kids sent copies of the scrolls to his partner in Cairo, we need to get her out but we haven't enough room on the plane... yeah... yeah... right" he put the phone back in his pocket, "Okay kid we are getting your partner. Where is she?"

"The Four Seasons"

"Nile Plaza?"

"I think so?"

"Then I suggest you get your head down, it's a four hundred mile drive"

I woke with a jump. It was still dark but in the distance it was possible to see the slightest glimmer of the raising sun. I never quite took in just how beautiful this country was driving past stretches of green fields, houses built on top of houses, the Nile sweeping off into the horizon. Splashes of pools, used to water the fields further off were scattered among the greenery and the odd donkey sat waiting for the sun to rise yawned and wheezed. There was something very biblical about this place.

"Hey kid, if you need some water there are a couple of bottles in the back. And some food, I could only get some crisps, it was the only thing sealed"

I took some time to study him as the light slowly crept across a wizened face. It was a scraggy beard; left to grow wild on what I think was a stark and aggressive chin. There were a lot of lines on his face, defining a harsh set of cheek bones and a Roman nose, and long shaggy hair pulled back with little care and looked like it hadn't been washed in weeks, maybe months. It was now that I noticed his left arm, the one closest the window and furthest away from me, was heavily bandaged. "You alright kid?"

His voice was like a chainsaw, or as if his voice box had been pulled from his throat, dragged across a dirt track attached to a rally car, and then put back in. "Yeah… what happened to your arm?"

"Oh" he said looking at it briefly, "That… that kid is age creeping up on you"

"How old are you?"

He scratched his beard in thought, his voice also had an accent, I was no good at accents but I think it was Yorkshire. "Y'know kid I don't know, I think I'm forty six now.   And I'm strapped up cos of Rheumatism, bloody shoulder and elbow kills in the morning. Think my doc said it was tendinopathy but I can't remember"

"Sounds painful"

"It is… just something to do with my tendons or my muscles. I just try to ignore it now"

The road ahead of us just kept going as the Land Rover seemed determined to head butt the horizon. The ride was bumpy but above all it was the most uncomfortable seat I had ever sat on, I squirmed a little and the man turned to me. "We will get out for a walk around in a minute, these seats are a pain in the arse but you can't beat an old fashioned Land Rover for cutting across the country"

Two hours later and the sun had risen to a point that everything was clear and bright, an orange glow lending itself to the water pools scattered across the landscape. Farmers began attending to their sweeping fields, and donkeys screaming at the top of their rather irritating voices. We stood by the roadside, or what you could call a road anyway, it was more of a dirt path widened to accommodate two cars. I pulled out my lighter and stared at it depressingly, I really wish I had some cigars. "Oh thank god for that! It didn't say you smoked on your file…" he said reaching into the Land Rover through the window, pulling out two… *cigars*! "…You want one?"

"Oh god yes!"

"I lost my lighter a week ago, I've been dying for one and probably why I hit your professor as hard as I did, those withdrawal symptoms make you do some crazy things. I tried smoking a banana leaf two days ago"

I lit his cigar and then lit my own and then I felt the urge to ask the question. "What is on the scrolls?"

He physically sagged. Then took a really long drag on the cigar and blew out, somehow the world bent in around him, silhouetting him in a perfect hue, behind him the giant orange sun surrounding him like a protective orb. "I'll be honest kid, I don't know"

"*You* don't know? How do you know they are so important? How do you know they will kill us all?"

"It's something to do with that scroll you found under Karnak kid. There is something on that manuscript they don't want you to know"

"What's it all about though? I don't get it? Why kill for what's written down?"

"That's like asking the reason for most wars kid. There is a way in to that library from a tunnel in Luxor Temple; it's a long walk but a lot safer than the way you took. I think Mayweather wanted to make sure that it was discovered at last, it stops anyone else going in there now." He knows Mayweather? "Stops the likes of me and you from snooping about, trying to find answers, it will be the most secure place in the world right now. I tried to go back to Karnak but it was sealed up good and tight, I think this is where your Alpha bloke will come into it. I think whoever this guy is, he knows about the scrolls and wants them for himself. For what purpose, I don't know, until we can fathom out what the hell they mean"

"That still doesn't explain why they would kill me!"

"Doesn't it? Listen kid, whatever is on those scrolls is worth five million pounds to this Alpha bloke and the MI: 5, well, I think they know more than there letting on. They wouldn't follow Mayweather without a damn good reason; they wouldn't send you in for the sake of sending you in"

"But why kill me?"

"Jesus Christ kid! Why do you think I put that scrambler on your room when that bastard Mayweather was there with you? So the MI: 5 wouldn't hear any of it, that's why! They will kill you because you know something nobody else in the world except for one or two people know. You have seen information that somebody out there wants to get to the world! And MI: 5 can't let that happen because they know what it will do. There not evil in this, but they will kill you to protect this information. I don't want that, I wanna find out what the fuck this thing is and end it and you can help. All I can be thankful for is that the bloody Americans aren't in on this yet, if they got involved we would all be up shit creek"

"But I don't know what it means!"

"No but you saw the symbols didn't you?"

I couldn't deny it. I did. Several times in the library and in the scrolls, a white throne. He was right. "What is it that is so important?"

"I don't know kid, I wish I knew. All we have is what we managed to steal from MI: 5, *'And I saw a great white throne, and him that sat on it, from whose face the earth and the heaven fled away; and there was found no place for them. And I saw the dead, small and great, stand before God; and the books were opened: and another book was opened, which is the book of life: and the dead were judged out of those things which were written in the books, according to their works'*

What that means I don't know yet. That's why we need to get back to England and find out. The MI: 5 think it was something to do with the bible, and being written in Aramaic supported it, as it was the language they used around the same time as the supposed birth of Jesus Christ"

"So it proves the existence of God?" I said, "That would explain why they want to keep it secret doesn't it?"

"Yeah, I know" he said, "That's what I thought too. Putting this out in the public, the idea that Jesus Christ and God actually existed would bring the crusades back. Catholics and Christians on one team and all other religions on the other. It would be a Holy War to end all Holy Wars. Proof that there is only one religion would not go down well in the Muslim and Islam communities"

He was right. This information was worth killing for. A small number of deaths to prevent millions. It would discredit every other holy book, defy all other religious monuments, turn religion into myth over night and suddenly you have a reason for mass war. Faith is so strong that it causes wars that sometimes don't end, culture and religion go hand in hand; imagine telling the Indians that the cow they have been keeping sacred for thousands of years is about as sacred as a mosquito. "C'mon kid. I know it's a lot to take in, hopefully when we find out what the hell that library is, it will open up a few doors for us"

It was five hours later and we finally started to come into Cairo, the city that never sleeps. It filtered through the streets like a disease, spreading out into the country bit by bit taking lane by lane and road by road. Its how most big cities become big but to see it in progress is a strange sight, it's like seeing a virus multiply through a microscope but on a much bigger scale.

He pulled up next to a bridge and turned to me, the blinding sun surrounding his head like a halo. "Round the corner is the hotel. I don't know what to expect, I am hoping he will be safe and sound but if we find nothing, we have to accept they are dead and move on, okay?"

"It's a she… and she won't be dead, she wouldn't let herself die"

"You really care for her don't you?"

"Wha-? I don't know what you mean; she's my partner that's all"

"Yeah"

We made our way over what the sign said was Kasr El Nil Bridge, a wave of smog hovered over the air and for the first time I noticed just how bad the pollution here was. It was so bad it was difficult to make out the Opera House that my mystery partner had pointed out to his left. At the end of the bridge where huge buildings, on the left was the Egyptian Museum, sat amongst the throng with pomp and circumstance and to the right a Garden City, as it called itself. It's not what the English would call a garden.

Beyond it though, on Corniche El Nil, sat the Four Seasons Hotel. It stood, loud and egotistical, behind the Nile in front of it. Small water fountains planted in the Nile dancing around the hotel; if it was a human you would say that it had an inferiority complex. It was a beautiful hotel, there was no doubt of that and I am sure that everything about it is luxurious and smart but there was something so typically American about it, it seemed to be screaming at the world, look at me!

"Ready kid?"

"Yeah I guess"

"Are you ready?" he said. It wasn't an invitation to say 'maybe' or 'I guess', I had to mean it.

"Yeah I am"

"Right then. Good luck kid, I'll meet you at her room"

"What? Aren't we going in together?"

"Dressed like this kid, you gotta be kidding me; at least you look like you've come from England. I look like I've lived in Siberia for a couple of years"

"Well I wasn't going to say anything…"

"Funny kid. I'll see you in your partner's room. Just be careful"

He jumped out and I lost him only seconds later in the crowds. He was good, whoever he was. I stared up at the hotel; suddenly it felt a lot more daunting than it did a few minutes ago. I shut the Land Rover door, and stared up at the cameras that glared rather purposefully at the entrance, this was more like it! This felt like a mission, this had the hallmarks of a rescue mission; I used to love these in training! I straightened my jacket up as much as I could, I had a feeling I had wet patches under my armpits and a strong suspicion I may be on the smelly side but confidence was everything. You appear confident and people buy it, the professor taught me that...

I pushed through the giant entrance doors and into the splendorous hall that was the reception. There was a firm scheme of cream, vanilla and pine that hinted in everything that ordained the area, tables and chairs were sat neatly in the segregated area below the two winding staircases leading to a set of lifts. It was busy, staff were running around trying to keep tags on everything and you got the feeling very quickly that this place never stopped. It was almost alive; the reception was the heart of the hotel, pumping the staff around its ventricles and through its veins. It was then that my eyes cast over the marble floor and the giant mosaic that sat, spread-eagled and awake with a malevolent look of anguish, a picture of Nefatiti.

My mind shifted up a gear as I strode toward the reception. First rule of training, move the obstacle with a question. There was a register on the front of the desk, if I could find Carters name, it would tell me her room number and all would be fine! Yeah!

Move the obstacle with a question.

"May I'z elp you zir?" said the receptionist gowned in red.

Move the obstacle with a question!

"Erm..."

Move the obstacle with a question, damn it!

He looked at me squarely, and then smiled gently; there was something strangely un-Egyptian about him. Like my tour guide was definitely Egyptian, this man definitely wasn't. "Erm...I'd like to see your manager" I said, I could feel the sweat and the stench of fear seeping through my pores.

"X'zcuse me one momentz then zir"

He lurched into the back. I swung the ledger around to me and leafed through the register as quickly as I could, scanning the pages for Carter. It quickly dawned that there was no way they would book her in as Carter, shit! But there was a Jennifer Meak staying here, room 405. Meak... an ex-boyfriend huh?

I made my way to the staircase quickly, not looking back until I was stood in the lift starting down at the reception seeing the receptionist arrive with a confused looking manager. Phew! That was hard. As soon as it came to it, my brain emptied. Nothing but a blank field of wilderness and the odd tumbleweed scattered by. I was beginning to comprehend that training meant absolutely nothing.

I realised quite quickly that this floor was more than I expected. This was because it was a Royal Suite floor. Vanilla colouring ran down the corridor, highlighted by the royal red carpet and chandeliers that glistened in the wall light.

403... 404... 405. I knocked on the door and didn't know what to expect.

The top lock clicked open.

I mean, what if she hits me for jeopardising the whole mission because of some random man coming out of nowhere and telling me everything we have done has been for nothing but our own deaths. How would I feel?

The middle lock clicked open.

I'd feel bloody confused. I know that, but I'm sure if I explained everything to her, she would understand, I mean I'm saving her life. If what that man said was true anyway...

The bottom lock clicked and the door opened.

There she stood, slightly thinner than last time I saw her with a look of pure surprise and bewilderment. It was possible to tell that she had not left the room for a few days, not just because of the trays of food behind her but from the rough and ready look that she had adopted. "What the..."

I pushed her inside and shut the door behind me. I went straight for the bathroom, under the bed, poked in all the dark spots and all the hiding places, I didn't want anybody in here who shouldn't be here. All the while behind me I heard Carter, "What the hell are you doing... you should be in Luxor... what happened the Mayweather... why haven't you said anything in your room... well that's obvious really... why didn't you phone me... I've been so worried about you..."

It was then that I felt her arms wrap around my back and hug. I didn't know what to do, I just stood still for a moment, enjoying the touch of affection and then turned to her as she brushed aside a tear. Then slap me.

"You could've rang and told me you were on your way here!" she shouted, "I thought me and the agent they were sending were going to pick you up!"

"Agent they were sending? When?"

It was as if Hollywood had written the script. The knock was loud and the door opened, in walked the professor with a grin of iron. A purple eye stared at me and Carter as the world slowed down, I gazed at his hand reach into his jacket and removed a pistol. All I could do was grab Carter and go to ground as the noise erupted around us. The sound of smashing glass and the harsh raw power of a bullet muzzle, it was like an explosion in my ear drum, the scream of Carter and the feeling of pain rifling through my body. I could feel the hot lead singe and wiggle through.

A hand took my own and pulled me with surprising force to my feet. "C'mon kid, we gotta get the hell out of here now!"

I looked down at the dead body of the professor and felt my torso and the small graze where the bullet had scratched the surface. He spun me round to take a look, "Phew, another second and you'd have been dead" he said casually, all the while throwing something underneath the computer equipment that Carter had been using. Then scanning the room, seemed to find what he was looking for, a long thin tube.

"How –?"

"Through the window, set up a bungee up top and swung down, glad I got the right room… now *come on!*"

I led Carter to her feet as she gawped into my eyes. "I know this is weird. But you have to trust me…" I said to her feeling I couldn't even trust myself never mind ask somebody else to.

She nodded through a sting of emotion and we stormed out of the room. A gun shot echoed from down the corridor, more agents were after us; my mystery friend pushed us back in the room and used the doorframe for cover. He span out, ducked, rolled and shot all within seconds and pulled himself back up, beckoning us to follow him. We did, it wasn't as if we had a choice right now.

We charged down the corridor. A padlock on the fire exit was blown away and we flew head first down a flight of stone steps. We picked ourselves up, charged down in a blur of panic and consternation; it was no longer scary or fearful but emotional and filled with aura. It felt as if we were both coming out of a coma, the world was brighter and instead of seeing darks we could only see lights. Outside, the afternoon sun smashed against us, the Land Rover sat waiting and without chase we ploughed on, heading for Cairo airport.

There was peace for a few minutes. He had lit a cigar and held it outside the window with his left arm, occasionally wincing from the pain his rheumatism was giving him. Nobody had followed us. I wasn't as surprised by this as I would have been in any normal situation but the explosion from the hotel was probably enough to keep everyone who was caught in the area, in the area.

Carter was curled up on my knee, arms around my neck and legs tucked in, like an adult baby. She had cried a little, but it was sporadic crying, the kind you do when you don't know what you should be doing because you have never been in this situation before. She looked up at me, and asked the question that I had been wondering since I first met him. "Who is he?"

"I'm assuming you mean me love. Just call me... Wolf for now"

Wolf? "Why did my room explode?"

"Because I threw a small charge underneath all your stuff"

"And why did you do that?"

"Because if I didn't, then the MI: 5 and whoever else was there might have found that information and used it. All I needed was that..." he said pointing to the long tube he threw in the back, "...now we have that we can start to decipher it"

"But we work for MI: 5! Don't we?"

"The man who just knocked on your door was going to kill you. MI: 5 want you dead. You and Banner here know way too much about this scroll, these are the most important discoveries made in the last thousand years. There is a chance that they could prove the existence of Jesus Christ and God himself"

She smiled, and then laughed. It didn't last long as Wolf's serious face didn't flinch. "What you're serious? Don't tell me you believe this rubbish Banner?"

I didn't move. I didn't look away, anxiety dashed through my body but I still managed to say, "Everything he has said so far is true. It all links, he has saved my life more than enough times now. MI: 5 want to kill us"

"But we don't know anything! We don't know what those scroll mean!"

"You both saw the symbols on the scroll" said Wolf, "With a little digging you both would quite easily find out it is something to do with Jesus Christ and God. You both know it was written in Aramaic, linking back to AD and especially that area of Bethlehem. You both know the government have hold of copies of a document that could have been written by Jesus Christ"

"I think I remember seeing a film once about the lost gospel of Jesus?"

"This isn't a gospel... as much as its cliché... this is much worse. I think this proves something much more than Jesus, I just don't know what"

Carter sat in silence for a while and Wolf seemed to enjoy it. He smoked the cigar like someone who needed a bit of stress relief; it was hard to believe he was forty six, but right now, there was a lot I was finding hard to believe.

CHAPTER 4
IT'S NEVER THAT EASY

I had been told to relax, and this was a very difficult thing to do when you are squashed between a surprisingly bulky Yorkshire man and an unsurprisingly bulky woman who you had just risked your life to save without knowing why. As it was, it was exactly the same plane as I had flown over in; it just felt this time that I had less room. Wolf was at the right of me next to the gangway, and Carter stared out into the quickly dimming landscape. Right now, the only thought that ran across the back of my eyes was, 'Five hours of this?'

What genuinely surprised me was Wolf. He looked like a scruff and yet nobody said a word to him, nobody searched him; they just let him through at the terminals. He had an aura; it was the only way to explain it. It surrounded him and made people think they had stepped on his toes when they were only a few feet away from him. He was an immense man, he had muscles, but not in a body builder perfect peck sort of way. His muscle was real, like a quarry worker who throws blocks of stone around all day and then wonders why all those weightlifters struggle with lifting those little weights on the TV. I couldn't remember now if he worked for the SES, he hadn't confirmed it had he? He just asked me how I had heard of them; Wolf seemed to know a lot more than he was letting on.

So… the days unfolded in front of me like a newspaper, flicking through the pages of information (Not a tabloid paper then) and glaring at the facts. What had happened so far? My old professor works for MI: 5, *worked* for MI: 5, and was sent to watch me and to eliminate me depending on what I found out from Mayweather who is a mercenary agent doing odd jobs for serious cash. If I found out anything to do with this hidden library or this silly religious stuff, I was to be killed. What possibly can be so damn important to the MI: 5? Even if it was evidence that Jesus Christ lived, could it really cause so much controversy, is the world so devoid of religion nowadays that we don't really want to know if it really happened? If that's the case, isn't all religion simply mythology, and if that's true why do we persecute people who challenge the idea of religion? People like Greg Graffin, Keith Ward, Edward Taylor and Emile Durkheim who are oft criticized for their views when really it's just commentating on mythology like any scholar of Greek or Roman or even Celtic mythology. There were so many pieces missing, Wolf had all the corners, and probably all the edge pieces too, I just wish he would tell me.

Instead he just sat there, staring at the TV screen watching Top Gear sat in the middle of the gangway and occasionally groaning at the people walking past blocking his view and knocking his arm. One thing about him that did scare me was the obvious anger being permanently held back, ready to be unleashed on some helpless person. Actually, staring at him and seeing just how good he was, made me far less fearful of getting old, I had previously been quite a chronophobic but seeing just how impressive Wolf was, was a reassuring sign that age is not the end.

"I've never seen that before" said Carter almost out of the blue. "I thought they had to be so far apart"

"What's that?"

I looked over and stared at the blinking lights in the clouds ahead. It was another plane, I turned to Wolf but he was already gone.

"Oh shit!" was the only thing I could say, "They don't want us to get back to England, why is it never that easy! Wait here"

I got up and followed the line of amazed passengers who were shocked at something, possibly the sight of a steaming Yorkshire man flying through them with a careless disregard for whoever he knocked over on the way. The cockpit door was wide open with several air stewardesses stood hovering round the joystick. Wolf was stood, arms stretched out, giant shoulders hunched up while he rested on the centre console. "What's the score?" I asked

"There is no Captain, no assistant. The planes being controlled by remote, which means we are in deep shit kid" he said turning,

"What do we do?"

"Prepare to be boarded" he said storming out of the cockpit and pulling apart cupboards used by the air stewards. I looked around the cockpit, blinking lights, dials flailing and switches and levers meant absolutely nothing to me. The only thing I did recognise was a simple flashing light with a sound wave symbol, it just stood there amongst all the others, patient and willing to be used. I pressed it.

"*Ah. At last, someone has discovered the loud speaker. I did think momentarily that the crew would never uncover it. Good evening gents…*"

I turned to Wolf who had stopped rifling through the cupboards and was listening intently. "*Now let me guess who is on the plane that I need to worry about. There will be Jonathan Banner, just been brought into the MI: 5 am I right? I thought so; no doubt you will have left your partner at her seat, the strangely attractive Rose Carter. Now, there will be another won't they. A man I am so looking forward to meet…*"

Wolf looked at me, and then out of the window at the plane that had come very close. From where I was I am sure I could make out a door opening. *"Would any of you do me a favour? Please open your cabin door, do not panic, the pressure will not be lost. We have a highly technological bridge coming your way. Just please make sure your passengers are well away, we do not want any civilian casualties do we?"*

"Who are you?" I asked to the dismay of Wolf. He pulled out three parachutes from the cupboards and put them on the floor before disappearing into the bowels of the plane. *"Ah. I am so glad someone has decided to speak. Is that you Jonathan?"*

"It's Agent Banner"

"Excellent. Here is what we want to do. We want to link our two planes Jonathan, so that you, your partner and your friend can all come on board my plane and then and only then can that plane land safely. Sound like a deal, three lives for the sake of three hundred?"

"I just want to know who I am talking to first"

"They call me Alpha, and my friend Mayweather here is dying to see you again"

Alpha. The bastard was over on that plane, so close I could touch him, the answers were all on that plane but I knew as well as Wolf that if we got on that plane, we wouldn't come off alive. Staring down the gangway I saw a flash of red, and then the idea dawned on me. "You have got to be kidding me"

"What? Hey kid, if you wanna live this is the best chance you have got"

Carter was behind him, already wearing the life jacket with a reassurance that everything was going to be okay. I suddenly felt like a wet blanket, but this was crazy! Everything about this was nuts! An expanding bridge from plane to plane was bad enough but this was almost suicide! "Look. I've seen these bridges before, if you jump and thump your legs down, the fabric tears and we escape. We have a parachute each and a lifejacket each, where we land, who knows? Just for god's sake, unstrap the parachute if we are gunna hit water a couple of feet from the ground, I don't want you trapped underneath the thing. It will be a lot safer than here though, I can tell you that"

The heavy loading door swung open. There was no wind, no rush of intense raw air but just the calm tranquillity of peaceful flying. The danger suddenly sped into my head, that being, we were about to walk along a fabric thinner than hair 10,000 feet above ground, and at about

500mph. Carter looked up into my face after Wolf had passed me, "I thought you were braver than this?"

Wolf had stepped out, bouncing on the spot as if on a bouncy castle. Each step he made sent a bullet through my heart.

Carter followed.

Then I stepped out.

It was a strange feeling. It was a transparent tube, made from some sort of plastic, and held along the top by what looked like a long metal shaft. I could feel myself on the precipice of death, being tertiary to Wolf and Carter was not making things any easier and I was beginning to feel tetchy. Wolf motioned me to shut the door behind me, it was like trying to push a donkey up a flight of stairs, but eventually it gave way and shut. Ahead of us there was someone in the opposite planes doorway and it wasn't Mayweather. This man was built like Wolf. Giant like, as if he was built of different clay to that of the rest of us, a man radiating the kind of power only kings can dream of. I wouldn't forget those eyes.

"*Now!*"

I wasn't sure I had heard it because it all happened so quickly. At first it just felt like we had been hit by a blustery wind but then, it changed. It was a blustery wind in a rush, and it was in a rush because we were falling faster than any car could every dream of moving. I heard the scream of Carter before it faded away to be overtaken by the fury of the winds howl, wailing vehemence at me. The plane above us disappeared through the clouds and then, out of nowhere Wolf and Carter flew past me, parachutes launched and propping up the sky.

I pulled the cord. The zip of wind. The noise of flapping fabric and then the gentle caress of the breeze, as if I had been in and out of a hurricane within the last microseconds. There was a pop, a final gust of wind, and then I flew within an inch of Wolf and Carter. The ground was yet to appear but Carter seemed in good spirits from what I could see and even scarier was the sight of Wolf with a cigar in his mouth. The sea closed in fast, the clouds parted, Wolf and Carter flew by me without a parachute so I unbuckled and fell quickly at the deep blue, piercing the water as straight as a pencil. I emerged looking around, Carters head bobbed up. She slapped the water and screamed, "How awesome was that!?"

Wolf rose as if pushed by something from underneath the water and then seemed to be fiddling with his lifejacket. Mine and Carters were fully inflated and keeping us bobbing about in the freezing cold water, but Wolf was having trouble, blowing furiously into the tube to blow it up. He finally seemed satisfied and looked at me, he gazed at the sky for a moment and then turned back saying "I don't really like water"

There was a brief second, the kind of second that comes and goes in a blink of an eye that suggested there was the smallest element of fear. It didn't last long. Fiddling about below the waterline Wolf produced a soaking wet mobile phone. He looked at it through bright red eyes; the salt water was starting to sting. "Does that still work?" I asked

"Water proof tech, excellent contribution by the Japs"

A few seconds later his face rose in a delighted way, Carter looked at me obviously astonished. "Need a pick up Bingham... Yeah I'll explain when you pick us up... where about's? I don't know? Shouldn't my tracker say it?... I thought the Med was warmer than this, Jesus; anyway pick us up mate... See you in a few hours"

"The Med? As in the Mediterranean?" asked Carter

"Yeah" said Wolf, "We will get picked up in half an hour"

"Where are we going then?"

"Back to Albion"

It was awkward now, it had fallen through the window of adrenaline and the real world came to. England brought back many old habits, the old girl had taken so many hammerings over the years that it was starting to look like amateurish DIY. It was hard not to like her though; England was like one of those old ladies steeped in history who can tell you what it was like in the war. Normally the old ladies you call Grandma and who started their sentences with 'Back in my day...'

Right now I was sat with Carter and Wolf in a cold room surrounded by metal walls. It felt like a prison and yet Wolf was reassuring me that the holes in the wall were gently sucking and regurgitating the harder polluted Egyptian air into something that won't have us vomiting in the next twenty four hours. I don't think it helped dropping into the middle of the Med but sometimes you just have to do these things to keep reminding yourself you are an international spy, and although we were James Bond wannabes, it was still good sometimes to try. And when things get as monotonous as these, you realise just how much James Bond has been lying to you.

Two mind numbing hours later we had been led through to an office room. It reminded me very much of the MI: 5 building but this place was somehow, well, smarter. Everything was wireless, everything was cream and everything else was oak. Through the blinds and lancing sunlight, the skyline was new to me, it was less smoggy than London, the buildings were as tall but there were more mills, or what used to be mills. There was something definitely industrial about the place.

The door swung open as a flustered man, sweat forming on his brow, walked in with a laptop under his arm, he put it in front of him as he sat down. "Ah, still alive eh?" he said looking at Wolf, "Go get a shave and a shower. You look like you haven't had one in days!"

"Alreet Bob... oh and its weeks"

Then were left alone with 'Bob'. As he set up his laptop he spoke, his strong voice stank of years of good breeding. "So I heard he took you two for a swim?"

"Yeah" said Carter, "Don't reckon much to the location though"

"Just off the coast of Rhodes they picked you up wasn't it? Ah... it's booted up"

He spent a few seconds gazing wide-eyed at the screen before looking up at us with intrigue, or so it seemed. "Full names please?"

"Jonathan Henry Banner"

"Rosemary Louise Carter"

"Date of births?"

"Third of the third eighty three" I said

"Fourteenth of the eleventh, eighty two"

He squinted at the screen, padding his pockets in the vain hope of some glasses, he must have forgotten them. "Are you Jonathan Banner of Isle Close Bristol?"

"Yeah..." a record of everybody born. Impressive.

"And Miss Carter, are you the Rosemary Carter of Queen Street Plymouth, or of Gladstone Taunton?"

"Gladstone"

He flicked through what seemed like pages and pages of prompts before finally settling with a finalising dramatic tap of the mouse. "Right then!" he said, "The big question. Do you want to join?"

"Join what?" said Carter, "You haven't told us where we are yet?"

"There is a good reason for that Miss Carter which you will find the answer to shortly. I must explain the terms and conditions of your admission before you agree, is this okay?"

We both nodded our heads in a perplexed and above all suspicious way, I felt like Alice in Wonderland, deciding whether or not to find out where that damn white rabbit went. "Right, here goes. Upon your agreement you will be declared dead. You will have very little life outside of work, few friends, you will become little more than a ghost, and you will not exist. Life as you know it will no longer exist. Parents, friends, colleagues, everyone will think you were KIA in your previous adventure into Egypt. You *must* not return to your hometown for ten years, you *must* not make contact with your family; doing so will result in immediate termination. You will be trained to a level far above that which you are now, you will be tuned to perfection, your bodies will be as perfect as they can be and then allowed to evolve as you see fit. You will become subhuman; you will be elite, a perfect specimen of homo-sapiens.

Your salary compared to that of MI: 5 will double. You will be given a free, full tech, fully secure, rent excluding flat in the city. What we ask of you, is a twenty five year contract, a will to do whatever is possible, a declaration of loyalty to the crown and a signed copy of your birth certificate of which I will explain after you have agreed"

I looked at Carter who was preparing a response almost instantly. "What if we don't accept?"

"You will be shipped back to MI: 5"

"Sounds fair. Who are we joining? How do we know you aren't evil terrorists?"

"I can assure you we are not terrorists. And I can assure you even if you think our methods may sometimes be evil, we are always doing things for the greater good of England"

Double wages, a luxury flat in whatever this city was, all the training and mental stimulation I needed was sat right in front of me. Carter didn't look so sure, but I had a gut feeling that this was the same group who wanted me two years ago, the same group who hacked my computer. I don't know why I know, or how I know, it was a gut instinct.

"I'll do it" I said

I heard Carter gasp as if not expecting such a quick answer. The man known as Bob smiled gently before turning to Carter, she breathed in deep, I never noticed before just how much, erm, chest she had. "Why not"

"Right then" he said slamming the laptop shut, "Let's be on"

He led is out and around into what can only be described as a command centre. A giant screen, about the size of a house, dominated one wall with a very detailed map of the earth sprawled on the centre. Every few seconds someone would touch a part of the screen, which would zoom to that point, in crystal clear quality. Google Earth; eat your heart out.

There were ten computers, all manned, in front of the screen. The dim room was making my eyes water. It was like the first few seconds of the bright lights of a gig after being coated in darkness for the previous half hour. "This is where we run from. This is where every piece of information is gathered, processed and stored"

"Stored for what?"

"Reference"

He led us through the only other door across from where we were and into a sprawl of corridors leading left, right and straight on. "Agents like yourselves will only be able to access your own units. Except for the offices, medical bay and the equipment shed. The offices are straight on and then left, the equipment shed is straight on and right, straight on is the Action Unit"

He gave us both a key card each. "To your left is the Recon Unit and right is the Ghost Squad. Carter, you are in Recon. You will head under Ian Jordan who is Captain of the squad, your computer abilities and undeniable resilience in the face of danger will be a credit to the Unit"

He turned to me, his ghost white eyes analysing every muscle in my face, I don't know what he was looking for but he seemed to think he had found it. "You, Banner. You will be in the Ghost Squad but more commonly known around here as the Action Unit. You will take orders from… Field-Marshal McCloud"

That name! Steeped in history, from the records of what he was supposed to have done in Guatemala with the army, earning him the instant promotion to Colonel, then after the Falklands he became one of the youngest Brigadiers in the British Army before his rise to Field-Marshal and eventual KIA. Of which everyone knew wasn't true, he was immortal!

The door to our left parted in the middle like on the Starship Enterprise, I can't believe they have things like this that actually exist. From the parted doors lay exactly a parted fringe, childhood curtains still clinging on to a man who looked in his early thirties.

It must have been that which left the bad impression because the rest of his was fairly inoffensive. He just looked like a little boy with wrinkles. He walked over, his fingertips locked together, with a gentle sense that the whole world was surrounding him and could wait for him to walk over. "Ahh. Is this my new recruit?" he said, eyes like needles lanced at Carter.

"Yes, this is Private Carter"

"So excellent to meet you. I am Ian Jordan. Captain of Recon and Information. If you will?"

He gestured Carter forward, his presence surrounding her like Dracula's cape.

Then they were gone.

It was so sudden, even though she was behind some tacky parting doors I felt like she was gone forever, at the other side of the world. It felt like a movie cliché, I wanted to put my palm on the door and find she was doing the same on the other side. Did I miss her already? No, it must have been that we had been through a lot together the past couple of days. That was it. I don't like girls that big anyway! Psshh, I could go to any nightclub anywhere and pull any gorgeous girl, Carter was no oil painting, and yet…

I didn't know what to expect when he led me through to the 'Action Unit', I still didn't quite understand everything what had transpired, although the first thing I noticed was the no-nonsense of the doors. Recon had parting doors; this Unit had a barricade of steel and metal and screamed at the world to try its luck.

I swiped the key card like he asked and a retina scanner slid out of the metal. He motioned me toward it and it read my eye, the door opened and I stepped inside. "This is where I leave you, it was a pleasure…" he said shaking my hand, "I have no doubt I will never see you again"

The mass of metal slammed shut narrowly avoiding our hands and then he had gone too. I was alone, I felt naked, as if I had been born into a new world kicking and screaming. There was a faint hint of blue everywhere, a hue emanating from every corner and it was only now that I heard the fans, high above, enormous industrial fans, each the size of elephants, being dwarfed by the size of the room.

This was like a factory, it must have been a warehouse at some point, it all seemed so used, and the bright red girders holding up the roof were a big giveaway. "I'm glad you signed up," said a voice that echoed around, it was hauntingly familiar. "Welcome to the SES kid"

Then as if by magic he was stood in the middle of the room, his arms stretched out wide; a glaring sense of pride on his clean shaven chin, his hair cut short with a stylish gel spike at the front. "Wolf?" I said, "You're in the Action Unit too?"

"Yeah kid" he looked around, "Come stand here and watch"

As I stood next to him I could feel eyes following me and when I stood next to Wolf I couldn't believe what I was seeing. In front of me were at least twenty men, all camouflaged into the wall, from one angle completely hidden, the next angle as visible as a whale in a bathtub. "The SES is the best in the business. We don't take shit, we deal out a lot of shit and if we can't do the job then nobody else can"

"The SES?"

"Yeah. You made it kid"

The rest of the Unit stood down and waited in a line, disciplined and standing to attention like the terracotta army. "At ease lads" he said, "Get your sens home, I'll see you int morning"

The group left after some contented mumblings leaving me and Wolf in the room. There was an awkward silence cut short by Wolf flicking a lighter shut after his cigar flared up, "I would offer you one but you're not allowed to smoke in here"

"Won't Field-Marshal..." I revelled in the name. I was working for a living legend, an English hero, a man feared by even the greatest of villains and heroes alike "...McCloud be annoyed?"

He puffed out a bellow of smoke saying, "Come on. I'll introduce you"

It was a small office at the back of the factory floor containing a simple table with a very luxurious chair behind it. There was no one here, just the soft eyes of a middle aged woman in a photograph on a table. It looked like it hadn't been touched for months. "McCloud has two offices, this one here he never uses and one in the offices he never uses"

"Doesn't he even have a computer?"

"His assistant Bingham- Steve Bingham does all the computer work. McCloud just likes to be in the field, feeling the wind in his face..." he looked up staring at the ceiling but from Wolf's eyes, I bet it was something much more, "... feeling gods grace float across his skin, becoming one with nature... ahh... I miss it..."

His face flashed back from his reverie to the present and for a few minutes all I could hear was the slow burn of the cigar in Wolf's hand. Then he started, "The SES, or (S)ecret (E)nglish (S)ervice was formed in 1887 shortly after the assassination attempt of Queen Victoria on her Golden Jubilee. Back then, it was a secret group of police who worked solely for the Queen, cleaning up situations that have thankfully never seen the light of day. It hasn't all been plain sailing; we had an opportunity to assassinate Hitler in 38' and didn't take it. We had Saddam in chains in 89'"

"What about Bin Laden? Nobodies caught him yet?" I ventured

"That's because he doesn't exist kid. America needed someone it could hate, something for the public to despise, so they created a lie. Now it's a myth, who'd know?"

Now I had been in the room a little longer I could take in the little details (Or lack of), the layer of dust caressing the table, the bin with nothing in it, no paperwork anywhere. "I know what your thinking kid. Its all bullshit, nothing like this can exist without people knowing, blah blah! But it does! It's far more real than anything you can imagine. The Queen is our boss, and when she goes a convenient letter will find itself on the Princes lap. We survive because without us, its chaos!"

There wasn't even a clock! "Why me?"

"Because I don't like MI: 5 killing its members to preserve there information. It's a huge waste of time and effort. Plus I've wanted a new recruit for some time"

"So it wasn't because I was special or anything?"

"There are no special agents. Just good and bad ones, there are no heroes. War is not a glorious thing and even if you win, sometimes the sacrifice you make means you may as well have lost"

There was something about Wolf that made him endearing but right now it was impossible to find. Every achievement by this country he had managed to make seem wrong in one sentence and there it was; a pang of realisation, he was talking morals! Something I never wanted to have, something I didn't think a good soldier needed, looks like I was wrong, again!

Wolf sat down in the chair and flicked the cigar into the bin with a satisfying ping. "Three reasons you're in the SES. 1, you're English, only English born men and women can be appointed. 2, you trailed an excellent agent for days on your first mission with few nerves and thirdly…" he stood up, rested a giant hand on each shoulder and said, "…you know a lot more about the hidden library and those scrolls, and that's what we are going to investigate"

CHAPTER 5
THE TEMPLAR CONNECTION

There seemed to be a quiet emphasis on simplicity here at the SES building. Rooms were fairly sparse, and typically followed a pattern of magnolia walls with what Wolf had said was 'sunburst-orange' swirls, the effect wasn't what the designer had in mind. Apparently, it was conceived to bring the best out of people in each room, colours to inspire and cheer up, I just wanted to vomit. This room was no exception, and carried on the garish tradition to the letter, the only difference being the small rubber plant in the corner.

I'd been here for near three hours now sat with Steve. Wolf had told me that Steven Bingham was integral and that he will one day inherit the SES, but for now he was simply Wolf's assistant. He was the brains behind Wolf's brawn and yet on first look you wouldn't have thought it. Where as Wolf had the impression of working strength, the kind you get naturally inherited from your father who worked in quarries, Bingham was definitely a man made build, the kind who are born pumping iron. Even beneath his shirt and tie he rippled with a muscular superiority.

"642AD?" he said

"Yeah, that's when she said the scrolls were moved there"

"Hmm"

I had filled Steven in on the entire trip to Luxor, explaining the conversation I couldn't quite catch on my phone, the talks at dinner, how scared I was and more importantly the actual raid on the hidden library itself. He had told me they were aware of something being beneath Luxor but was quite happy to leave it there as it was doing nobody any harm. I was amazed at how much was actually hidden and monitored by this group of people, so far I'd head counted no more than thirty and it seemed like half the world was under there protection, it was quite stunning.

Bingham was sat opposite me with a laptop. We had named the whole thing Operation Luxor, simple but accurate. Steve had told me point blank that they had no idea what was going on, that as far as they were aware there was no motive and they were simply trying to find out who knew about the hidden temple. He had figured that whoever knew of the temple was going to be responsible for a lot of what had happened, hopefully it would work out as simple as that. As for Mayweather, he was forgotten about as a needless pawn that was going to collect five million for one days work, if we managed to catch him, it was a bonus. Steve saw me watching him, his face fixed on the laptop screen. "I'm scanning the SES database for anything relating to that year. History always seems to give good answers. We can learn a lot from history, so McCloud always says" the screen flashed up a few windows, "Hmm, there are less than I thought"

He clicked very purposefully through a selection of menus. His eyes widened, "How many scrolls were there? Were they old? Did they look old?"

There was a quiver in his voice, I could feel panic. I felt like he was gunna grab me by the shoulders and try and shake it out of me.

"Yeah they looked ancient, why?"

"I don't believe it. Do you know what it *might* be?"

In a flurry of excitement he searched for his phone padding every pocket before finally finding it, dropping it, picking it up and ringing. "McCloud! Get down here. This could be the discovery of the millennium!"

I stood side by side with Wolf. McCloud couldn't make it apparently. Both of us were gazing alarmingly at how excited Bingham was. His eyes were wide, his skin was pale and it looked like he would pass out at any moment. He looked like he had taken a shot and was now coming down, it was scary. "I think Banner has stumbled upon something, something fairly legendary"

"Go on"

"Your gunna love this..." he said looking at Wolf, "...In 642AD, a strong Muslim army led by Amr ibn al 'Aas sacked Alexandria after the Byzantine army was defeated at Heliopolis. And according to Legend, the commander asked a certain Captain Umar what to do with the famous library. He said, 'They will either contradict the Koran, in which case they are heresy, or they will agree with it, so they are superfluous'"

"Ok, that makes sense, what's that got to do with the scrolls?"

"Think about it. You're the history man!"

You could tell Bingham was enjoying this, it reeked of an assistant finally gaining the advantage over his boss, and Steve seemed determined to enjoy it. "They burned everything in Alexandria, everything to do with God, Jesus Christ, everything!"

"Are you telling me..." a cog was starting to turn rapidly in Wolf's head, "...Oh my god it can't be?"

Bingham nodded. His grin getting wider and wider as it looked like it might just separate from his face. "Are you telling me that this kid has been to the Lost Library of Alexandria?"

The grin didn't shift; I didn't quite understand the magnitude until Wolf saw my puzzled face. I wasn't aware up to that point that I was so easy to read, I didn't know what my puzzled face looked like. "The myth of what happened to the library of Alexandria is so messed up I don't think anyone else knows the truth"

"Anyone else?"

"We have something at the SES nobody else has. Something that archaeologists would probably wet themselves at the sight of. Tell him the story Steve…"

"Right then. It's a long one but here we go. In 1884 nine officers and ninety two soldiers lost their lives in the Sudan of action and disease. We know this because a small amount of men managed to break free and make it to Philae Temple where this exact message is chiselled into the side of the temple. What was also found at the site was a set of scrolls all written in Latin and brought back with the few surviving officers. Now Captain Darley and Major Atherton never knew what it was they had found. And neither did the army and when the SES was formed, the few scrolls they had brought back were given to us as our 'baby' if you will. Unfortunately at the time, we were so obsessed with the countless assassination attempts of Queen Victoria that nothing was ever done about them. In 1965 though, Mark Williamson, the old head of the SES had the case reopened and they managed to trace it to being written, we assume, by the Templars and told a story of a site somewhere in Egypt of a temple dedicated to the saved scrolls of Alexandria Library"

"Nobody knows who moved it. Or how they knew that the Muslims were gunna burn it down. And until now, we had dismissed those scrolls as myth, along with the whole story. But actually finding it… wait… when you went to the Library kid…" he said looking at me. His body language said nothing, but his voice asked as if pleading, this was strange; he wanted an answer from me that I didn't know I could give. It was as if he could crack the whole case if I said the right thing, suddenly, the weight of fifteen hundred years rested on my shoulders. "… was there a Templar cross?"

There were a few moments of buzzing silence. The buzzing from Bingham's laptop was deafening now, almost like someone had given a bee a megaphone and had focussed solely on this room. "A Templar cross? Is that the one that broadens out at the corners?"

"Yes" he said swiftly and sternly.

"Yeah, I saw one in the Library"

Something clicked in his head. It was amazing to see, the internal workings, flashing up, down, left and right before finalising on one central point that was the answer. "It all makes sense!" he screamed

"What!" shouted Bingham on the cusp of ecstasy.

"The Catholic paintings on the walls of Karnak Temple, the Templar crosses chipped into the bloody pillars! It's true! It all adds up!"

Wolf looked like he would faint at any moment. I had seen that look before, on the faces of champions, on the faces of people who had been trying all their lives at something and have now finally achieved it.

And then it sank like a concrete slab. "No wait" said Wolf, "It's too early for the Templar's. They didn't really come about till the first crusades in the 1100's. 1096 if we are being picky but ordained by the church in 1129"

"So it can't have been them" said Bingham solemnly, "But there are Templar crosses in the library! Why would a Templar cross be somewhere that has nothing to do with the Templar's?" in defiance.

"I dunno" Wolfs body language clearly taken aback, "But as much as I would love this to be yet another Templar conspiracy, it just can't be"

They both stood, coming down off the bridge of ecstasy and now riding a giant wave of disappointment. I didn't really want to chip in with anything but unfortunately I had to add my own point. "What are the Templar's?"

Wolf looked at me in disbelief before saying, "A Templar Knight is truly a fearless knight, and secure on every side, for his soul is protected by the armour of faith, just as his body is protected by the armour of steel. He is thus doubly-armed, and need fear neither demons nor men"

"They started out as a group of nine men who helped escort pilgrims to the Holy Land. However, they have become objects of mythical obsession over the years as defenders of the true teachings of Christ and guardians of the Holy Grail if you believe some modern fiction"

"So if it wasn't them…" I said, "Who was it? And who else knew of the Library, why did they want those scrolls so bad and why now?"

"C'mon kid. I've just been on the biggest high of my life and now I am being ripped off it all in the space of two minutes. I need a few minutes. In fact…" he said as if remembering something, "… I need to report to medic. We will hopefully have the results of the translation of the scrolls and after that we will meet up and discuss it all again. Bingham, get some sleep, I know you've been up all night mate. Kid, meet me at reception in a half hour. I'll show you your new home"

When Wolf had brought me through the city my industrial leanings had proved correct, as this was Leeds. Situated in the heart of Yorkshire, it had become the counties capital after a wave of incredible financial backing bringing about the headquarters of nearly all the biggest companies in the Northern Section. Leeds and its surrounding areas had become financially viable by the mills and quarries that I saw dotted around and the amount of mines and closed shafts was incredible. The city seemed to grow around its past, spreading like a virus throughout its landscape. Unfinished skyscrapers hogged the skyline away from the small businesses, men and women with suits wandered the streets passing the odd coin to the stray homeless. It was like being in London twenty years ago.

When we were on the outskirts we arrived at a smaller town called Morley that was sat around ten miles from Leeds' city centre. It was a mining town from what Wolf was telling me, built on the foundations of the old coal mines, now shut down at the north and south of the town hall. The town hall itself was fabulous. Made from sandstone from the nearby quarry and built in the early nineteen hundreds, it was positioned and dignified in a way that many other town halls had never managed. The bell struck seven times and the dusk of the day was already forming in the red skies when Wolf removed a small remote, pressed a button and pulled into a slowly opening garage.

He threw me the keys as we got out. "Here you go" he said, "Your new car"

I looked down at the keys and then at the car. Curving around the lights like a wave the chassis slithered like a snake across the wheel arches, at the back, huge chunks as if it had been battered with an axe split the bright red paint job apart. "It's a TVR Sagaris. It does the job, should I say it did the job. Before TVR went bust,"

He led me up the stairs and using a keycard swiped through each and every door before reaching what looked like his destination. "There is no lift in this apartment block. Just stairs, the reason being that a lift is easy to hide in, there are too many places for people to enter if we are ever found"

He swiped another door and walked in. It was dark, until Wolf used the remote again, and the blinds started to ascend. "Right kid" he said as I took the surrounding room in. As the red sky lanced through the blinds, the flat came to life. A long white leather sofa sat opposite a 40'inch plasma TV that was bolted to a waist high wall that itself, held a sheet of pale blue glass that separated the living room area from the kitchen. I could also hear the air conditioning kick in. "This is your flat. You are on the tenth floor, one below me. Bring who you want back but never, and I repeat *never* allow them to stay in here without you. There are cameras everywhere, hidden from you and anyone else who makes it in here. Everything is sent wirelessly back to Leeds HQ and recorded onto a hard-drive for our own records. Living room, kitchen, bedroom… I'm sure I don't have to tell you how to use anything"

I was temporarily speechless. "Oi kid" he shouted

"Huh? Yeah sorry"

"Clothes have been provided but I'm sure you would prefer to get your own. Do what you will with the clothes we have given you, there not cheap but I know they are not for everyone's taste"

"Right"

Wolf looked at me and just for a moment there was a deathly silence, broken by Wolf saying "Right then kid. That's me done. Be downstairs at 0700 and you can take me to work, I left my car back at HQ. That way I can show you were we are"

"Wait a minute. Its only just past seven, you fancy a drink?"

"Not yet kid. I only drink in Morley but I don't fancy it tonight. Its been a long day and I got some reports to write up, looks like me, you and Bingham are on this case on our own"

"Oh. What do you mean you only drink in Morley?"

"I mean what I said"

"You mean you have never drunk a few beers in say, Watford or Soho?"

"No"

"What?" I was shocked, "I'm taking you out one day"

I scanned the English northern cities and only one sprang to mind straight away. "We can go to Newcastle for a night out!"

"Right. Okay kid. Whatever you say"

And with that glimmer of sarcasm he left.

I couldn't remember the last time I was left on my own for this long. *I had made it.* That's what he had said to me. It was strange how isolated I felt now I no longer had Wolf next to me at all times. A dark desolation I had never felt before, creeping on me like a vine lingering up the side of a house and before you know, it has taken over. Was it fear? No, not fear. This was next to fear, a not so distant cousin who came to see you once a decade. It was concern, anxiety and agitation all wrapped around in a consternating bubble.

My head rose almost instinctively from my pillow and scanned the room. Eyes darting into the corners, deciphering every morsel of darkness to make sure I was not being watched. It was silly; this was the most advanced secure flat in all of England. Nobody was going to get in, and yet... the agitation came in, itching at the back of my neck. A lump in my throat the size of an apple hindered my breathing, my skin prickled and I felt a ghastly wind rush through my body before everything was nothing and blackness took me into sleep.

As we drove before dawn through the streets of Leeds we came to a high rise building seemingly made of glass. "Every window is bullet proof" said Wolf, "And mirror tinted, it's possibly the best looking safe-house in the world"

The buildings façade promoted a fictional record company called, "Hell's Records?"

"Yeah we need something to keep the truth a secret. There is even a real recording studio down in the cellar too"

Holding my key-card to the scanner it buzzed me through into a reception. The marble floor reflected the ceilings lights but most of all, shone the receptionist's reflection straight at me. Looking at her head on was no better. "Good morning Dora" said Wolf saluting theatrically.

"It's not now you're here" countered Dora, a beehive sat on her head, "I could think of much better mornings"

"It's just an expression love"

We both scanned in, and then Wolf turned back to Dora. "Oh, just keep a track of that black Lexus, registration X372 0NJ will you? I think we are being followed"

I could see the smile strain across his face from here, every one of those seventeen muscles trying to defy his mind. Sporting a gun metal grey suit, Wolf oozed the kind of masculine toughness that was almost impossible in a normal man. When he was in the field he was a gruff, rough and ready brawler, out in the real world he was a mass of cultural civilisation, I guess, the perfect operative.

As we headed up the stairs, I couldn't help but say "I didn't see a black Lexus?"

"You gotta open your eyes kid" he said to me sternly, as if passing on knowledge, "It followed us last night back to your flat as well"

At the top of the stairs Bingham stood, tapping an impatient shoe. His thin but wild black hair pulled back into a ponytail and the look of utter frustration clouded his face. "Why haven't you been answering your cell?"

"It's called a mobile Steve. How many times do I have to tell you? And I didn't answer it 'cos it was turned off. I had some news, wanted to be alone for a bit, that's all"

"Typical!" stammered Steve, "We have some news on the pictures of these manuscripts"

"Considering it was from a phone and a rush job, there is a little to go on"

"You mean you can translate it?" asked Wolf

"God no" shouted Professor Stignan, a round man shaped like an egg. He had a gap between his gleaming front teeth, it was difficult not to notice when his thin, expertly trimmed, goatee highlighted his mouth so much. "There is no doubt the text is Aramaic. But it is the symbols which have intrigued me. The text is far too blurry for us to read. Had the camera been of higher pixel standard we would have been lucky"

"Good old MI: 5" rapped Bingham

The room was very much like a surgery, but for anything except people. It was divided by a wide table at which we all stood at opposite ends staring at the pictures laid upon. Glaringly hot lamps throwing as much brilliant white light as the sun in summer.

Using an infra-red pointer he began highlighting parts of the photos, the little red dot flickering in Stignan's grasp. "All this writing is indecipherable" he said zipping the little red dot across the photos, "But this symbol in the top right, do you see it? Hidden almost?"

It was there, veiled like a small red berry in amongst a forest of black thorns, none of us had seen it. "We blew the image up several times but could not determine exactly what it is. We believe though through sheer guess work, it is a book. Or at least a symbolisation of a book. Our educated guess is it's a kind of insignia. All scrolls or books relating to this library carry this seal"

"Wait. How can you know that?" asked Wolf, "From one scroll?"

"We don't have just one" beamed Stignan suddenly brightening up, "We have it from two"

"What, which one?"

Stignan, glorifying in his moment of pleasure, followed our gazes along the infra-red path to the far wall that lit up, as if it knew we were talking about it. "The Atherton Scroll, as we call it, also bares this insignia"

"So it's all linked" said Bingham, "Ha! Who'd have thought a scroll found in 1884 would become part of this!"

"What is strange however is that the Atherton Scrolls are written in a form of Latin" said Stignan, "The Atherton Scrolls seem to be mainly bible quotes"

"Bible quotes?" stammered Wolf, "Which one?"

"Erm… I have one nearby" said Stignan scouring across desks in the darkness behind us, then he emerged reeling off the quote, '*And I saw a great white throne, and him that sat on it, from whose face the earth and the heaven fled away; and there was found no place for them. And I saw the dead, small and great, stand before God; and the books were opened: and another book was opened, which is the book of life: and the dead were judged out of those things which were written in the books, according to their works*'"

Wolf's face cracked into a smile. "The same one we intercepted from MI: 5. Seems there is a link here bigger than even we know"

"What about that though" I said, snapping myself out of a deep reverie of information, "What about that throne, it's mentioned in both scrolls now? And the depiction of Jesus? That has to mean something?"

"The 'White Throne' as it is called is the symbolisation of the kingdom of god in Christian Eschatology. The image of Jesus we think just solidifies this idea; if it *is* from the same time as the Atherton Scrolls that means it is easily in the ages of Christ, meaning it wasn't enough just to depict the White Throne because people would not understand its meaning at that time on its own. No, I believe Jesus' face is there to associate them together"

"I thought the Atherton Scroll's were written by the Templar's?"

"No. I believe this to be false now" snapped Stignan

"We need to know what it says" said Wolf, "Can't we get *someone* who can read this?"

"Its difficult sir" said Stignan, "The Vatican banned all people from trying to translate Aramaic. The Vatican themselves are the only ones able to read it"

"Are you sure?" said Bingham, the light glaring suddenly in his face, "I'm sure there must be someone?"

"I have tried once, but I shall try again" said Stignan

Wolf walked away, his arms crossed, the cogs in his head prominently turning. "You sure there is no professional in the world who can read Aramaic?"

"I can't promise you that nobody can read it. Some boffin in his garden shed can probably do it, but as for a professional who can be hired for help… not one"

"Steve, Banner" said Wolf. He said my name, he didn't call me kid. I didn't know whether to be happy or worried.

"I don't like the idea of them bastards beating us to the translation. I get the feeling this Alpha guy, whoever he is will have no problem in translating this scroll. It wouldn't surprise me if he knew what it said before it was stolen which leaves us at a great disadvantage"

"What do you want to do?" asked Bingham, seriousness carved into his face, "We don't know where Alpha is; we don't know where Mayweather is. We don't know how to translate the scroll. We are losing here…"

"There is only one thing we can do" said Wolf, "We need to get a translator"

"Oh yeah" I said, "And what are we going to do, check Google's language department?"

"Don't try sarcasm kid it doesn't suit you"

"You're thinking what I think your thinking aren't you?"

Just for a moment I needed to make sense of the sentence just said by Bingham, and then it occurred to me. "The only way to get a translator…" I said as the idea seemed to flow from Wolf's consciousness directly to mine, "…is to go to the source?"

"We need to go to The Vatican"

It's not a well known fact that the Vatican City is not just a city, but a country as well, ran by the Holy-See and headed by the Pope. What the Vatican held were the secret archives, which were not as clandestine as the Vatican would have you believe. Anybody with access to the net can view the Parchment of Chinon and have a read through Catholicism's darkest hours.

The midday Italian sun was doing its best but the cumulus was having none of it, bullying its deep and dark clouds across the looming horizon. I had never been to Italy, and stood in St. Peters Square surrounded by culture and civilisation, I could finally see what all the fuss was about.

Wolf and I were playing the typical tourist card dressed in shorts and t-shirts holding a digital camera and attempting to blend in. Urban camouflage an essential part of the SES, that's what Wolf had said. Wolf was busy snapping away, pictures of escape routes and architecture of passing tactical advantage.

Analysis can save your life, that's what Wolf had repeatedly told me on the plane across from Leeds/Bradford. I had a nervousness I hadn't felt since Egypt rise in the bowels of my stomach but was comforted by Wolf's presence. "Get anything?" I asked as the sun managed to crack a single cloud and caused me to raise an arm in shade.

"Not yet" said Wolf, "I am thinking more than looking. None of it makes sense"

"What doesn't? They would defend the Vatican well you know, you can't just think yourself in"

"No not that. This whole situation" he said resting the camera on its strap across his muscular neck, "Does it seem odd to you that we have held the Atherton Scrolls over a hundred years and the MI: 5, at this *exact* time, have sent a message to itself writing the only part of the scrolls we have actually managed to translate? Something just does not add up"

We both stared intently at the Vatican Palace through St. Peters Square and knew what we had to do. "Unless it's what MI: 5 have managed to translate from the new scroll, its just they say the same?"

We both stayed silent a moment. The dark clouds above us making me feel more hemmed in and stupid for saying something blatantly wrong. I seemed to have a real habit of coming up with stupid suggestions when my back is against the wall. Then, Wolf reached into his pocket and produced his phone. "Bingham... are you at a computer, good... check that quote on the net. I'm curious... it's what? ... Right cheers"

"What is it?"

"It's a bible quote alright" he said putting his phone back in his pocket, "Revelations 20: 11-12 apparently"

"Does that change anything?" I said feeling completely plebeian.

"I don't know yet" he said back to me, "I think as soon as we can get the bastard things translated we can stop using pure guesswork and actually make our move. Whoever Alpha is, I get the feeling he is already more than one step ahead, and I don't like it. Anyway, have you figured out how to get into the Vatican Palace yet?"

"What?" I said shifting my feet awkwardly as I felt someone brush past me in the busy Square. I looked around but only blank faces stared back in my direction, I guess it was nothing, when I looked back Wolf had gone.

Urgency flickered up. Panic stricken I looked left to right; the crowds had parted and were starting to fill in again to my right. I filtered through the last of the closing path of pedestrians but there was nothing. Nothing at all. Birds flew above me in a 'V'. The noise of people, the whisperings of conversation, it all crowded my brain. Consternation took hold of my lungs and squeezed. What had happened to Wolf, where had he gone? The lump in my throat grew to the size of a grapefruit.

Nothing but the rapturous crowds now filled the air, the smell of chestnuts hung onto the breeze; the first spots of rain began to fall. I pushed on through the crowds as they started to move out, looking for anything resembling where Wolf had gone. Then a strong hand gripped my shoulder and it dragged me through a few people bumping through the Italians with a satisfactory elbow. Wolf looked at me through happy eyes, "Are you ready?"

"What?"

"*Are you ready?*"

"For what?"

"Follow me"

He pushed past the last of the crowding members of public and jostled into a small café that was sat behind the square. Winking at the waiter on the counter we sauntered into the back area and with an ease that suggested much planning in the few minutes that he had abandoned me, pulled down a ladder on rollers and began to climb. "How did you know?" I said

"Know what?"

"About these ladders?"

"I didn't. I just had a look around, it's amazing what you can find when you actually look"

We eventually made it to the top of the deceivingly long ladders and crawled along a narrow crawlspace. Ahead of us was a small circular window rimmed with delicate and precise woodwork. "See that?"

"See what?" I said

Then I traced his finger along his line of sight and saw, as tiny as a fly, a claw protruding from the Vatican Palace. It was as if it was left for us. "It's a way in"

"It's an old satellite hook?" I said managing to squint it into shape.

"To you its an old satellite hook, but you know what it is to me kid?"

"Do tell…"

"It's a shining hook of hope"

And then the rain came down, heavy as hell, filled with sleet and hardened with fury, it was as if the weather knew what we were to do.

Bingham had sent us over the equipment that Wolf had ordered from the SES. I still didn't know exactly how this was going to go but in all honesty I don't think Wolf did either. I wish I could know more about him, where he came from and what it was that inspired him to be who he was, to gain the skills he possessed, to somehow be the best there was. Until I met this McCloud that is.

We had set ourselves up in a small hotel just outside the Vatican City itself. Night was approaching and had brought the rain with it. Angry thunderclouds, deep and nightmarish hovered with the tenacity of a mischievous god. I understand now why the Greeks and Romans invented such fabrications; the sight of these clouds would be enough to sway even the most fervent of non-believers.

A flash of lightning lit the hotel room. Wolf gazing into the steel trunk, it was as if he knew that I was staring at him. "What?"

"Oh, nothing"

He held up what looked like a pistol with a grapple on the front, and that's exactly what it was. Night vision goggles with several switches for different effects, some flares and some extra ammunition got thrown onto the bed, he gave me the slightest of glances, "You sure you up for this?" he asked me

The beginning of the mission, fear drumming on my chest, anxiety rising out of the depths of my stomach into an apple sized lump in my throat. The perils of Egypt once again danced along my eyes bringing back the full terror, only the sweet smell of tobacco slipping between Wolf's lips brought me from my reverie. "Yeah, I'm up for it"

He flashed me a wan smile. "Here" he said handing me a cigar, "For victory" he said lighting it. "I thought you were supposed to celebrate with cigars *after* you've won?"

"That's an American tradition. You know how backwards they are"

Up on the roof of the café on the outskirts of St. Peters Square I felt at the mercy of the gods and their tormenting skies. Raising the grappling gun, Wolf took aim and then moving with every different gust of wind, he fired as the grapple whistled through the air finally clamping onto the satellite hook. "Lucky shot..."

"Yeah"

He pulled the rope taught, and wrapped it to a long ago sawn off piece of washing line pole. "Your gloves will protect you. Don't worry about the smoke, its natural"

"Smoking?"

Falling backwards off the edge of the building he disappeared into the darkness with the taught rope flexing and bending with his weight. The wire made that noise, only made by metal when it is wobbled in such a way, as the cable finally restored to its original shape. He had made it.

I knelt down. Gripped the wire, held hard as gravity took hold of me swinging me around and then without any warning or caution, I began sliding down. The landing was not graceful in the slightest, as I hit the ground with a thump I felt Wolf drag me up one handed on to my feet as we slammed our backs against the wall of the palace.

A flash of lightning lit Wolf up like a streak of wet leather. The sneaking suits we had been issued with in our accoutrements felt foreign, tight on the torso but easy to move in, the rain made us squeak. The rattle of a paint can echoed in the rain as we sidled along the outer wall and Wolf sprayed a smartly concealed camera I myself had failed to notice.

Wolf had told me that, where we were, was the least guarded part of the Vatican. He had also said, there were only two or three guards in this area, as if this was not going to be a problem. I followed Wolf around the corner of the building, the rain smashing against us, lightning streaks randomly illuminating us up like fireflies. Ahead of us the palace laid, its giant red doors gaping wide like the mouth of a satanic beast. The nightmarish clouds threatening to suffocate the building, being propped up by the torches that floodlit the aisle of the bailey.

The Vatican Palace was an 'E' shape looking similar to the old Duke courtyards of England in the Elizabethan age, someone told me the building was in the shape of an 'E' in honour of the Queen, if there is any truth in it I've not heard it since. Wolf looked ready to move when through the thrashing rain, I heard a mechanical whirr from above, we were stood in a cameras blind spot, just waiting for us to move, I diverted Wolf's eyes upward and he graciously sprayed a quick burst of paint across the lens.

The lightning lit up the front of the palace again; it was a beautiful building, home to the pope and the Holy-See as well as the house of all Catholicism. Heaven, I thought, the very notion of what this building stood for made me sick, and yet, in our grasps we had the potential to prove belief in God, I don't know if I want that to happen. I don't want to be a perpetrator in a Holy War or a Jihad or whatever they call them. The whole thing reeked of a bad ending and we needed to keep things quiet, keep it insular.

Wolf gave me a nudge. There were two guards, dressed in black and doing a regimental walk around the gardens perimeter. Then, he darted his eyes to the wall further down and jutting out of the wall, harnessed by strong looking roses, was a trellis. He used his fingers to gesticulate that he was going to the trellis and that I should bring down the two guards. Before I could protest he had gone, silently, nothing but the sound of the rain pounding down.

I could feel my breathing rise, tension building, and the scent of blossom managing to break through the torrent. Lighting flashed the guards up, just another human being doing there job just like me, just another man in the wrong place at the wrong time. I patted my sides, two silenced pistols holstered and ready but not for now.

Don't forget to count your bullets when you shoot, you never know when having one bullet left will save your life.

The guards met in the middle of the path leading from front door to gate, I could see them chatting, making small talk, probably talking about their wives, there kids, maybe even that they hate there jobs or that they don't feel safe and that they wish they weren't here. I wish that too.

As soon as they turn around I move. At that point it's the longest time until they see each other again. Then in the others confusion I will jump him too! Yeah, that's what's going to happen, calm breaths. Relax, think blue skies and green fields, and think sheep and little lambs prancing. A ferocious burst of thunder erupted and the guards turned. I dashed forward, a black shadow lit up in the misty rain-sogged floodlight. I wrapped my left arm around his face, my right arm around his neck and tightened. The guards panic sending a tremor through his body, nerves splintering, the dreams beginning to overcome him. He went limp. I dropped him with a careless thud then turned, charged and with a theatrical jump came down hard with a sweeping forearm to the back of the second guard's neck.

The night went silent. Just the rain and the hum of the floodlights echoed in the air. It was then I realised I was lit up, and ran flittingly back to the wall.

I slowed my breathing down, in... out... in... out... Took a gulp of saliva and lactic acid, swallowed it, to lubricate my dry throat and concentrated hard. I stared back at the two unconscious bodies drenched by the rain. They would wake up soon, quicker because of the rain. I sidled along the wall to the red door, the gate to hell, or heaven in this case and noticed a palm reader. I dragged one of the surprisingly heavy guards over and his palm gave me admission. The door creaked shut behind me as I stood in a massive hall, surrounded by darkness, dripping rainwater onto the smooth marble floor. I stepped forward and heard a buzz, then saw a small red dot, and as my eyes adjusted to the gloom I noticed a camera lens. Seconds later it disappeared behind a puff of black smoke and the Wolf shadow beckoned me on with him.

I trudged across the hard floor, fully aware I was dripping rainwater in every single footstep. This was a home; it didn't seem like anything secretive would be housed here, or that the whole of Catholicism saw this as the holiest place on earth, until we stumbled upon an entrance buried into a corridor wall, its position given away by a camera seemingly glaring at nothing. After disabling the camera with a whiff of black, the wall gave way with a precise nudge at what must have been the hinge.

The first step was wooden and slippy from the thunderstorm, and it led down, deeper and deeper into the hot kiln of the building. Sweat poured from my forehead, from nerves and the steaming heat. The anticipation of what was ahead fuelled my flame of adrenaline, following Wolf deeper passing torch after ancient torch before we came to a shiny clearing. Embedded in the old stone arches, completely juxtaposed to its surroundings was a smooth metal door, a keypad on the right hand side, taunting us with impossible glee. Above it, the symbol of the Vatican Secret Archives, a circle holding two keys crossed, the keys to paradise, interweaved with a crown and bearing the Latin 'Archivium Secretum

Apostolicum Vaticanum', was embossed into the steel. It looked well used, and Wolf didn't look like he was going to be put off. From his belt he removed the night-vision goggles he was so insistent on bringing, and put them on, fiddling with a few of the tiny levers and switches on the bridge of the goggles. He stared at the keypad for some time before saying, "We need to be careful. Someone has just passed through here"

Then without much hesitation or problem he began tapping the buttons in. "How do you know?"

The steel door began to part, a bright artificial light filtering through the middle as we both flattened ourselves to opposite sides of the door. I didn't know what to expect, what I was going to see, this was the most secret location in the entire world. A place scholars have wanted to explore almost as much as the Library of Alexandria, I felt privileged that in the past week I had had the pleasure to see them both. Nothing prepared me for the sight. It was without a doubt one of the most beautiful and ornate 'cellars' I, or anyone, had come across. The walls ordained with frescoes of stunning quality, centuries old, and renditions of the bearded God reaching out to mankind. Strong acid smells hung in the air, hovering over rows and rows of bookcases shrinking into the distance surrounded with a blue hue.

Around us, magnificent frescoes, ones that I recognised, the crowning of Charles IV, the donation by Emperor Constantine, all telling the stories of the Kings and Queens of Europe and the influence of the Catholic Church. You could even argue that no King or Queen has ever ruled; that all of Europe was controlled by the Church. That was a much different argument.

Wolf looked around, not at the beauty but looking for someone, he knew what we needed to do. Find someone, get them to cooperate, and go. Or if it came down to it, find someone and take them against their will and get the scroll translated at last. The scroll was the key to everything and if Wolf was right, we were already a step behind Alpha and whatever he was trying to achieve. We skulked through the Piano Nobile room, shelf by shelf. Now we had our guns in front, Wolf leading the way, allowing me to keep our rear secure. When I tapped his shoulder, I passed him leading into the next room as we rotated ourselves like this through a damp dingy corridor that led us to another room, this one continuing the same theme of detailed frescoes with more Kings through the ages lending themselves to the Church. There was someone in here, a book held in front of them, turning the pages with a set of tweezers, the creak of ancient parchment hiding each of our footsteps. Wolf looked at me through his black mask, only his eyes were visible but it was enough, he nodded his head. I could feel my heartbeat erupt again, the target looked like a monk, a long red cloak concealing there body and covering there head. I lowered my gun, took another large gulping breath and expelled it silently. I took a step forward, "Accendete, potete ora andare"

I flung myself back behind the cover of the bookcase, trying hard to keep my breath in, Wolf looked at me in shock, I tried a quick glance around the corner and now, standing where the monk had been stood was a woman. Wolf glared at me in confusion, I shrugged my shoulders, Wolf gestured me back in. No hesitation this time, I crept a foot around the corner of the shelf, the woman in plain sight. There was something strange, she was not like the monk, she looked like... well an archaeologist. Khaki shorts, showing her long tanned legs toward her white wool socks and Dr. Marten boots. A sleeveless black top, cut in a perfect relaxed round neck blossomed into a sweet smelling head of hair. The adrenaline roared through my body, my fingertips ready to shoot licks of flame. I gripped hard around her mouth with one hand, then wrapped another hand around her midsection and against the resistance lifted her from the floor and backed away as silently as she would let me. I moved back, her body convulsing with terror. I could see Wolf's eyes watching her, then him trying to communicate. He raised his finger to his mouth, *shhhh*, but the resistance didn't stop, he pointed at her then made a talking motion with his hand before pointing to himself. It was like trying to gesticulate with the deaf when you don't know sign language.

He indicated me to move back, back through the last room and into the staircase we went, letting the huge steel doors shut, then blocking the stairs with his ample frame he removed his mask and gestured me to let the woman go. I still hadn't seen her face, but she smelled beautiful. "Che cosa lo pensate state facendo?"

"Do you understand Italian kid?"

"No"

"Hmm"

She made a run to try and get past Wolf but he politely nudged her back, then even before she knew she was going to scream, Wolf nodded to me and I put a strong hand around her mouth again. He stood up; there was something in Wolf's demeanour that told me he was dying for a cigar. I knew the feeling. "Do you understand English?" he said as straight as he could, trying to rid the strong Yorkshire accent from his tone.

I felt her nod. I felt her relax. I also felt her become more reassured almost instantly at the thought of talking. I didn't think this was the way hostages were supposed to act. Another acknowledgement from Wolf and I let her go. "What are you doing here?" she said to our surprise in full English, no accent or hint of the Italian she was speaking only moments earlier. "What the hell do you want? I'll call the guards! You're gunna pay for this! Please don't hurt me, I haven't done anything wrong!"

"Whoa, whoa, *whoa*" motioned Wolf with his hands. "Just shut up will you. We are not going to hurt you. We are not going to pay for this. You won't call the guards and I will tell you what we want"

She changed posture. Putting her hand in her pocket, I watched it intently and saw movement, I reached down, pulled her hand out and found a phone being used, and I ripped it from her grasp and saw the video phone transmit a guard's face right at me. "Shit! Wolf, we gotta go!"

"Knock her out! We will take her" said Wolf pulling his mask on and pulling the slide back on both his pistols ready. In that moment she turned to me, her face pure and soft with the hint of red cheeks, her eyes surrounded with thick black eye liner, her forehead hidden by a swirling black fringe with flashes of dark brown and lips so full and soft you could use them as a pillow. She was beautiful! "Can you translate Aramaic?" I asked her softly.

"What the fuck you doing! Come on!" shouted Wolf wanting to go, the stairs ahead of him willing him on. "Knock her the fuck out!"

Through those pliable eyes she looked at me, surprised at the question, she gestured yes, and then stretched a hand out. As I went to solidify this show of trust, within seconds she had unsheathed my gun held it at my head and I saw her eyes roll to the back of her skull. Wolf staring at me with remorse, "I told you to knock her the fuck out"

"You didn't have to pistol whip her!"

"What else would you have me do; you nearly lost your head!"

Bang! Above us the door to the steps was being charged down. The thrash of shoulder on stone was loud and echoed down the wet stairs. "Quick open the door!" shouted Wolf as he threw the goggles at me. I put them on quickly as Wolf kept an eye on the stairs, gun aimed up and straight. It all came together as I looked at the keypad in thermal vision.

The goggles had several different functions and the thermal was bringing up the numbers he had typed in earlier, traces of his heat slowly fading away at different levels of temperature. "That's very clever" I said turning with a smile then remembered where I was.

I keyed in the lightest numbers first and the door began to part. I grabbed the girl off the floor and gave her a fireman's lift onto my left shoulder freeing my right hand for my gun. Wolf backed through as the chant of the Italian guards plummeted down the stairs with fury and anger. The doors began to shut, Wolf waited, gun at the ready, the guards reached the bottom step, Wolf fired, dropping one, a hand falling between the doors before being crushed and snapped clean. "You lead kid, I'll cover the rear"

I dashed forward, the woman's boot catching a bookcase, no longer relying on stealth, just trying to get out, to get to safety. There had to be another way out of here, another exit, somewhere we could use to extract ourselves. My thighs and hamstrings began to burn; the acid building up in my body, oxygen struggling to get to the muscles that need it most, even my heart began to ache!

I charged on, the frescoes now of little importance other than a blur that whizzed past as we bolted straight on. A man, dressed in a long red, monk-like, cloak stood in my way as I forced head on, "Move out of the way!" I screamed at him.

He froze in fear, hands up in the air, and then a right hand clutched a set of rosary beads on his chest and with a well timed kick sent him flying into the bookcase to his left. The next door was shut, a sturdy looking wooden portal, and another boot… *crash!* The door exploded into an array of splinters and dust, the next room was the same, filled with ancient paintings, all dating from the earlier centuries. I stopped, looked around, felt my breathing catch up with my body, the blood in my veins on fire, it was no longer an ache, my hamstring felt torn, felt as if it was going to come away from my leg at any time.

"Come on!" pushed Wolf and I started again, pushing onward. I could feel the life returning to the woman on my shoulders as she groaned painfully in my ear, the kind of groan you get from those alcoholic nights out on the town. Where next? Stairs! I rushed them, the second upper floor awaited as I powered my legs up toward it. The bookcases were the same as downstairs but encased in glass safes, far more secure than the documents downstairs it seemed. The light grew dimmer up here but the sound of rain became more acute, we were getting closer to the top. I hazarded a look behind me and Wolf fired a shot down, there were guards on our tail now! A bullet hole formed ahead of me in the wall, I turned quickly out of the line of sight as I heard another scream. I ploughed forward but my thighs were starting to give in, no, no! Not now you can't!

A hard left led me down another corridor, all the same, information stacked higher and higher. I tried to take my mind off the pain. By thinking of what could be written on these scrolls, on these documents older than time, secret information regarding the Templar's, the ancient popes, what really happened all those years ago. It wasn't working, the pain was rifling through my body, being kept at bay only by the burning rush of adrenaline. Another set of stairs ran up ahead. I hit them hard, running with the last bastion of strength I possessed, and made the top, dropped to one knee and picked up again running for the window ahead. The third floor, The Tower of Winds. The window glared at me, taunting me, sitting there with the laugh of an infant finding what it was seeing so funny, the pathetic Englishman running for it. There were more people up here, more scared than a threat but in my tired state any of them would have been able to push me over. We passed through the Sala Degli Apostoli, there was nothing left now, nothing but a bright white light starting to give me tunnel vision. The window… I could feel my body beginning to shut down, to stop the pain. The sound of gunshots behind me spurred me on further, panic struck my body and now there was nothing from my mind, my body was running itself. Clinging on to its final reserves… The next room went by, the Sala Degli Patriarchi, all sense of thought had gone… The Meridian Hall… The window… I had slowed down next to the window that when I hit it, the glass didn't break. When I turned to try again, I hit Wolf who forced me through and we all fell into a great heap on the palace roof in a barrage of glass and rain. Wolf was on his back, every guard that showed its head had it taken off in a flash of red. He threw his guns to one side and grabbed mine off my lifeless body and used them instead, the guards ceased, had he got them all? I tried to move but I was empty. Not even adrenaline could keep me going now. The burn in my muscles was eclipsing the flame of my body; the oxygen had long since smouldered away to nothing.

There was urgency in Wolf as he grabbed hold of my sneaking suit, pulled me to my feet. I fell down but he did it again and again and then grabbed me once more and screamed in my ear, "Banner! You stay with me! I've got the girl, just run!"

The order touched something in my head that even I didn't have control of as my legs began to creak into action again. My knees shrieked in revulsion at being asked to move again, my hamstrings tried not to snap as they rotated themselves again. Both my gastrocnemius muscles told me to stop. No! I focussed ahead of me; I was not letting Wolf down! No way, no how! A tenth wind hit me, the tunnel vision cleared; I could see what was ahead of me now, even through the driving rain. Two miniature domes (Miniature compared to the giant one behind us) were positioned at either side of us, I risked a look back, and Wolf was fighting on with the woman on his shoulders and waved me forward. I stopped at the edge of the Palace, down below the small courtyard before the square. Wolf dropped the girl as softly as was possible from over six feet, and looked down, "Throw her down to me, and then you follow"

"It's a..." I looked down and couldn't even begin to judge the distance; my head just simply would not compute it. "...long way down"

Wolf was already hanging off the edge when I said it. "Just do it"

He dropped to the ground, moments later a thud. I looked over and he stood beckoning me to drop the girl, this felt very wrong. I picked her up and held her outstretched with both arms, in my arms like a baby. She was so slender and light. I took another look at her face, and felt a rush urge to kiss her before pushing it quickly to the back of my head. I shut my eyes and dropped her. A gunshot echoed through the air and woke me out of my thoughts with a jump; I flung myself onto the ledge and dropped to the courtyard floor with a hard thump, then rolled so my knees didn't end up through my shoulders.

"We need a car!" shouted Wolf, "There are more coming, I saw em running through the palace. They think we are still in there so we need to be quick!"

I could see Wolf labouring as he hitched the woman onto his shoulders again and we ran right, in between the pillars lining St. Peters Square and into the streets themselves. The rain was furious now, the streets looking more like rivers as we trudged through them trying to escape from the clutches of the Vatican Guard. "Doesn't anyone in this fucking country own a car!" shouted Wolf as we rounded another corner onto another empty street. "We need a miracle" I said, almost losing faith in the mission.

"We have just broke in to the house of the pope, gods right hand man on earth, and shot about eight men dead, kidnapped a researcher in there and are now trying to get away unharmed. Do you really think god is going to give us a miracle?"

We took another left turn, almost back on ourselves but the gamble paid off when a black Mercedes was parked half on the pavement and half on the road. "You were saying?"

"That was luck. Not a miracle"

"Whatever"

The door gave little resistance when hit with the butt of a gun. Wolf jumped in the drivers seat and popped open the boot. "Stick her in it"

"What, we can't?"

"She tried to shoot you in the head last time you were nice to her now stick her in the god damn boot kid!"

I didn't like it but I did as he said and put her in, just as I shut the boot I saw her eyes flicker open and a wave of guilt came over me. The guilt disappeared in a flash as a bullet starred the rear window. I turned and saw a group of black shadows running towards us; I ran around the car jumped in and Wolf floored the accelerator. The car jerked under the tired legs of Wolf as the Mercedes groaned down the streets, we took a hard left and then saw in the rain soaked haze the flashing of red and blue lights. "You have got to be kidding me" shouted Wolf.

The Mercedes ploughed on, the windscreen wipers flashing back and forth giving us a glimpse of the streets ahead of us. He flung the car around a right corner, the back end spinning around in the rain, before shooting rain behind us into the windscreens of the cars behind us. We powered on, behind us still more police cars, and now the sirens were loud and close. I felt claustrophobic from the rain punishing the car, trapping us inside without a sight of the outside world; Wolf seemed remarkably calm despite the situation. "Here" he said tossing me a silenced pistol he had taken from me previously, "Four shots left, make em count"

He brought the electric window down on my side and I leaned out and came back in wiping my face instantly. The side mirror cracked as a bullet trashed it. "There shooting at us?" I said

"What do you want them to do kid? Kiss us goodbye?"

I leaned out of the window, sat on the door frame and for the first time could take in the streets without feeling like I was being hemmed into the car. High orange looking buildings looking like they were holding up the rain sodden sky, the clouds as heavy and monstrous as they were earlier. The red and blue of the police cars lights reflected in the mist, the harsh torrent of the river street flung up bouncing on the bonnets, the spray from the road crashing into my face, obscuring my vision. I could hear the bullets whizzing by in between the sirens, I had four shots. *One.* A bullet speared through the air and hit the windscreen starring in on the drivers side, the car starting swaying from side to side. I leaned further out, holding the windscreen arch, my body stretched out fully and with my arm at full extension I shot the front tire. *Two.* The car dropped on the blown tires side, must have hit a hidden grate under the river that was the street and stopped suddenly, the back of the car raising and looping up and over crashing to the street sending an enormous wave toward me.

I jumped back in through the window. Took my mask off, used it to wipe some of the rain that had managed to seep through and tried to see through the rear window but the crack was too bad. The lights still flashed around us, reminding us they were still following us; the rain not letting up. Wolf pushed the car as hard as he dared in the rain, powerslid around the next corner and ahead of us I could see in between the interweaving wipers, the border. "Keep your head in" he said

The barrier to Italy burst into splinters. The Roman streets were far more congested as we joined straight onto a busy street, weaving in between the pedestrian speed traffic. It must have been nearing dawn now, commuters heading for work or university. We assaulted the traffic ahead of us, sparks being dampened by the rain before they've got a chance to shine, the sirens behind us sifting in the traffic with us. "I've got an idea" I said, "Keep the car straight"

I leaned out of the car again, narrowly avoiding a giant artic truck that was at the side of us. Two shots left, I made sure I counted them. *Three.* I shot the right tire of the car to the left of us. *Four.* I shot the left tire of the car on the right of us. With a predicted swerve the cars came together converging into one, blocking the path behind us and then being separated by the police car that barged in between the two of them; flames bursting out from underneath the bonnet before grinding to a slow halt.

"Nicely done. Shame it didn't blow up, not very Hollywood are you?"

I could feel the smile through his mask as the electric window went up. The rain was not ready to stop yet but it shouldn't matter now. He pulled off the main road, bending the car around and into a petrol station.

He pulled down his mask and got out into the cover of the petrol station roof; he backed onto the car and seemed to be taking a breather before leaning inside asking "Check the glove box. He must have a cigar somewhere"

I did as he asked but there was no sign of anything. He got back in and shut the door, rubbing his eyes and then opening them as wide as he could, trying to stay awake. It was a delayed reaction that hit us both, the fury of sleep was beginning to take hold even though we still had so much to do. "We need to swap cars. They will be looking for this one"

"I was thinking that" I countered, "But we need to do it without anyone seeing us getting her out of the back of the car"

There was nothing for a moment. The rain was finally resting, turning from the relentless torrent into a calm drizzle, the remnants of the night starting to peel away. Then my head was next to the gear stick, the noise of the car being peppered was all I could hear, the windscreen shattered and fell upon us in shards. The gun fire stopped, Wolf pushed up sending glass flying out through the holes and tried the ignition which started with a splurge and a grumble. "It's that fucking Lexus!" he shouted, "Someone's been following us all the way! How many bullets you got?"

Another thrashing of bullets collided with the car, the noise so loud that I could barely hear what Wolf was saying. "Empty!"

"Shit!" and slammed hard on the accelerator seeing the destroyed Mercedes gallantly trying to force itself on through the petrol station. It crashed itself out onto the street that was just off a main road, as if it was being newly built leading along the closest thing Rome had to a country lane. Plots of land that had started spawning new homes lined the streets, a digger, forklift trucks, pallets of bricks and a wagon carrying a load of timber stretched along the pavement.

The rain had left the street as slick as ice, floating along the new tarmac. The Lexus behind us was finding it a lot easier to do so than the battered Mercedes. The car spluttered on, turning left into a new patch of road that was unfinished. The underlay of the tarmac was shooting stones of tar up into the bullet hole ridden Mercedes, "We need to hide! We can't do anything in this hunk of junk!"

The tarmac ended and turned into a dirt track that the Mercedes was not enjoying in the slightest. This was not the ideal surface for either car, but the condition of the Lexus was allowing it to catch quicker than we had hoped. The wind from the culmination of the rain was blowing tiny shards of glass into the car, I could feel them sticking to my face as I put my mask back on. Wolf didn't have the same luxury, every corner; every rev of the engine was pushing more and more into his face. We burst through a chain link fence, a pole from which flew in between me and Wolf and back out through the rear window and toward the Lexus that bounced off its bonnet. Our back bumper dropped off into the path of the Lexus that ran over it turning it into a crumpled mess. The Lexus was tearing up the dirt, enjoying its brief foray into the world of off-roading; the Mercedes was not enjoying it anywhere near as much. The engine was starting to splutter, the tires looking more and more worn, it was ready to give in. I knew how the poor thing felt; I was ready to do the same.

Wolf tried everything he could to push the Mercedes on and on and at the same time trying unsympathetically to out manoeuvre the Lexus behind. I wanted this to end, why didn't I keep at least one bullet in the fucking gun! "I got an idea kid. But this may hurt a lot"

He pushed the Mercedes on toward the wooden skeleton of a house with a nearly finished roof. He looked at me and I nodded back to him. We both lowered our heads into what you would call a recovery position on a plane. Then I saw nothing but heard everything. The crack of wood, that uncomfortable noise when wood is bent the wrong way, the squeak of nails flying and the roof coming down with a rush of wind before everything settled into a relaxing hum, the dust settling, resting on our heads. The top of the Mercedes had been completely bent out of shape; we both started kicking at our doors, finally breaking free into the shell of the house, gaps to the outside only once every few feet. The skeleton of the house had caved in to make a fairly sturdy shelter, we both assumed positions with our back to the makeshift walls, hidden in the darkness.

There was nothing for what felt like a century. I tried to keep my heartbeat quiet because I felt like it was going to explode from my chest, my legs were still aching and didn't like me standing and the dust felt like it had settled on my lungs. There was a creaking of wood and a bit more of the roof fell down, a permanent dribble of debris filtered down at my side like a trickle of water. The cloudy dust swirled in small cyclones in the places where air had managed to get in, the plan was good to say it was made in the head of a man outrunning a new Lexus off-road in a bullet filled Mercedes that was losing parts as it went along.

We both saw a shadow emerge in one of the areas by the mini-cyclone. There was a tense few seconds. I reached down for a shaft of hard lumber that had snapped in the collision and kept it held up, ready for him to walk in. Wolf seemed to be psyching himself up too, his fists curled round ready to smash. The shadow seemed to be taking a long time, I wondered who it was? I wondered if it was Mayweather, out for revenge. Or was it Alpha? Then something completely unexpected happened. The plan hit a snag. Our punishment it seemed for trespassing on god. A package slid along the dusty floor and settled next to the car wheel with a thud. The shadow disappeared and Wolf flung himself on his knees next to the package. He threw me it and he ran for me sliding along the ground, his feet already half way out of the shelter. "Come on!"

I looked at the package. *C4*. With a twenty second timer already down to fifteen. I thought about the girl in the back of the Mercedes and jumped over the car to get to her hearing Wolf in the background shouting for me to leave her but I was not going to let an innocent die like this. She hadn't done anything wrong; she was a nothing in this whole process. 'She doesn't deserve to die!' I was telling myself

Did I feel guilty? I didn't know what it was but in that moment of epiphany I managed somehow against all physical strength to pull the boot lid clear of its lock and see the *very* conscious woman raise a boot to my face. I pushed it to one side and despite a furious combo of punches to the head got her to the small gap in the shelter, pushed her through and just as I got my legs free the thing erupted. I jumped over the woman, covering her completely from the volcanic swirls of raw orange and yellows. I could feel the burn on my back from the nearby flames and as timber and flaming balls of dust landed around us, I somehow managed to pick her up, shell shocked and disorientated toward Wolf.

We looked back, the fires burning strong, crisping the timber to a cinder. Thick black smoke rose high into the Roman sky, we quickly pushed on toward the far end of the plot of land that was being developed. Hoping that the explosion would be enough for our follower to assume our deaths, the shelter exploded again, this time the smell of diesel expelled into the air following the liquid flame that boiled over and flared into nothing.

The dawn was beginning to break as we walked on, every few seconds having to push the woman on further. We had no idea where we had been driven to, I could hear cars deep in the distance driving along main roads, and it all seemed so harmonious as if the world was playing us a mechanical melody. "Any idea's Wolf?"

"We need to find out where we are"

"What about your phone?"

"It got smashed in the jump from the palace. There is no way of getting in touch with Bingham until I get to a phone"

"Wait please" said the woman, her first words since Wolf had knocked her out, "I need to rest, please"

Wolf stopped, didn't turn but just sat down and motioned to me that we could. I was amazed at how far we had been driven out of the Vatican; we were now in the vast green fields on the outskirts with little sign of human activity at all. Wolf was studying her all of a sudden, I hadn't noticed but I think he had seen something, something I hadn't. It didn't take him long to speak, "You know where we are don't you?" he said assuredly, "You've known all along but haven't said anything"

"What do you expect me to do? Help?" she said coldly

"So where are we?"

There was a pause, I don't think she wanted to tell us, but common sense prevailed. She had just journeyed with Wolf through the entire Vatican Palace, been thrown off the Palace itself and been involved in a car chase followed by surviving explosions. Safe to say she must know we don't want to kill her. "Are you doing this because you know who my father is? I only found out a few years ago, I didn't know who he was! I didn't know he was that important!"

"Calm down" I said, "We don't know who your father is. We just need someone who can read Aramaic"

At first tears had begun to swell but when I told her we didn't know her father she relaxed. She was understandably shaken, but then from a deep resolve she said, "My father will kill you when he finds out. He can do that, just because he is... who he is... doesn't mean he can't"

"Who is your father?" asked Wolf sternly, "Because I will kill him before he gets me"

"No you won't. He is more protected than anyone else in the entire world"

"Look I don't care who your father is" I said, "Where are we? I ache, I want to go to sleep and I'm pretty sure I've torn my hamstring. I want to go home! Where are we?"

"We are in the forest to the east of Via de Valle Aurelia. My house is only a mile north, I will let you use the phone there if you let me go" she said

"No" said Wolf, "We will use your phone and then you will come to England with us and you will translate what we want you to translate"

The idea of translation crept into her head and avoided the mess that was panic and fear and came out of her mouth as intrigue. "Translation? Of what?"

"A scroll found in the last remnants of Alexandria Library"

"What? No, I don't believe you"

"We think it has something to do with proving the existence of Jesus Christ" said Wolf, "So are you in?" he said pulling down his mask revealing his face, he offered her a hand.

She studied the face he offered her. His aged and weathered face, the face of a thousand battle fields, a face of pure unrivalled pride and determination, he willed her to shake his hand. She shook it. "What's your name?" he asked

"Charlie. Charlie Lambent"

"Well Charlie Lambent. Lead the way…"

Charlie held her word as she led us to her small apartment on the outskirts of Rome, just east of Via de Valle Aurelia motorway. It was the kind of place you expected more from a student than from a researcher at the Vatican. Obviously being an examiner for the highest power religion in the world was not a way of generating a good income. Wolf remained untrusting despite Charlie offering us full use of the flat and when he found a pair of kinky handcuffs that Charlie insisted she didn't know about, he chained her to the bed. It was only now I noticed the tattoos on in the underside of her wrist, one on each arm, a tulip shape, purple and beautiful. Wolf was sat down on a long red leather sofa stubbed with cigarette burns and what looked like knife slits testing the phone and ringing out. "Sorry about this, he isn't the most trusting"

The kitchen was situated in the corner of the room with a sink, cooker and four hobs, one with a pan of recently cooked tomato soup covered with a strip of cling film. There was an attempt at corresponding kitchenware with a chrome kettle, toaster and bread bin and the sight of the kettle was enough for me to get excited. "Anyone want a cuppa?"

"I don't have any teabags"

"Doesn't matter then"

Directly adjacent to the kitchen was a small TV on a cluttered stand scattered with beer bottle prints and that horrible ring from the bottom of a coffee mug. Scattered pirated DVD's and an aged looking CD player that looked like it had seen much better days made up the rest of the corner. In a strange way this room felt lived in, it felt as if it had been struggled in and above all it felt like it had a purpose and a spirit, not like my new place back in England. The other two corners held the bed and Wolf, sat on the phone arguing respectively. Charlie was asleep.

I didn't really know what to do or say so I backed myself onto the door and felt paper ruffle. It was an old film poster, some Italian film that I had never heard of, and then the phone slammed down in the corner, Charlie jumped. "Ten minutes"

"Who are you guys?" said Charlie, "Why have you picked me?"

"Don't get all full of yourself love" said Wolf, "We didn't *pick* you. You just so happened to walk in just as we wanted someone and forgive me for asking but you don't exactly look like a normal Vatican student. What were *you* doing in there?"

"I get in because of my father" she said, her mouth stretching into a thin line, "He gets me in almost anywhere I want. He is ashamed of me I think"

Wolf's persona changed now that the stress was gone and we were on the verge of being picked up. He had finally relaxed. I sat on the bed next to Charlie and rested my legs that were continuing to shriek at me in agony. I knew I needed a few days rest but I also knew I wouldn't get the luxury. "You don't happen to have any cigars or cigarettes do you?"

"No" she said, her face lighting up, "I don't smoke"

"Damn it. I thought all Italians smoked"

"I'm not Italian… Well I am but I wasn't raised here, I was raised and educated in London so I guess I lean more toward Britain than anywhere else"

"Not a bad thing" he countered, "So who is your big important father"

"I'm not sure I should tell you"

"I'm sure you should. I wanna know who I am dealing with"

For a while nobody said anything because the conversation carried on with hard gestures and eye contacts. Charlie did not want to tell us who her father was, that much was for certain but deep inside she felt we would find out eventually so why not tell us now. "I am…" she began as hesitation crept into her voice, "I am the popes dirty little secret"

"Your dad is the pontiff?" I shouted jumping to my feet in amazement, my legs dropping me back down. "You are the daughter of the pope? Seriously?"

"See I knew you'd be like this!" she said starting to move before being held back by her restraint, "Now you know why I was there. I am not supposed to tell anyone, I told him I wouldn't but he doesn't care. He just fobs me off with money, dirty money brought in by the church"

"Of all the researchers in the world kid you had to grab the one who could get us in trouble didn't you?" said Wolf giving me the sarcastic look that I was beginning to get used to.

Above us we all heard the blades of the helicopter at the same time. "Well Miss Lambent, which is obviously not your real name. How do you fancy helping us proving that your father is in the right?"

"What?" she said as Wolf made his way over winking at her and unlocking her handcuffs. "What do you mean?"

"You will see"

CHAPTER 6
THE SECRETS OF WOLVES

Sleep had been a luxury I simply hadn't had so when the opportunity arose I planned to take full advantage of it. I decided not to go home in case there was some great breakthrough in the investigations but Charlie had told us it was going to be slow work so Wolf figured if it was slow for us it would have been slow for Alpha too.

As I woke I pulled myself up so that I was sat staring at the white walls of the medical bay and a short man in a white coat looking at something on the wall. He turned, "Ah. You're awake"

I looked around a little more as he started a steady walk in my direction. Behind him the pictures he was looking at seemed like detailed analysis of what I think was my legs. It was then I stared at them... "Jesus Christ I got fucking needles sticking out of my legs!"

"You're muscles were badly worn. Especially the Gastrocnemius, Soleus and Extensor digitorum longus muscles. So much so I thought I should try something a little different"

"My legs have got fucking needles in them"

I heard a set of doors open behind me. The doctor looked up and saluted, his small round face blushing in the cheeks like he was nervous or uneasy around the man or woman who had just entered. It was Wolf, only Wolf would have the nerve to smoke in the medical bay and sure enough the cigar came into my vision seconds before he did, once more clean shaven and looking a lot better for a shower. "How you doing kid?" he said with his back to the bright white walls. My eyes felt funny like I had never used them before and they were struggling to adjust to any kind of light. "I feel a little groggy, and I've got needles in my legs"

"Yeah I noticed that when I came in. This your idea?" he motioned toward the doctor with his cigar and a casual smile, "Acupuncture is supposed to be good for the muscles. Never tried it myself. How does it feel?"

"You're enjoying this aren't you?"

"Yes. Is it so obvious?"

As Wolf and I talked the doctor had made himself busy by putting on some latex gloves and was beginning to gently remove the enormous needles that were currently jarring with malevolence from my legs. It was funny how I was willing to drive my muscles into the ground and now felt funny about them being stabbed with needles, there was something about the holistic treatments that I didn't really like, possibly because they had all the scientific fact of a leprechaun. And yet, so did God, didn't he? Where was the proof? Sure we have a book telling us about things but who was to say that if the world ended a single copy of Lord of the Rings would survive and suddenly we all believe in the fables of Frodo. The world was too open to seduction by romantic ideals, a place where even the maddest man can be an inspiration. A cacophonous needle broke from my leg shaking me from my thoughts. A wave of cigar smoke overwhelmed my senses; I suddenly felt a great urge to have a smoke like I hadn't had one in days. "Have you got another one on you?"

"Sorry kid" he said taking another long tempting drag, "None till you up and about. You have been out for a while"

"How long?"

"Nearly two days. Charlie seems to have taken a shine to you, seems to think you're a hero and I'm a bastard. Something to do with me wanting to leave her in the car boot when it was going to go bang, you know what women are like"

Sometimes sarcasm just wasn't funny. "Is she making any progress on the scroll?"

"She is having more luck with the Atherton Scroll than the pictures. She said the pictures are really poor quality. I am kinda hoping that just knowing the Atherton Scroll will help us catch Alpha... the bastard. Won't raise his head for a minute for me to rip it off his god damn shoulders"

I turned my attention to the doctor again, his jerking reaction making me feel a little on edge like he was nervous about treating anyone. He looked relaxed enough, from his balding head around his blushing red cheeks and dedicated smile, until you saw the quiver in his hands, it was as if he had hit the bottle really hard the night before. Wolf was stood like an old drill sergeant from those ancient war movies, he was stood with his left hand on his hip, right hand holding his cigar and staring with the kind of surprise to suggest he didn't really know what he was looking at. He turned biting down on the cigar he raised to his mouth. There weren't many people who could pull off wearing a suit and smoking a cigar as well as Wolf, the black pinstriped suit with grey shirt and grey and black tie was smart and modern.

The doctor had finished removing the needles from my legs and in a bid for freedom I swung them round. As soon as my feet hit the floor my muscles screamed, a violent tremor shuddering up my bones to my spine. "It might take a little while for your muscles to warm up again. I suggest a bit of yoga" said the doctor. Wolf gave him a look and then a nod and the doctor departed with a neurotic wave and disappeared completely out the door. "Nice bloke" I said, "Bit quiet?"

"Dr. Hawks… nervous, it's the only way to describe him. He's been here longer than me. I'm trying to get him kicked out but the powers that be seem to like his new age methods. Acupuncture, herbal teas… all that bollocks"

Silence filled the room only broken for the slow burning cigar that Wolf eventually extinguished and placed in the bin. His whole manner reeked of class, of a power that was far beyond that of anybody else around him. Mayweather had it as well; I wondered if I would ever achieve it? If I would ever become the sort of person that people called the devil. I still remembered the fear in Mayweather's eyes when he had seen Wolf in front of him, how he vaulted the barrier. That was true power; to make your enemy quiver at your name, at the very sight of you. Would I ever be like that?

"Come on kid" said Wolf "Let's go see how *she* is doing"

"Any luck with anything?" said Wolf as he led me into the briefing room that me and Carter had started our SES journey. How was Carter?

"She has managed to translate a great deal of the Atherton Scrolls, seems we were translating it wrong. We thought it was Latin, but it was a different dialect of Aramaic" said Bingham standing like a schoolboy who had been disturbed from doing something he shouldn't have been doing.

Charlie turned and shot me a wan smile. Her eyes looked drained and her complexion wasn't what it was when we kidnapped her. She ran her fingers through her hair and let it settle in a mess, it was stupidly sexy. "There all bible quotes" she said. "Every one of them"

Wolf and I moved forward to look at the translations scribbled in black biro across several sheets of A3 paper. There was a lot there; at the top of the page were a series of boxes with interpretations of our own language. It was like a key. "Its just a scroll with loads of bible quotes on them, no link to God being real, no significance that warrants all this sleuthing you have been doing."

"What are the quotes?" asked Wolf with a look of disappointment stretched across his face.

"Well this one underneath that symbol of a throne. That just says *'And I saw a great white throne and him that sat on it'*. Erm, this one says, *'Just as the weeds are collected and burned up with fire, so will it be at the end of the age.*

The Son of Man will send his angels, and they will collect out of his kingdom all causes of sin and all evildoers, and they will throw them into the furnace of fire, where there will be weeping and gnashing of teeth. Then the righteous will shine like the sun in the kingdom of their Father. Let anyone with ears listen!"

"Which means?"

"It's from somewhere in Matthew's gospel. I've heard my father talk of it before"

"Why? Why would he talk about this phrase? And why is it on the Atherton Scrolls? There must be a reason somewhere!" said Wolf clinging to desperation.

"Look if there is I don't know okay!" said Charlie back to him, "I'm tired. I'm Cranky. I need sleep and some makeup and a flipping shower! I've translated all that for you! Can you just give me a day before I start on those shitty pictures?"

"You've got your day" said Wolf, "Banner will stay with you. Bingham, I need to talk to you in private"

"Oh before I forget" said Bingham as he stood about to walk with Wolf from the door, "Dora told me to tell you she has the activity of that car following you. Says its interesting"

"I'll have a look. Kid, watch her"

"What do you want me to do?"

"Take her back to yours. And get her some make up"

"Out of my own money?"

"Well I aren't going to pay for it"

With that he left slamming the door. I turned to Charlie, her face a picture of sleep deprivation; she managed a faint smile before huffing with fatigue. "Suppose your coming back to mine then"

For some reason I was receiving the silent treatment from Charlie on the drive home. I couldn't put it down to nerves because she had seemed quite composed. Nor could I put it down to lack of trying on my part as I had attempted on numerous occasions to get the conversation rolling. Upon arriving in Morley I put the radio on but that went down about as well as playing Satanic Rock Music in Church.

After parking up and ushering her into my apartment I could sense a little unease surrounding her like an aura. Perhaps it was fear that kept me from getting too close to her but as she stood in the threshold of the kitchen/living room divide with her arms crossed looking curiously around the room I felt a strong urge to hug her. I managed to resist until at last she spoke asking for a shower. I nodded and showed her the bathroom. I threw a towel in for her and heard the whoosh of spray as I sat down with a thud, the relaxing feel of the white leather needing into my back. I hadn't spent much time on my own lately, either being with Carter or Wolf and now Charlie and I was beginning to miss being able to do my own thing. The whole investigation was now playing a small hidden swansong in my head, a tease, and a way of shouting at me that we were missing something or misunderstanding it. Nothing had made sense; a scroll from over a century ago listing bible quotes, us being chased from the Vatican, the clandestine haunting of Karnak Temple, every religion was crossing over. Wolf was lost, as was Bingham. There short-lived link to the Templars there only real breakthrough and even that had been dismissed by Wolf himself. Charlie had later disregarded it due to the lack of any Templar seal on any scroll, but the splayed cross in Karnak had to mean something... surely!

There was a knock at the door. I was cautious as being in an SES stronghold building I hadn't expected anybody being able to access without the correct SES identification. I was right and shocked as I was at the sight of Carter at the door; I managed somehow to ask her in. She sat down on the sofa in her hands a folder, strapped in red, like some top secret work. "So how are things?" she asked, "I've missed working with you, Ian's a bit of a creep"

"Yeah" I said, the nerves threading through my body making me jerk and twitch at the slightest noises. It was like a heightened drunkenness. "He seemed a bit like that. Can I offer you a cuppa?"

"I'd like that"

I made my way over and then heard the shower squeak to a halt. The water stopped and the boiler shuddered, I'd completely forgotten about Charlie! I looked at Carter who smiled back. Make-up, lipstick and a smart suit, hair tied back... what must have been a new bra. She looked excellent. Was this what I thought it was? Charlie sauntered lazily out of the bathroom, a towel wrapped sheepishly around her midsection and hair left to hang. Even without make-up she looked stunning and I found the dark almost Cleopatra eyes were not for show but real, she was like a dark princess, a typical bad girl but born like it. Carter's face dropped, "Oh I didn't know you already had company. On second thoughts I won't have that cuppa. I've got work to do anyway" she said lifting the folder up, "I'm sure you two would like to be alone"

Her eyes fixed on Charlie and the look was like that of a wolf from hell. "I'll see myself out"

The door slammed behind her. I glared at Charlie who with the slightest glimmer of a smile shrugged her shoulders and turned to go back in the bathroom. I made chase for Carter dashing down the steps. I could feel the endurance of the past few days kick into my hamstrings. I found Carter before the front door and she turned as I shouted for her and then tried to open the door but she dropped her folder, blank sheets fell out. "It's not what it looks like y'know" I said as I knelt down to help her pick up the paper, "She is helping me and my boss figure out the translation of the manuscripts!"

"I knew I was stupid coming here" she countered. Her eyes were red as if she had been crying and her mascara had run. "But I thought we had fun, we trusted each other and we looked out for each other. I shouldn't have come.... I feel a fool"

"Don't feel a fool! I haven't stopped thinking about you since you went through that door!"

She pulled herself together impressively like only a female can, rising above the pressure and the tension and rallying around that pure feminine desire to retain dignity. "Well why haven't you called!"

"You think I haven't wanted to? I've been in Italy! I've been running from police shooting out tires and escaping explosions!" It all sounded like a film, "I thought you would have moved on. I didn't know you felt what I feel!"

"And what feeling is that?"

I don't know what made me say it. It might have been because stood in front of me now was the only woman who had actually come back to me. Who didn't do a runner after a few days. Who came back and who had left her mark on me without even trying. It could also have been that I had grown to like her from her fears of needles to her unbelievable courage in jumping out of that plane when she had told me about how she was not keen on flying. But despite all this I said it anyway, "The feeling that I really like you. That I want to see you more and that if I am lucky, we might be more than friends"

Breaking through the tears that had started again I thought I saw a thin smile, no thicker than a line from a biro. Her face beamed and the aura of a thousand Aphrodite's clustered around her, she hugged me, her grip as tight as the day when she clung to me in fear for her life in the hotel room. Her hair was like silk, her skin soft, the feeling of her breath on my neck was like lighting a match in my heart. We stood apart for a few moments when she glanced at her watch, "I need to go. Here is my number okay? It's my SES phone; you should be able to ring it"

"Thanks" I said and then reached down to kiss her.

"Let's just take it steady okay? I'm glad you feel the same, I really am, but lets wait till we have some time together"

"Okay"

She gave me one final hug and left the building climbing into a brand new waxed Ford Mondeo and driving off down Queen Street.

Walking back through my door Charlie had managed to regain some dignity by being dressed and finishing the cups of tea I had started to make before she had come out of the shower. "I hope I didn't cause any trouble? I didn't mean to"

"No its fine"

It was strange, before she had gotten in the shower I had wanted to hug her and now I wanted nothing to do with her at all. I would have a word with Wolf in the morning. She handed me the cup of tea and I took a long gulp from it. It was good tea. "I've also put some food in. I hope you don't mind?"

"No, that's fine as well. You can have the bed tonight; I'll sleep on the sofa"

"Thank you" she said and then made her way over to the settee. She sat down, legs hitched and crossed and rested her cup of tea on her legs as she tied her hair back. "I'm sorry I haven't been talking too much. I am not normally surrounded by so many people. I'm normally surrounded by researchers or monks and no one speaks that much, I am not used to so much conversation"

"It's fine. Honestly. I am normally on my own anyway; it makes a change having so much company"

"So what's it like?"

"What?"

"Being a spy" she said lifting the cup of tea again, "It must be exciting?"

"It has its ups and downs" I said and that was pure truth. "But most of the time you're stuck in limbo. Always on the verge of something and never quite getting there"

"Sounds frustrating. Not at all like my job, discovering new things everyday"

"What is your job?"

"I am a theologian"

"I bet your dad was happy?"

"You don't know the half of it"

She shifted her legs and rested her feet along the floor. Just above her ankle sat another tattoo, a set of hollow stars. "You're gunna have to explain that a little bit"

She sighed heavily like expecting the request but not really wanting to answer it. "Basically my dad was... taking advantage of certain privileges. Before he was even nominated for the pontiff he, erm, indulged in cheap women. Guards and close knitted security kept the whole thing under wraps of course. As soon as he became pontiff he started paying women off to keep them quiet. He is not a man of God. It is an insult to call him so. He is just some randy old vicar who struck it lucky"

There was a perfectly timed ping from the oven. She jumped up, mug in hand and headed for the kitchen with a relieved smile. It was obvious she disliked talking about her father but how could I not? This is the sort of thing privileged only for the spies of this world; this was not the sort of gossip you got with Heat magazine. She came back with two plates, passed me one and sat down again. Steam rose from the ready made oven meal that had surprisingly tasty looking roast potatoes, mash, Yorkshire puddings, a sprinkle of peas and sweet corn and a few sliced carrots to add to the colour. The whole thing was topped up with light gravy that was giving off a delightful aroma.

It didn't take long for the both of us to wolf the food down; I couldn't remember the last time I ate anything and the satisfaction I gained from devouring the meal was rivalled only by the feeling of that I had discovered for Carter only hours earlier. Charlie looked satisfied despite leaving half of the meal on the plate. I felt inclined to talk to her, every time she spoke she gave more and more sensationalism it seemed untrue. "So why the English accent despite being an Italian?"

"My mother was English" she said as if this would end the conversation and satisfy my question. It simply fuelled my curiosity further.

"And she raised you? How did you end up in the secret archives of the Vatican?"

There was another sigh. "My mother was from Newcastle. From what I can gather she was a working girl okay? She was in Italy, and she was 'hired' by my father. She threatened to tell the whole world when my father became popular. He shut her up by paying her off. The Church has deep pockets"

"And you? How did you end up here?"

"I wanted to research. I have always been interested in religion. I was heavily inspired by the kind of music I was listening to and the books I was reading. I studied Greek Mythology to a degree level when I was fourteen and then began listening to music that spoke out against organised religions, and then that led me on to the Church and how they controlled the masses in the Middle Ages and so I ended up here. Always wanting to know more"

"How did the Pope find out about you?"

"He always knew me" she said before rubbing her eyes with the palms of her hands "He said he had followed me growing up and had wanted to help me"

"Wouldn't that be dangerous to him?"

"I have no interest in money or ruining his life. My mother now lives better than the Queen so people have told me. I have no interest in her and she gave me up for adoption as soon as she got hold of the money. That's when my father brought me to Italy into the care of a foster family"

"That's a hell of a story"

"So what's the deal with you? How did you get here?" she said obviously ecstatic at the chance of a change of subject. "There isn't much to tell. I was bred to be a spy since High School, after that I moved to an MI: 5 training college and studied moral ethics. My professor then tried to kill me so I left MI: 5 and moved with these guys"

"Who are 'these guys'?"

"We are just the shadows Charlie. That's all I can tell you"

"What about that Wolf? He seems an interesting guy"

"Yeah" I said without giving anything away. She had just told me her life story; all I could do is tell her that Wolf was just a man, just another average Joe on the street who meant no harm to anyone other than the bad people of this world.

"Anyway. If I am going to get anywhere with that manuscript tomorrow I think I had better get some sleep" she said. "Good night"

I wished her good night and watched her leave for the bedroom and shut the door behind her with a soft click as if she didn't want to shut it too loud. I glanced at the clock; 23:01. I put my head down, and felt the angels carry me to slumber.

The morning brought with it a new sense of optimism that had been missing from the corridors of the SES over the past few days. Dr. Stignan had joined myself and Bingham in the computer labs as we intensified our search to try and find a way of clearing up the pictures that I had taken of the scrolls. If only I had taken my time with them! I had all the time in the world when I had them. Mayweather didn't come until the night and I took the pictures as if I had only seconds to spare. I had hours!

Dr. Stignan had come up with an excellent idea through the night after being called to operate on an awkwardly positioned hernia on one of the other agents. He said that in order to gain its position in the body he had worked out the size and typical shape of a hernia and compared it to the most common cases. He then judged that the small piece of hernia he could see in his patient correlated with other patients he had seen before. Therefore on comparison it would have to be the same size, because the sides of any other hernia of that size would not have been able to support it and would have burst. He then put this theory to Bingham who reasoned that if they could take part of the text from the scroll I had taken a picture of and compare it in every angle and position with the ones from the Atherton Scrolls eventually we would have a perfect copy. The process however was taking a long time, and patience was high on the agenda. "Where is Wolf today?" I questioned

"Oh he is at the med bay" said Dr. Stignan, "He prefers to see his own GP"

"I thought everyone saw you Dr. Stignan?"

"Not everyone" said Bingham, "I prefer my own GP also. It is not an insult to Dr. Stignan who is a fabulous practitioner; I just prefer to get access to my doctor at all times and without having to wait in line. Dr. Stignan's expertise is sought after so much it is difficult to ever see him"

"Who was the guy who worked on me?"

"Oh Dr. Hawks? He's a bit of an odd one. Prefers holistic remedies to normal more scientific approaches. I know McCloud wants him thrown out of the place, but he is like part of the furniture"

They had sent Charlie to a room of her own down the corridor and had told her the floor was hers to explore at her leisure. It was a surprising change of attitude although I had a feeling that it was something to do with Wolf not being here and that Bingham was running the show. Dr. Stignan left us telling us he had some work to attend to but what he had given us here was the slightest chance of getting the scrolls from Karnak translated before it was too late. "How long do you think it will take?"

"Hard to say. The first few will be difficult but I am hoping that as it goes on there will be a few repeats which will make it a lot easier" said Bingham. You could see the whites of his eyes had become infected by the red of tiredness, the computer screen had burnt a permanent image of a square in his retina and we all knew, eventually, the fatigue would catch up with all of us. "I am going to go check on Charlie" I said

"How did it go with you two last night?"

"What do you mean?"

"Don't act coy" he said as I stood with the door half open, "Did you, y'know... rock the Casbah?"

"Nope"

"What seriously?"

"Yep"

"Why not?"

"Because I think I found love last night.... And it's not Charlie"

I shut the door on Bingham despite his pleads not to and walked down the corridor to find Charlie drinking what looked like an ice cold glass of water. The condensation slipping down the side of the glass had also dribbled down her chin not before sliding along her lips, making them look red and luscious. I hated her, not because she was a nasty person or even because we didn't get along but I hated her because she was so beautiful I knew she could charm me into things I didn't want to do. It was then that I had noticed the change in wardrobe. Although, I wasn't sure that it would have been to her immediate taste. "I know what you're going to say" she said to me before I had managed to even open my mouth "I look like a librarian"

It was a stereotypical thing to say but on the terms of it, quite an accurate thing to say. A pale pink cardigan sat on top of a flowery blouse and a knee length skirt of black cotton wrapped up the image nicely. Interesting look. "That Bingham dropped me off this big suitcase of clothing. I'm happy to be out of those other clothes but look at me!"

"Any luck with the translation?" I asked trying feverently to change the subject.

"Yeah it's nearly done. It's all bible quotes by the looks of it"

"Great. When Wolf gets back we are going to have a look at the other scrolls. We think we have found a way to get a good clear picture"

"Sounds good. Just let me know when I can help"

I began to walk away when I felt a hand grip my arm and I turned into the eyes of Charlie once again. "Have you, erm...." her eyes darted around the corridor, a furious sense of self preservation hid in her eyes, "...Have you found anything else out about Wolf? I think he might be hiding something? Isn't there any files or anything?" she said whispering to the point of near impossible to hear.

"I am not snooping around on my boss!"

"Whoa okay I was just saying that's all. Sorry"

With that I turned and walked away but she had planted a seed in my head that was growing with surprising maturity. Who was Wolf? What was he hiding? She was right, through everything he had never told me his name, where he had come from other than he only drank in Morley. But if I had lived in Morley as long as he had then that is all I would do. Who the hell was he? A resurgence of will fired up in my soul pushing me onward toward the Action Unit and through the heavy set metal doors and through the warehouse into the back office. It hit me like a bus when I walked in, that instant feeling of nervousness; I was trespassing on Wolf's property, on his part in the company. Adrenaline flew through my veins ignited by the nerves and held in place by my fear. I was going to turn and leave but the computer sucked me in laughing at me when I sat down as the dust flew from the underused chair. The computer booted up and instantly wanted a password. Thoughts that I never knew I could think of came to me. If I was away for so long and had access to thousands of passwords and user details I would write it down. It was obvious he was never here, so he would barely use it, but when he *did*, where would he keep the passwords. That was when the only feature of the room leapt out at me. I remembered before he didn't even have a clock! Yet he had a picture and as I carefully removed it from its frame the passwords revealed themselves underneath.

I was in!

The windows lit up and left as it was loading what seemed like a huge database of information. I remembered what Bingham had said, they keep everything they find about *everyone* for reference. This programme was loading up information about everyone in the entire country! A tense minute later and it had loaded bringing with it the sweat from my brow that was now starting to run free. Folders and files littered the screen, everything from forms to be printed when needed to secret forms each with passwords of there own. I just wanted the database and the black background with bright green text flew up. It simply said name, and the block cursor flashed after it. My fingertips tingled with trepidation as I typed in the word Wolf.

W. O. L. F.

Disappointment flushed through me with the waves of Wolf's in the country. A Thomas Wolf, Henry Wolf, Theodore Wolf. None of which were what I wanted. Instead I tried my luck at McCloud but again it brought up no noticeable discoveries. "Try Edward Swinson"

I recognised the voice and my heart sank into my chest. The growling voice of Wolf echoed in the small room as the lining of light from behind the door frame was blocked with his presence. I typed it in.

E. D. W. A. R. D. . S. W. I. N. S. O. N.

There were several matches but at the side of the third one down were the word 'Alias' and the name Donald McCloud. The black background was swamped with bright green writing as I clicked on his name and suddenly a whole mans life was in front of me. Born on the 21st April 1962 in Morley, Leeds. Mother and Father both servants of the British Army, both achieving high ranks, a sister born in 1967. Both parents died in 1970 in a house fire, no arrests, no suspicion despite the door to the parent's bedroom being locked from the outside and the fire alarm working correctly. For a while there was nothing but rumour, he and his sister being pushed from orphanage to hostel to eventually living off the streets. His sister died in 1977, with a picture at the side from a journalist at the time who was doing a report on child poverty. A young McCloud looking swollen in grief. Patches of dirt on his rugged knees in what must have been an old camera as the still was brown and white. There was nothing for three years until he registered with the British Army in 1980 on the 23rd April; S.t Georges Day. There was a small note from an old Sergeant from 1981 remarking that the young McCloud had a 'knack' for soldiering, and that his dedication to the job was 'phenomenal'.

He was sent to the Falklands in 1982 and was on the front line leading a small battalion of men through rough terrain and in the words of his Captain, 'Single handedly saved the unit from collapse and brought about the end of the war'. His achievements were kept hidden. Only known to those around him as the 'Duke' due to his ability to arrive and sort out problems that no other military man could handle. He was promoted to Major and soon after received a commendation for work in the Middle East before being sent to Guatemala in 1984. Two years later he received the Victoria Cross for saving twenty five people from a terrorist targeted bus carrying foods and supplies; he was also ordained with a promotion to Field Marshall, the highest rank in the British Army. He was then officially KIA in the early years of the Gulf War, after which there was a side note declaring he had accepted the cover story with a final picture of his signature, the last as Edward Swinson. Then afterward a photo of the great man himself stood with the Queen and Prime Minister Thatcher holding the VC with pride and honour. Only then did the picture shock me. It wasn't immediate but it grew on me, the face looking at me and smiling a smile of pure honour and dignity.

"I was going to tell you after all this had blown over" said Wolf

"I can't believe it. I can't believe that him, that man in the picture....."

"I know" started the gravel voiced Wolf, "Bit of a disappointment eh?"

I looked at him for what seemed like hours. I could feel time ticking. God damn there should be a clock! "The name of McCloud is almost legendary, bordering on myth! Some people don't think he exists!" said Wolf, "McCloud isn't a man any more. The things he has done have made him more powerful than he actually is"

"Why didn't you tell me?" I said physically drained and emotionally weeping, "Why leave it for me to find out?"

"I didn't know what it meant to you. How does it feel to know?"

I stood up walking past Wolf and out the door. I didn't know how to react, I didn't know if that was the reaction he was expecting but all I knew now was after all this time Wolf had been lying to me. Wolf was McCloud.

I walked out into the midday sun as the heat scorched the skyscrapers and Lithuanian workmen beginning work and yet another building of wonder. It would probably be another block of flats, more places for the rich to get richer and the poor to watch in amazement as the very ground they walk on gets built up from under them. I took off my suit jacket and slung it over one shoulder as the elements of the last few minutes shaped and curved in my mind turning them into a Picasso painting. Wolf was McCloud, why did it bother me so much? Was it that he had lied to me? The one man who had persuaded me to join this SES was the same man who fronted it? Why me? Why save me in the middle of this whole affair? There were so many unanswered questions that had to be heeded but not yet. I had the strangest feeling as I walked down King Street, leading along a ring road of one way traffic and past the Metropolitan Hotel. It was as if someone had stabbed me in the back. It was red hot, stinging now and upon feeling the area in question there was nothing but skin and an itch.

I turned and as I did the rays of sunlight split my vision with a prism of colours above my retina. A horn echoed in between the buildings, another, and then another. A bus pulled around a black car swearing and irate. A black car, parked on the double yellow lines, tinted windows and a waxed finish, it was a black Lexus. The drivers side opened, my heart burst with anticipation, a pair of thick boots hit the pavement as a traffic warden from across the street dashed between traffic. The man stood out of the car, a black windbreaker ruffling in the light breeze. A pair of jet sunglasses covered most of his face and a thick untrimmed beard sat with the raw aggression of an arctic wind. The luminous jacket of a traffic warden flashed against the sun as he walked up to the strangely familiar man "I am sorry sir, you cannot park here! I will have to give you a ticket then you will be on your w–"

The mans sentence was cut short by the stiff rising arm of Mayweather. The warden fell to the ground in a mist of red tumbling onto the stairs of the nearby hotel. Even from here and through the beard I could see the smile, that look of the predator finding its prey vulnerable at last. Venturing out into the world without its master. I took a glance down the street, a few pedestrians looking baffled by the collapse of the traffic warden, some smiling and thinking he deserved it but the pavement ahead was not too clustered. The traffic lights where on red so if I went now I would be straight across, I noticed all this in a matter of seconds, I could feel the inner instinct of my survival coming into the fray, the ones Wolf, or McCloud had told me to hone.

I ran. It didn't take long for the adrenaline to flow, my legs pumping, and my heart throwing blood to the brain quicker than an Olympic runner. My knees started to loosen; my lungs began to take more and more air in. I charged across the street leaping over a car bonnet, sliding onto the ground rolling over and bouncing up as quickly as a horse jumper. The pavement carried on, the buildings and people I past where a blur, screams and sirens rang out into the street; I flew past the Irish National Bank and stormed across the road weaving between the oncoming busses. I managed a quick glance back; Mayweather was in hot pursuit, the windbreaker shed and glasses struggling to stay on.

With the gentle breeze at my back I powered on breaking into the main square where a spear of water lanced the sky in front of me. I dodged to the side of it into another and then the fountains sprayed over the top of me drenching me from head to toe. I shook my head while running; I couldn't let it slow me down. Mayweather was still in pursuit, his run graceful like that of a cheetah. I felt like an ostrich, running fast but awkward and as if my knees were bending the wrong way. I padded my pockets turning onto Bank Street, nothing except the card from Carter! Not even my god damn phone! I'd left in such a fury that I hadn't picked anything up! How could I be so stupid! I took another left which led me down an alley down the side of HSBC and charged down the incline till I reached another clearing. This time more secluded with only a handful of people about but the high rise buildings that surrounded us were full of people. No doubt the audience would be huge. I had to make the choice. I couldn't run forever hoping to tire him out. I was sick of running! Sick of being saved! It was now or never, if I got caught then he would kill me but if I got him.....

I turned and stopped on my back foot and Mayweather put the brakes on hard, his boots skidding slightly in surprise. We were in what I would call a governments attempt at an outside public garden, no plants but green shrubs, a set of maroon steel benches and a pleasant set of statues depicting a happy family.

I removed my pale blue tie, threw it to the floor and unbuttoned the top of my shirt. This was going to be an old fashioned street brawl, the kind you get outside pubs in the early hours where anything you find was a weapon. Mayweather had very little on underneath the now discarded windbreaker, a simple T-shirt with the slogan 'Do I look Bothered?' blazoned across the front. "You've got more guts than I remember" said Mayweather

We had attracted quite a crowd with our run and the healthier of the pedestrians had just caught us up completely engrossed on what was going on. They were in for a shock. I threw the first punch and it landed cold and hard along Mayweather's chin who stumbled back under the force. He lunged back, sluggish but powerful, I managed to jump to one side and parry the next punch from his left before landing a solid shot to his kidneys that curled his body into an inverted arch. Left arm hovering over the affected kidneys he took tentative steps back. McCloud would be proud of me I thought through it all, Mayweather was badly hurt, reeling from the punches I had landed. I could see a tear forming in his eyes, a swelling evolving around his chin. As normal with fights outside in the public, and especially in the north, the crowds were gathered around in a circle, a pit of human de-evolution returning to the primal roots of wanting to see someone get hurt, that raw powerful bloodlust that is inside every once of us. I screamed as I lunged forward, arms too predictable and slow as in one swooping motion he had grabbed hold of my right arm, twisted and threw me to the ground, jumping ferociously to the ground on top of me like a lion attacking its prey. His hands clung to my neck, his fingers the size of rolling pins as the air rushed out of my mouth. I couldn't breathe! Air, I needed air! Panic rifled through my body, seizing my muscles. I pulled at his hands but to no avail, I could feel it all slipping away as the fearsome grin of Mayweather leaned over me, spit slipping from his tongue dangling at the back of my throat. One last.... *push!* Knee, connected in between his legs, hard and he fell back yelping only to get to his feet again quickly swinging a heavy Dr. Marten boot into my chest. I flipped up, my legs rejuvenated and with fury charged at him headfirst lifting him off the ground and slamming him up against the statues of the children.

I unhooked myself from under his arms and aimed a straight boot in between his unresisting legs. I thought even if I lose this I can stop him from ever having sex again. It was then I noticed he wasn't moving too much, the dribble of red seeping gently from a bubbling lip. Then I noticed the finger poking through his chest. I turned to the side of him seeing that the outstretched arm of the smiling teenage statue was firmly through him, pointing through his chest at the building behind me.

The police picked me up ten minutes later, handcuffs in front, and arrested me next to the mob of city workers. I felt like I should say something meaningful, raise a fist and say 'Fight the Power', but common sense prevailed and I went silent.

I was currently sat waiting in a dark interrogation room with a single light bulb and the table in front of me. It was hard to get a sense of detail through the smell of old sweat covered with lavender air freshener and was enough to fuel my suspicion of blood on the wall.

It was now I started to think of options, contemplating who my phone call should go on. The SES would deny all knowledge, I couldn't break contract by even mentioning them. I couldn't ring anyone I knew as there was no one. Until I remembered that Carter had given me her number, that was an SES phone, she could collect me; there was just the little matter of murder hanging on my head.

An iron bolt slid across the heavy set door and light shone in. The silhouette of broad shoulders stood in the doorway and then a second set walked in with him. One of them shut the door, bolted it and stood back observationally watching his partner slam a thick folder down onto the table.

"You're dead?" he said sitting down.

He had slick black hair, but was as greasy as a burning wax candle. A thin moustache suggested more effort than the overall look let on. "I'm Agent Saunders. Behind me is Agent Wilkins. You have been a busy man Agent Banner... or should I say KIA Agent Banner. Death suits you"

"I want my phone call" I said sternly but with stark realisation I saw what this was. This was the MI: 5 finding me.

"No one you can phone can save you Mr. Banner" said Agent Saunders, "But we would enjoy a rendition on your course of events. You see, myself and Agent Wilkins here were sent after you. That is after Agent Clarke had reported ex-Agent Mayweather had hired help to knock him out on the boat. He went next to collect Agent Carter and then we had a body bag and a very large hotel bill. Are you with me so far?"

I nodded in inclined agreement. There was little point in contesting something that had been dragged through weeks of reporting, that sort of thing got you nowhere.

He made a scrunched up face like he had just swallowed a nest of wasps and the repercussions were stinging hard. Saunders suit was pitch-black, so it looked like white hands floating in the gloom. "We were ready to assume that you were either captured by Mayweather, or you had made chase, we were trying to help you until we found your new status very interesting. Tell me Jonathan..." he leaned with a hint of ferocity, his voice tinged with cold, "... how are you dead when you are sat here?"

"Zombification?"

"Do you think we are deaf, dumb and blind at the MI: 5?"

"No but you sure play a mean pinball"

Saunders sagged back into his chair, waved his right arm behind him, ushering Agent Wilkins forward who whispered something in his ear, shielding it all with his right hand. Then anger streaked across Saunders' face, "I know it was The Who!"

I wish I hadn't smiled. "You think it's funny?" snapped Saunders, clicking his fingers, a determined right hand of Wilkins thundering across my cheek. "Did you like that Mr. Banner?"

I raised a hand, gave Saunders a thumbs up. The fist came again, this time I dodged it, his knuckles cracking on the wall to my side. I lunged up, grabbed his wrist and span it round, a kick flick of my foot into his knees sent Wilkins face down into the table with a crack. As I reached into Wilkins' jacket a slurred speech hung in the air, Saunders knew how to end it, and most people freeze in the face of danger, Saunders pointed his gun at it. "Don't move another step"

Wilkins spluttered beneath me, a stray tooth sliding along the metal table. A trail of blood skipped along the surface, weaving in and out of the grime like the Thames.

"What are you going to do Saunders?" I said "Kill me?"

"Don't push me Banner. You are already dead officially"

"You don't have a licence to kill"

It suddenly dawned on me that I was turning into Wolf, McCloud, whatever his name was. Adrenaline didn't run yet, I was expecting it to kick in but the ignition didn't start. This would have got my blood running only a week ago, I managed to grip hold of Wilkins gun, my hands began to shake, Wilkins tried to get up, his broad shoulders forcing backward. As his head rose, I smashed it back down again and the resistance gave in.

It was now or never! I scanned the room, shot the light in one sweeping motion, shut my eyes and ducked.

I knew I didn't have long. A few seconds at most, I crawled along the width of the table and hugged the wall around to the door. The grey indentation of Saunders, stooped and swaying in the dark came into view. A long echoing sigh burst from Saunders mouth as the gun butt split Saunders in two. I quickly turned and unbolted the door, slammed it behind me and walked nervously but with purpose down the magnolia corridor.

The station was mainly abandoned but for the few stalwarts who would live here if there wives and husbands wouldn't order them home. I tried furiously to remember which way it was to safe-keeping. I needed Carters Card and that number, no doubt it was filled away but I needed to try and simply turning the corner brought results.

The holding area was busy. What day was it? I looked at the clock, it was five in the afternoon, and time had flown by. The football hooligans were in force and the flustered old policeman was twitching his moustache at the knob head fans screaming abuse and spitting out from their drunken mouths. Leeds United fans were guaranteed to get arrested on match day regardless of opponent or type of game.

A chequered capped fan gave me a window of opportunity and I launched myself at it, pushing open a side door and slipping inside, back to the shut door and lowered down to a crouch. The flustered policeman hadn't heard the noise above the drunken fuelled mayhem outside his booth. Another chav screamed out loud, his Burberry cap sent flying by an outraged policeman at the side of him. Suddenly a handcuffed pair of fists flashed out from behind the crowd and soon there was chaos. God bless Leeds fans!

The distraction was enough for me to take a good long look at the number tray my belongings were being kept.

No. 342.

The sorting system was idiot proof and I soon got to my things that simply involved the SES ID card and the card that Carter had given me the night before. I pocketed them and noticed as soon as I had that the hubbub had died down. "Hey!"

I saw the moustache before the man. Its silver length curling at the edges but the eyes above it were furious, a taser was whipped from his pocket and the old man charged.

Steady... He bore down the corridor like a bull

Steady...... The old man shouted at the top of his voice.

Now! I bolted to one side, took a step back and thundered a forceful blow up the side of the policeman's body. His skeleton shooting to one side in midair, curving in at the waist from where I had hit him and then he fell in a crumpled heap. I grabbed the taser, and ran back to the door to get out of the booth. I hit it with more force than I thought and fell through the door, rolling as I tried to slow myself down. I hit the far wall with a thud but this was no time to be weakening. I picked myself up, stimulated by the pain I could feel refreshing in my head, the fear was running now, the excitement gathering. Behind me I could see the MI: 5 agents, desperate and confused holding their heads in a tired bid to recover. They pointed at me, Saunders collapsing to his knees as he did so.

The doors to the outside world only a corridor away seemed now to be as far as the moon. The afternoon sun beating through the window, out onto the streets of Leeds. I took a deep breath, steadied and on the charge of the policeman made my dash.

Each step was suddenly like a burning ball of flame had erupted at the balls of my feet as I charged into Leeds City Centre. The sudden rush had dug into my heart, the fury of chase propelling me as I charged for the doors. I was there, the automatic doors taking there time to open but shut on the policemen behind me as I ran as fast as my legs could take me, left and into the bus station. Phone, phone, I needed a phone!

The crowds parted as they saw me coming except for one business man who looked out of place, he was on his mobile! With quick hands I pilfered the phone, his shouting from behind me merely an echo as I saw his briefcase slide past me in anger. The phone was brand new, touch screen and completely foreign to any kind of phone I had ever used before. I turned the corner and stopped, my legs thanking me a thousand times as the few fit policemen who had bothered to follow me further than the edge of their own building swept past. The stare of a small Jack Russell looked up at me, behind him his master, a homeless man in his thirties swallowed by a battered looking blanket. The smell was all I needed to know. I took Carters card out of my pocket and dialled the number. A small but crystal clear message prompt appeared on screen. NO CREDIT.

"God damn it" I said and then looked once more into the eyes of the cute old dog. "You don't happen to have a mobile do you?" I asked

"Erm..." a petrified hand raised from the pits of the blanket and the wave of toxic garbage flooded over me. "... I do?"

"You haven't got a home, a job or a life, yet you have a phone?"

"Erm..." the man seemed lost in a world of chemicals, drug use creates this, people who can only start sentences with the noise 'Erm' and can only end it when there brain clicks into the right gear. I despise drug users! "Can I ring off it?" I asked

"Erm... Yeah, I get a hundred free minutes a month"

"Excellent pass it here" I said as the man reached into the blanket and uncovered from god knows where a battered old Nokia which was absolutely perfect. I resisted the urge to wipe the mouthpiece before I rang but knew I would have some sort of disease later on. The phone managed to crack a buzz through the speaker and Carter's voice came into sound, her voice as pleasing a sound I had heard all day. "Carter it's me Banner. I need your help?"

"What's wrong? Where are you?"

"I've been arrested for killing Mayweather in broad daylight"

"Why on earth did you do that? The SES will kill you for that!"

"Not if MI: 5 get to me first. They know we aren't dead Carter, they know we didn't die in Egypt, they know we have ran from them!"

"Calm down" she said, "We have time. Where are you?"

"Leeds Bus Station"

"I'll be there in ten minutes"

The ten minutes felt like ten hours as Carters silver Passat screeched to a halt outside the station. I jumped in, head down and took the sunglasses and baseball cap that Carter had kept on the dashboard, the rush washed over me like a wave of relief, a pang of nerves returning every time we passed a pissed off looking police officer. "So what the hell is going on?"

"MI: 5 know about us. I think they must still have been following Mayweather and now I've killed the bastard they know about me too!"

"We really need to tell the SES about this"

"I know" I said glumly, "If McCloud doesn't kill me, it's going to make the job a lot harder with MI: 5 on our tails too"

"What is McCloud like when you properly talk to him, you know, away from the fighting and the saving lives?" she said dramatically changing the subject. The mood in the car shifted as she pulled onto the ring road and headed directly for Morley. Why did everyone think McCloud was some superhero!

"He is just a man. And a liar it turns out, Wolf is McCloud"

"Wow. Really? I would never have guessed that..." she said and suddenly I realised that there was a lashing of sarcasm eclipsing what she had just said. "You knew?"

"I thought you did as well! Ian told me"

"Thanks. You could have told me too"

"I thought you already knew!"

Carter's driving reeked of advanced training and it soon dawned that she had been sent on a lot more training courses and job improvements than I had. There was even a small stump nosed .45 pistol in a holster on the inside pocket of her custom jacket. This was a very different Carter to the one I went to Egypt with. The horizon brought with it the dome on top of Morley Town Hall, the Passat curving around into the underground car park underneath her apartment block only two hundred metres down the road. It was above Barclays Bank, surrounded by the same glass used at HQ, the black reflective glass that blinded you when the sun came out. "Come on; let's get you cleaned up eh?"

She led me through the security gates and doors around the back of the bank and around a spiral staircase that at the top opened into a beautiful open flat with a dominating window doubling as a wall. The afternoon sun now setting on a bright red sky, the claret shade turning all the white furniture pink. There was a distant but noticeable fragrance of deep lilies, a burning stick of incense smouldering behind thin gauze like cage and underneath a small but delicate rose sat on top of the centrepiece coffee table dividing the sofa from the TV. It all seemed so cliché, or modern maybe, but there was a homely appeal. Unlike my flat which I had only used for maybe a few nights, Carter had been living here, been working here and making it her home, and the aura of the flat made it feel twice as warm as it probably was.

She sat down, crashing into the soft leather sofa and after removing her jacket undid the top two buttons of the white shirt underneath. I sat down next to her and without a word she turned to me and kissed me. The kiss lasted a lifetime, enveloping me with a warm glow passing the gentle aura of her genteel self through her kiss as a line of saliva grew as we pulled apart before splitting at the end of her luscious wet lips. Shock rifled through my veins making them stick out like ropes. "What was that for?"

"I was worried about you" she said and then hugged me. "Do you know how long I've wanted to do that?"

All I could do was smile because my throat had gone numb. So this is what it felt like to truly feel something for someone? This is what all the love songs are about? This feeling of complete euphoria that sends shockwaves of tingling electricity down through your muscles and into your brain. "What are we going to do?" I asked softly. She stroked my jaw with one soft hand while she stared at me, resting the side of her head on the sofa. Her eyes were as deep as oceans; I could swim in those eyes! "Do we have to talk about that now?"

"But what if the MI: 5 find us!"

"Then..." she reached behind her, picked up a remote control and behind us a row of blinds began to descend over the Morley skyline. "...at least we will have enjoyed the last night with each other"

My nerves had well and truly shredded by the time the door swung open that I nearly jumped out of my skin at the very sight of an unshaven Wolf... or McCloud. In just a day he had managed to go from clean shaven to gorilla, the transformation was quite incredible. "You alright kid?"

"Am I in trouble?"

"For what? Killing a guy who chased after you? No kid, you're not in trouble, I knew the MI: 5 were looking for you but I didn't tell you because I didn't think you could do with that as well as everything else"

The door opened and Bingham, followed by Charlie, made there way into the room. The large oak desk sat in the middle of the room that had looked so daunting when I arrived here by myself was now swamped with people. Charlie put her arms around me from behind and planted a firm kiss on the side of my cheek, I didn't know how to act but I know McCloud saw my disgruntled look. "Did you get anything out of it?" asked Bingham

"What do you mean?"

"Any leads?"

"I was a bit busy fighting for my life" I said almost snapping it back at him. I didn't realise that the stress of the past few days had really built up as much as they had. I wasn't the kind of man to let my feelings explode but there are definitely a few small eruptions on the brink. "Tell us what happened then, you never know, something might come out of this"

"All that happened was when I left here; he parked up, knocked out a traffic warden and then chased me"

McCloud's eyes lit up. "What car was it?"

"I can't remember... oh it was that black Lexus"

"The same one that was following us the other morning?"

"I think so"

"Steve, get hold of Dora. She should have written down the registration number of the car a few days ago. We will see if we can find it anywhere, with any luck it has been impounded"

"Why?"

"Because you never know what people leave in there car. We can't get his body, but his car might just tell us what he was doing next"

I had to admit the whole process was swift and impressive. I had barely enough time to take a shower when McCloud came for me and now we were speeding into Leeds once again to the council scrap yard. Bingham had gained access to the DVLA, found the car had been towed and found its location. If nobody claimed it within two weeks the car would be crushed so it made it fairly imperative that we got there fast, because I also had a inkling that MI: 5 would be just as quick. "Open the glove box kid" he said, "There should be two ID's. Your Agent Kent, I'm your superior Agent Forsberg"

As the impound came into view the road got dustier and more torn up from the amount of heavy vehicles that had ploughed through the concrete. We took a hard left into the grounds and memories of Hollywood films portraying American scrap yards came into focus. The thin chain link fence plastered with signs warning of prosecution and two rottwieler's barking insanely at McCloud's comfy Mondeo. A battered caravan sat in corner of the site as McCloud and I stepped out of the car, a biting slash of wind smacked at our overcoats and once again I felt part of the fold, I couldn't believe the effect of a suit and tie, the power it can give you, it's a rush un-equal in the clothing sense.

The chain link gate slid across the automatic rollers as a wide eyed rottweiler snapped at our heels, a chain the size of an anchor keeping the dog out of our reach. "Can I help you lads?" said a scruffy man emerging from a caravan that looked part of the wreck. He was busy wiping his hands and then after he had, wiped his mouth and threw the towel away into the heaped mess of wrecked steel. I didn't think places like this actually existed outside of Texas but here I was on the outskirts of Leeds feeling transported back to the days of dodgy scrap yards. "Yeah I'm Agent Forsberg" said McCloud holding up the badge, "This is Agent Kent. Did you receive a black Lexus that was found on King Street two days ago?"

McCloud was good, his voice enough to scare the grubby man into submission even before the surly comments came out. The man pulled his baseball cap down over his eyes and said in a raspy tone, "Follow me"

As he led us through the complex maze of cars, above us sat an enormous crane and below it the compactor, the dusty road seemed to confuse the proprietor even though you got the impression he knew this place like the back of his hand. "So why is the MI: 5 involved? The owner try to top someone off?"

"Have you moved anything from the car at all?" asked McCloud

"No"

"Really?"

"No I swear"

"If I find anything missing from this car I will find you and get you locked up for a long time"

"I know but I didn't take anything I swear to you"

"Anybody else been interested in it?"

"What? I can't tell you that!"

"You can and will"

"Some woman rang up" he started with a sigh, "Saying it was hers, but she couldn't tell me the registration so I told her to buzz off, you know"

"And you didn't remove anything at all from the car?"

"No" he said and then waved an arm in the general direction of the black motor.

The Lexus looked like it had had a long journey before arriving here at the scrap yard. The arches were caked with hardened mud and the back window had the window wiper rainbow of cleanliness surrounded by thick build up. McCloud wasted no time and reaching down to pick up a steel rod that looked like part of the chassis of an old Suzuki, smashed the window to the drivers side and unlocked the door. "Check the boot kid" he said lifting a handle that triggered the boot to spring open.

The back of the car was filled with the usual garb and accoutrements found in the estate versions with a first aid kit tucked neatly into the felt folds, a metre of elastic rope with two hooks on each end sat next to it. A spare tire, rusted in the middle around the nuts, was waiting patiently in the middle with a few jugs of water. Nothing special. "Kid, we got something"

I shut the boot and walked around to McCloud who was sat with a freshly lit cigar in the driver's seat rolling a business card over and over in his fingers. "Name look familiar to you?"

I took it from him inhaling the wave of thick cigar smoke, "Laura Wood : Head of Force Security eh?" I said. The name was written in the font that made it look like it could be joined up, and was decorated with several golden badges all of which emblazed the name Force. Flicking it around there was remnants of what looked like HP sauce but could have been anything remotely the same colour. "Is this are next lead then?"

"Looks like it"

"There they are!"

We both turned at the same time to see the scruffy impound owner point two suited men in our direction. One was a bruised looking Agent Saunders and the other was the similarly annoyed looking Agent Wilkins, both of them with scowls enough to knock anyone off there feet. "Who are they kid?"

"Its MI: 5. They are tracking down the same leads"

"We need to get out of here then. And now"

Before I could answer McCloud was out of the car and running at the horizon of cars, the scream of the MI: 5 agents rang in my head as I followed McCloud pocketing the business card and pushing away the urge I had to turn and fight. Now was not the time, the time now was to run, you wouldn't get anywhere by fighting MI: 5 except pissing them off and getting another four Agents coming at you. A smart man knew to choose his fights well.

I followed McCloud who had banked left around a corner made from the wreckage of several dozen cubed cars, the sun lanced through the shattered windows, dust kicked up off each of our steps and looking back I realised we were leaving a very easy trail behind us. I backed onto the corner and looked around removing my pistol and then fired at the ground as the agents made their dash to cover. I took another shot to be sure and then ran for McCloud who was stood in wait; he outstretched his arm and fired as the agents skidded around the corner. A headlight shattered in the distance but retaliation followed with Saunders starring a windshield not more than a few meters in front of us.

As we ducked around the next corner McCloud looked at me with his back against the wall and simply nodded. He knew as well as I did that the only way to get out of here now was to stop them in their tracks. "I can't believe they are shooting us! They are only allowed to shoot if they feel under threat!"

"You've just shot at them kid! Is that enough of a threat?"

"Yeah but..."

"But nothing. We have got a lead but we need to get the hell out of here... *now!*"

As we caught our breath with our backs against the wall of rusted steel cars, now turned into cubes, the whistle of the wind carried Saunders voice. "We just want to talk to you Banner!"

"Well I don't want to talk to you" I shouted back, I could feel the bile rise from the pit of my stomach.

"Are you sure? I wanna know why you killed Mayweather Banner?"

I could feel McCloud behind me fidgeting with the wall of cars. Before I knew it I heard a grind of metal snap and a side mirror plunged from the depths. Using it, he peered around the corner, "Where is the other one?" said McCloud who turned into the face of the Wilkins who had crept around the compound and attacked us from the rear.

Wilkins curled a huge arm around McCloud's neck but as if by magic and a click of a finger the agent ended up the worse with McCloud reversing the move within the blink of an eyelid. He was that good. "It's no good Saunders!" I shouted, "We have your friend!"

"Let him go Banner. We just wanna know why you were betrayed!"

"What!?"

"We know someone betrayed you Banner. Someone ordered to have you killed and we don't know who"

"Neither do I!" I screamed

Saunders had seemed like a real bastard in the police interrogation room and now he was acting with the empathy of a vicar. I didn't know what to think, the cloud of doubt cast over my mind dotted with rays of sunshine saying that all this might just be true, if it was why would Saunders want to help me?

"What's in it for you anyway?" I shouted around the corner

"I wanna know why? Why get yourself put on the KIA list, why after completing your mission have you ran! What are you running from?"

"I am not running from anything!" I said bending my knees not once keeping my gun from the edge of the corner and then using the side mirror McCloud had dropped looked around the bend. Through the dust blown wind I could see Saunders creeping up on the corner with his gun drawn forward. "I am sorry Saunders" I shouted, "But you can't know anything"

As he took one step forward, I came down hard with the butt of my gun precisely where I thought his head would be and Saunders dropped like a sack of potatoes from the top of Big Ben. McCloud looked at me and then with a swift elbow knocked the other agent out cold, rifled through his pockets for his car keys and flung them into the compound scrapheap. "So they can't follow us" he said swiftly and then gestured me toward the exit.

We got into the car and with a ferocious rev of the engine McCloud threw the car out of the impound lot. "So where to now?"

"Simple" he said back to me, "We find out where this security firm is located and pay it a visit"

CHAPTER 7
DUFFTOWN

We'd Google'd Force Security and came up with the answers we were looking for fairly swiftly as the website gave us all the information we could possibly have needed and wanted. The company was set up in the remnants of the Second World War in 1946 and apparently was set up by an old American Sergeant who had become disillusioned with the state of life after he moved to London to be with his sweetheart.

The story was sentimental mush but clues leaked through the garbage with them saying that old Wol Wood loved the taste of Glenfiddich Whisky so much he set up the security firms modern HQ building up in the highlands of Scotland. In the small village of Dufftown.

It was that that made us set out and drive the next morning. Charlie came with us and sat in the back with me as Bingham drove with McCloud in the passenger seat constantly adjusting as he left his bandaged arm to dangle out of the window into the morning Yorkshire sun.

I had stopped at Carters the night before and managed to console her worries of Charlie coming along with us. She hadn't seen the need for Charlie, and to be honest neither had I, but McCloud's reasoning was that if anybody knew about secret clues hidden in code that was thousands of years old Charlie was better than any of us.

"I've never been to Scotland" said Charlie as Bingham guided the Mondeo onto the motorway.

"Oh you'll love it" said Bingham

"Yeah, it's got beautiful scenery.... and cows.... lots of cows" I said

"Sounds... nice?"

We didn't need to say it because everyone could hear the disconcerting groans from McCloud in the passenger seat. It was strange but we had all noticed how McCloud's breathing had gotten heavier as the past few days had become more and more drawn out, and that his arm was becoming more and more fragile in the mornings. A thick cigar smoke slid out through the window and almost fell onto the ground it was so convoluted. I like a smoke but not at 6am. McCloud seemed sucked into the fresh air of the open window, the yellow fields around us glowing in the morning sunlight. McCloud had said he had spent most of the afternoon yesterday in the medical bay, seeing his GP, which would explain the arm, and that was what was putting him in such a bad mood. It was mystifying in an awkward sort of way that after finally managing to get a hot lead that we were driving our way north and not only that, but seeming so relaxed. I could imagine the MI: 5 with this kind of lead and the whole place would be buzzing like a lake of water with live wires dangling above it. As it was, the SES building was the same as ever, a nice placid spring.

"Did you pack everything Bingham" asked McCloud waking from a painful looking reverie

"Yeah, equipment for the three of us. Don't think we will need it though"

"Better to be safe than sorry though"

"How's your arm doing?"

"It's reet. It's always like this in the mornings now"

Watching Bingham and McCloud talk was like seeing the old gents in the working men's clubs, recapping on the life they had had, fondly remembering things that should have been forgotten decades ago and underneath it all, the greatest respect for each other that nothing could interfere with. It was reassuring to see.

"Are you and your lady friend okay now?" asked Charlie out of the blue, McCloud and Bingham carried on talking as if she had said nothing. "Yeah she is fine now. I think it was just a shock for her seeing you in my apartment"

"Tell her I'm sorry won't you?"

"I will" I said. I had no plans to tell her, she wasn't exactly the top of Carter's Christmas cards list right now, "Who is working on the scrolls since your here?"

"Since they haven't managed to decode what the photos say yet, they allowed me to come with you. They should be ready by the time we get back"

"Oh"

I had nothing else to ask Charlie. For the rest of the trip she just sat there with incredible beauty oozing from her like a waterfall of paint, she was quite something to look at; shame a mannequin had more personality.

Scotland had leapt at us fairly quickly as the hills started to spawn, it seemed sometimes at random, and McCloud turned into a grumpy old bastard. Charlie had been fairly dormant since we passed Newcastle and not been too impressed by the Angel of the North but when she saw the heather filled hills she suddenly sprang into life. "It's as if there is no civilisation anywhere, you can't see any towns at all, just landscape!"

"Of course you can't see towns" said McCloud bitterly, "There are too many fucking hills! England is just as beautiful, just as stunning but because we had the know-how and can-do attitude to grow and expand we get told our land isn't as nice. Five minutes ago we were in England, now since we passed some incredible invisible dividing line we are in stunning fucking Scotland! You know why you can't see towns and culture? You know why?"

The anger was boiling in his voice. "Why?" I muttered

"Because there are so many fucking hills you can't see anything else! God damn it!"

Silence brewed in the air like a teabag left in a cup for over an hour. Then the services sign flashed and McCloud's anger erupted again, "Lets all have a break. I need a new tin of cigars anyway and if they give me any Scottish fucking monopoly money I really will hit the roof"

We had passed Keith twenty minutes ago and were ready to stop and ask for directions when the Glenfiddich Distillery came into view and suddenly the small village of Dufftown spread out in front of us, and so did the rain. I was as surprised as McCloud when we had travelled this far north and not caught sight of anything more than a few drops in the wind, but now here was the storm bubbling over us like a pan of hot water on the brink of overflowing.

Dufftown seemed to be just one street as the Mondeo cruised along passing shut down shops, a couple of small museums, a flower shop and a fish and chip shop. Then dead ahead of us was the centre, it was quite easy to distinguish, there was a big tower in it. Standing at well over fifty feet the old stone tower was the closest thing to a landmark that the town had, and yet McCloud had to make a comment. "It was a prison before"

"What? Why, looks like a lookout post to me"

"No. Look at the windows. If it was a lookout post they would be arrow loops for the archers. Those windows are square with bars across them, that is a prison if ever I saw one. Nice idea, having a prison for the centre of your town, wonder whose idea that was!"

McCloud's disregard for anything remotely Scottish was bringing a dampener down on the morale of the car and yet as we drove on a little bit further past a lavish looking golf course, we found the building we were looking for. Splattered on the horizon worse than a pylon in the middle of the Sahara was the Force Security building proudly displaying its logo for the highlands to see, a building built out of glass it seemed, quite the opposite to security really.

Bingham parked up the Mondeo in the company car park and turned handing me a card bearing my name and title relating to Hellz Records. "This is your alias" he said, and then handed another one to McCloud. "Same names as the MI: 5 aliases'?" I asked seeing I was once again Mr. Kent.

"Yep. The names are safe and secure"

McCloud muttered something under his breath and pulled himself out of the car using the doorframe to support his rheumatism stricken arm. "Follow McCloud's lead. Charlie and I are going to scout the grounds, see if we can turn anything up on them"

So out we went, standing on the precipice once again of a mission that lay ahead. The past few days were awash with the amount of content that had filled them, thoughts of Egypt were now like a distant memory and all of the previous exploits seemed to lead to this. I looked at McCloud who stumped out a cigar on the floor and in his face I could see that he had been here thousands of times before, sat on the edge of the mission thinking if I do something wrong here... I am going to die.

He turned to me and in his eyes I could see something I hadn't seen before. It looked like fear but it wasn't for what was ahead of him but fear of something worse. His body physically sagged and then, as if putting his work face on, put his jacket on to hide the bandaged arm and we walked across the stoned courtyard into the building.

We both had to wipe our brows from the rain, our fringes flicking away flashes of rainwater onto the smooth marble floor. Amazing what could cause a compensation claim nowadays. The reception had style and class but very few people. An ornate reception made of what looked like real oak was the only feature and was positioned opposite two wood ordained elevators flushed into the wall. The receptionist looked happy enough to wait for us to sort ourselves out, this despite us dripping water all over. Behind the wall he stood in front of I could hear a toilet flush and seconds later a security guard walked out and sat down on a chair next to the elevators which somehow I had failed to see.

At last the receptionist took notice of us, although he seemed more bothered with what was on his computer screen than us. He was hard to describe as weedy was the wrong way of putting it, there was definitely muscle there, or at least the potential of muscle, and his cheeks were chubby yet his figure was quite slender, he was a quandary. "Can I help you two gentlemen?" he said. When he talked, all you could see was teeth, bright white and completely nicotine free. His Scottish accent was fairly light which was a good thing, I didn't fancy the argument he would have had with McCloud otherwise.

"We are here to see Laura Wood. About the security for Hellz Records in Leeds, we booked an emergency appointment last night" I said looking at McCloud who had turned and been out stared by the giant security guard. Being in Scotland was seemingly putting him on edge, or was there something else; it was hard to tell sometimes with McCloud. The receptionist began typing away on a computer that had been set flush into the desk, "Ah yes. Miss Wood will see you in a moment. If you would like to go to the fifth floor, our doorman will see you there safe" he said and gestured the mean looking security guard toward us. "Here are your guest passes" he said passing us two passes that could be clipped onto our shirts, "And have a pleasant talk with our chairwoman"

It seemed strange to me as we headed up the elevator feeling the floors zip by us that a security guard was a doorman and briefly lost track of what I was doing and nearly asked him if he earned two wages but McCloud's look and the fierce black eyes of the security guard made me think twice. The elevator doors opened out onto a shimmering room filled with bright lights trying there best to push away the sight of the rain behind them. Once again the walls were glass and the far partition to our right was tinted but there was obviously someone in there, that was when the elevator behind us shut and we had little option to sit and wait in the snug black leather chairs. It was like a foyer for a hotel but without the magazines scattered around and then the far door opened and a tall elegant lady reached out her hand in greeting. "Good day to you both" she said shaking my hand and then McCloud's, "I hope you have not been waiting long?"

"No, we have just arrived thank you" said McCloud managing to hold back some of his aggressive voice.

As she invited us in to the office I knew I had to keep a clear head but up here in the Scottish mountains McCloud seemed to have lost his. Since leaving England he had seem somewhat erratic or distracted or maybe it was just my imagination.

It was then that I realised the horrific truth. I had seen this woman before, she was the one from the Forgotten Library, it was hard to tell in the face but when she spoke, that pure slice of evil tinged onto the end of everything she said this was her. She was the one working for Alpha!

The office was large and quite spacious but filled with Egyptian relics and memorabilia. The desk was made of solid sandstone and I had images of how amusing it must have been for the workmen to lift it into this floor, even the floorboards looked like they were sweating. Anubis' carvings were scattered frequently around while the wings of Horus were carved intricately into the walls. Parchment rolls descended from the roof hanging onto the ground and words and deeds painted in true Egyptian colour and dye, it was very impressive. Yet McCloud had already made his way to a drawing on the left wall; to something that looked like a table or a graph but was labelled in a language not familiar to me. "Ah I see you like my office. I have enjoyed many a trip to Egypt; I am a great fan of their mythology"

"I can see that" said McCloud, "But this is not Egyptian is it?"

"No" she said hesitantly, "This is the Sephirot, it is from the Jewish Kabbalah. It describes the ten ways in which God can manifest himself once again. In Keter, Chokmah, Binah, Chesed, Gevurah, Tipheret, Netzach, Hod, Yesod and Malkuth. This is based on the teachings of Rabbi Moses ben Jacob Cordovero but there are others of course"

"Of course" countered McCloud who then looked at me. It was time to act and without a word I took my place at the door and guarded it. "So I understand you want a new complete package for your studios?" she said with ice cool calm, when you talked to her you could feel the wind blow past your ear.

"Yes" said McCloud as sternly and woodenly as possible, "But I want to clarify a few things about your company first. I have fallen victim of poor security records before"

"Of course"

There was a silence in the air that wasn't there before; it wasn't the silence you get from nobody talking. It was the silence of nature holding its breath for the next line. "What would you like to know?"

"Have you any dealings with terrorism?"

The question hung in the room like a bad smell, it was as if McCloud was ready to give himself away without a moments bother, it was as if someone had taken from him the shrewdness that had made him so successful. I knew she was bad news and I knew she was our only real link to who Alpha was but to openly verbally assault her was not going to work. What was he doing?

"I can assure you Force Security has no dealings with terrorism"

"What about you yourself then? Does Laura Wood herself have any links?"

She took her time with each question, studying each one before giving back an answer. "I do not quite understand what you are getting at Mr. Forsberg?"

"Been to Egypt lately?"

He knew. McCloud had sensed it as soon as he saw her that she was the one from the hidden library in Luxor but the aggressiveness was uncontrollable. Why was he like this? I could see the cracks in her demeanour start to open, she was nervous. "I love Egypt as you can see. But I haven't been there for many months"

"I think your lying"

"Who are you? I do not like your tone Mr. Forsberg"

McCloud burst from his chair, gun whipped from his holster and facing forward. "Tell me where Alpha is now!"

The crackled face distorted into a perverted smile, she had him, and she had him good. Why had he been like this, why had he been so obvious. "Now I understand Mr. Forsberg, or should I say Mr. McCloud. And is this your pet here, Banner was it? I can't remember. I must say you had me well and truly fooled for a moment there"

McCloud's face exploded at the seams, anger was starting to boil over in his veins. Steam looked like it was ready to fly from his ears! "Tell me where he is! What is he going to do?"

"He is going to bring a great justice on this world. Gods Love will rise again!"

The door behind me nearly flew off its hinges; I pushed back at it trying in vain to hold back the force pushing from behind it. I thought I was winning until from a side door, set flush into the wall guards flooded in. McCloud span his gun round but to no avail as a small shiny tranquilizer dart penetrated his neck. I didn't have a leg to stand on, I moved from the door as McCloud took a heavy fall to the ground, and then without feeling a thing, I fell asleep.

The guards jabbed us in the back through a thick forest, past several large houses made from what looked like cinder blocks and then deep again into the forest following the mild little stream that weaved in and out of the foliage. We eventually came to a small outcrop chained off with the most flimsy looking piece of chain I had ever seen and they propped McCloud against it. "This is the Giants Chair" said Wood, "Not many people know of its origins or its meaning. We let people keep the myth going, let them think its paganism. We welcome the myth; they are very good at hiding truth"

"What the hell are you talking about?" screamed McCloud, a bust lip bleeding rapidly, making him spit to even get the most simple of words out.

There were two bodyguards that looked like trolls holding McCloud at each arm, hoisting him a few inches off the ground. For me there was just one. I couldn't help but feel a little insulted by that. "We are the Calivari, Mr. McCloud. Much like you, we are hidden from history, hidden in the depths of myth, hidden by the mystery and the scandal. We are the true believers of Christ"

"Bullshit!" shouted McCloud. In his voice the quiver of fear of the unknown. "We would know about you, we know everything!"

"Not us" she said calmly, "Our history is secret only to a selected group who are direct descendants of the original few. The few who had to flee their homes taking with them the infinite knowledge of our Lord God and build a whole new temple in his name"

"The hidden library?" I motioned. She turned to me as if remembering that I was actually there. "The Temple le Calivari" she said with pride. It was such a strong sense of pride that it rolled over you like a strong aftershave, you could taste it!

"We were the ones who had to flee our homes in the middle of the night. Taking with us all the scrolls we could carry, all the books filled with knowledge and run south, away from the Muslim onslaught on our beloved Alexandria. We marched south for seven days on the brink of death, when we found a temple. Abandoned and seemingly worthless, dedicated to gods impure and wrong. We desecrated them, chiselled their faces and found to our reward a feast of wild animals to save us from starvation. God had rewarded us for our hatred of the other gods. Fuelled by this we started to paint our words and teachings on the temple walls, the very same you can see today if you ever visit Karnak Temple.

As the years passed we became unsettled and at unease until the early 1300's when everything had changed. Unknowing to us at the time, the crusades had come to what was considered a conclusion well before that, in 1199. Our enemy had been destroyed, the Muslims held down by the strong arm of God, defended by the Knights of the Temple. And it was the Templar's who took us to safety away from the parched lands of Thebes, to Britannia, and to Scotland"

"There is no way the Templar's would have taken you so easily!"

"Of course not" countered Wood to McCloud; who's pent up rage was worrying even the guards now, "The Templar's were not fools. We gave them the Scroll of Aranius to prove our knowledge of God was not a falsehood. Which I believe your country found nearly five hundred years later"

"The Atherton Scrolls?"

"We promised the Templar's all the knowledge they could ever wish for in exchange for safe passage. They took us to a castle here in the Scottish Mountains and the Calivari's have not looked back since"

"Of course not. The Templar's were abolished in 1314, I bet not long after you arrived in Scotland"

"Brilliant how an idea like Baphomet could so easily be understood"

"You did it?" questioned McCloud, "You brought them down?"

"Amazing really. How a few well placed images and half truths can make people turn" she said and it was then that I realised what McCloud was saying.

It was this Calivari group that had brought down the Templar's. Carving images of a three headed god called Baphomet and placing them in areas of Templar worship would be more than enough for the Pope and King to round up the Templar's. Charges of worshipping satanic imagery and strange acts had brought about the burning of every Templar on L'île aux Juifs in Paris in 1314. The burning man Jacques De Molay being the last, leaving behind secrets so unparalleled we still don't know them today. It was the tale that was told to so many children in French schools, the jealous king who wanted the wealth of the Knights of the Temple or the Templar's as they later became known. Then at the height of their power they were persecuted for trampling and spitting on the cross and worshipping this grotesque idol known as Baphomet, a statue bearing three bearded heads or in some cases, four feet. Phillip IV of France had them all arrested on the 13th October 1307 where under extreme torture many of the Templar's admitted to the crimes and more including homosexuality. The Pontiff, Pope Clement V officially dissolved the poor knights of Christ in 1312 and Jacque de Molay, the last Grand Master was burnt at the stake in the March of 1314 where in his final words he cursed the King and the Pope that there death shall follow his in the year. Scarily, they both did.

"And the money?" asked McCloud. He turned his head, looking behind him over the edge of the Giants Chair. It was so quick I don't think she saw it.

"Money?" asked Wood

"You can't have reached this position of power as refugees from Thebes. You knew where the Templar treasure was didn't you?"

"Nobody to this day knows what happened to that treasure. The myth is that a group of surviving Templar's managed to move it all and hide it before anyone could find it. This is a half truth, there was a group who took it, but it was not the Templar's, it was the Calivari and we used it to build our fabulous empire!"

"You lied to history" said McCloud, "You are forgotten and lost in the arcane pages of history because you fucked over the group who helped you"

"How dare you" she said walking up to him, "We did what we needed to do to survive!"

"Nobody needs to kill thousands of Templar knights in falsehood to survive!"

"I didn't feel a plebeian like you would understand. Now I know I was right"

As she turned around a rugged looking Land Rover tore through a patch of grass not far from the edge of the forest. "I will leave you now" she said

"Wait!" shouted McCloud, "You said that this Giant's Chair was not pagan and that it was hiding the truth, if I'm going to die anyway. What is the truth?"

She let out a wry smile, as close to anything remotely pleasing about her entire posture and said "It was the pit of abyss for the Calivari. If you survived the fall you were forgiven for your crimes"

"Did anyone ever survive?" I asked

"No"

With that she was gone. The Land Rover tearing off with only the furious noise of its terrible engine surrounding the Scottish highlands. McCloud winked at me as the two guards holding him seemed to concur what they were about to do. As soon as they moved McCloud burst into life.

McCloud seemed to twist his body around himself in a way that I never thought possible; squirming under the arm of one of the aggressors he delivered a punishing kick to the back of the guard's leg, chopping him down, before pushing his head over the loose railing. My guard abandoned me to charge at McCloud but as he did I tripped him up, his head landing on a pointed rock and spraying blood like a fountain into the stream below. The final guard had just stopped and watched, frozen with fear as a trickle of urine soaked the inside of his right leg.

McCloud had turned to him with his whole body giving off the complete impression of being pissed off. The right arm of McCloud curved back, a thump with as much fury as a raging tiger was armed and ready, charging with each muscle being tightened like arrows in a bow when out of the wilderness the whirr of helicopter blades flashed over. The trees rocked with the wind, leaves flashed across our faces and then the huge shadow of a helicopter lashed across the floor. I looked at the urinated guard; eyes flashed blue, "Give me your gun!"

"I don't have a gun! You killed John who had the gun when you threw him off the chair!"

McCloud's look said it all. Just as he was about to say something the machinegun fire broke through the trees and smashed down on the ground like hardened rain drops. We both dived for cover as we saw the last guard obliterated by the shells, his bullet riddled body flailing into the waters below. The fire ceased momentarily and McCloud managed, "We need his gun from down there. I'll distract the chopper and you run down and get it!"

"How the hell you gunna distract it?"

"I don't know yet just do it!"

"What do I do when I've got the gun?"

"Aim for the fuel tank..."

The gunfire flashed across the forest floor again pulling up soil untouched for centuries. Then McCloud dived out of cover and ran into the open, his screams loud and brash; a cocky streak of insults splaying from his mouth like a boxer before a big fight. I stumbled over to the edge of the chair, the lip steep and the overhang too deep for me to swing down and into it. I managed to lower myself so I was hanging off the tiny lip and sidled across feeling the ancient stone crumble with my weight. My suit was tearing, my trousers were already tarnished in the knee, my arms were feeling the strain of the past couple of days and when I finally made my way to an area I could descend, I needed to rest. But the sound of incensed random gun fire spurred me on, I couldn't let anything happen to McCloud, I don't know what I'd do!

The sound of the bullets smashing into the ground was like a wooden plank slapping against wet concrete. I managed somehow to slide down a further six feet putting only the pleasant soft water stream between me and the now very deceased guard. Half of his head was missing and his arm was very much broken, twisting in a completely involuntary direction, but I guess this was the least of his worries. I reached into a holster on the inside of his jacket and pulled out a small snub-nosed .40 trying not to meet his glaring stare. The gun wouldn't have stopped a dog, never mind a helicopter. I span the barrel round and only four bullets from the six capacity barrel were loaded, either two shots fired or two for me and two for McCloud just in case the sacrifice hit a snag. The wild screech of the helicopter charging across again woke me from my reverie; I dashed out across the stream and into the light drizzle. McCloud was on the other end of the field some four hundred metres away and running for his life diving behind makeshift cover as the ground grew in small volcanic eruptions. I looked through the sight of the gun, the range was too far and there wouldn't be a chance in hell of a clean kill. I leapt forward, McCloud weaving in and out of the rocky outcrops occasionally diving into the heather. I could see his lips move in my direction but the sound of the chopper was blanking it out. The grass was cut up, the soil flying around getting caught in the wind; I steadied the gun only moments before the chopper sent another wave of furious anger, unleashing its payload of shells onto the ground. Rocks obliterated into pieces and then just as we were exposed for the first time I managed a single clean shot. The tiny bullet pinged the fuel tank; a slow drizzle of red diesel spilling across the lavender heather. "Quick!" shouted McCloud as he charged at me pushing me out of the way of oncoming lead.

McCloud thought fast and his lighter was soon out, the wind of the helicopters blades blowing the lighter out but McCloud angrily lit it up again before igniting the red line of diesel. A trail of fire flew through the air lit by oxygen and pummelled the fuel tank that swiftly exploded bringing the helicopter with it.

We dove for cover but finding none could only lie on the ground with our hands over our heads. I dared to look back over my shoulder as the smell of gas blew in the breeze; debris hammered into the floor, thud after thud of steel, the grass charred and the whirr of the blades... then the ground shook as the remnants of the chopper smashed heavily into the ground.

I turned around into the worst sight I could have imagined.

McCloud was face down into the heather, a stray grass root tickling his nose, his charred face a sign of a huge wave of red hot energy blasting against him head on. What was worse was by his knees, half of the helicopter blades had sheared loose and landed right next to his leg. I couldn't tell by just looking if it had taken his leg off or just brushed it. "McCloud..." I muttered pushing against him.

My whole body ached. I checked his pulse and he was alive, thank god. He groaned, and then with an ounce of strength tried to push himself off the ground. His left arm spasmed and sent him crashing back to the ground. I pocketed the snub-nosed just in case. "I can't feel my legs kid, go get some help. Get Bingham"

"I am not leaving you"

"Yes you are. Go get help or we will both die here!"

"You wouldn't leave me so I am not leaving you" I said helping him up to my level, his legs refused to work as the helicopter blade pulled away. I ripped off my jacket and tied it neatly around the heavy wound, it looked like it had torn cleaned through but right now that was the last of my worries. I hoisted him up into a fireman's lift position and managed somehow to get into the forest again.

I couldn't put him down no matter how heavy he was. He was muttering, I tried to keep him talking but it was impossible as the pain ebbed away at his consciousness. I put him down as we reached the stream; I washed his face clean with the soft water trying to somehow rejuvenate his body but to no avail. Once more I lifted him up into position and carried on, having to arch around the Giants Chair where the hill wasn't so steep. My thighs burned with the reminder of carrying Charlie through the Vatican, this time carrying an extra ten stone was making my eyes pop. The incline started to level off and I was able to arch around the edge of the forest past a wide open field that led to another hill and thought of what McCloud had said, 'You can't see anything for hills' and he was right.

For what seemed like hours I pushed on occasionally swapping shoulders with the unconscious McCloud but still not able to lighten the load. We came out to a road leading south down back into Dufftown when I heard a car rampaging up the road toward us. I readied the snub-nose ahead of me through bleary eyes, I thought I could make it out, it was blue, a pale blue... I blinked hard trying to free from my eyes the best sight I could.

I lowered my arm as the car skidded to the side of me.

It was Bingham's Mondeo.

I managed to lift my head enough to look into the eyes of Bingham whose assured face was the nicest thing I had seen in hours. I knew he was talking to me but all function had been lost in my head except for my eyes and even now they were beginning to curve inward. White light began to filter through them until everything in my sight looked like it had been smeared with Vaseline. I could just about feel someone pulling my arm and then a soft biting sensation and like a torrent of water flushing out my system every sense jumped back in one swift motion. Sound crashed against my eardrum, the smell of heather burst into my sinuses and then down in my arm was the sight of the adrenaline needle. McCloud was on my lap, half dead and out cold and Bingham was asking Charlie to open the door. "We need to get him help and quick" said Bingham who didn't want to look at McCloud's legs. Every time his eyes past them he shook his head.

Bingham grabbed him off my lap hitched him up and staggered with him toward the car and put him on the back seat and then looked at Charlie, "I'll be back soon. Stay off the road and hide..." he seemed to remember something and reached into McCloud's pocket, "...keep this tracker. We will know where to pick you up"

CHAPTER 8
DARK SECRETS OF THE PAST

"Things are far worse than we ever thought" said Bingham as he sat at the head of the table, his fingers arched together in front of him like an upturned 'V'. The room was littered with people I had never seen before but were all called together from different departments within the SES. Expensive suits, neat trimmed beards and enough aftershave to drown an elephant in. There was a big breakthrough in the case and it was time to let the whole Agency know.

He handed out an orange envelope to each individual and on first inspection it felt like nothing was in it until we opened it and a picture fell out. I could tell before I had seen the picture that the photo was bad, the looks on every face was enough to tell me that. The shock, the horror, it was one of the most vomit inducing pictures ever seen if I was to read the faces of the men. I turned it over and saw past the guards, past the surrounding foliage and straight into the eyes of the President of the United States.

"President Andrews was seen entering the Force Security building in Dufftown Scotland at 16:46 only minutes after the capture of Donald McCloud" continued Bingham, "We have great concerns regarding the Presidents appearance at the location but we have strong suspicion that the President of the United Stats is indeed the Alpha who we have been searching for"

There was a hush in the room. Everyone fell quiet as if stricken by paraplegia, outside the window behind Bingham I could see the storm clouds brewing. Death was on the horizon.

"How is McCloud?" I asked to try and break the silence.

"On the plus side Field Marshall McCloud is in full recovery. He has a broken leg and torn ligaments but they have repaired them in surgery and his rehabilitation is so far successful"

"And the scrolls?" I recognised the voice. It was Ian Jordan the head of the Intel Department and Carter's boss. His greasy hair was slicked back and he reminded me of the images of Dracula I had imagined when I was a kid reading Bram Stokers classic. His voice was like a very bad Mel Gibson impression.

"We have a small team working on the translation as we speak. The poor quality pictures have been set in super high resolution allowing our computers to educationally guess there symbology. A Miss Charlie

Lambent is leading the team and we hope to have results in the next twenty four hours"

"Who dropped the ball on this one then hmm?" said Jordan, "Why was an assault on the Force Security building sanctioned without the knowledge of the Intel Department and indeed if they are as seriously linked with this Alpha, surely we should have scoped the place out first?"

"As the case stood. McCloud and I felt the best course of action was to act fast; your Intel could have taken weeks. We needed to know and now we have the evidence we need to link it all together"

"But you still do not know anything Bing-Ham"

"We know something is being planned" I snapped back in the middle of the tiny argument breaking out between the two. "We also know that history has taken us for a fool. The Templar's were betrayed by a group called the Calivari's after they had given them safe passage from Luxor to Scotland. It's the same group who are coming out of the woodwork now and they are planning something big!"

There was a rapture of laughter and for a moment I felt crowded in to my small chair. The grins became wider and wider, aiming at me, my confidence shattered and blown away. McCloud wasn't here to back me up anymore and right now I felt almost afraid, but I had to stand firm. "You explain it all then!" I screamed back at them in desperation, "You tell me why a hidden library has been discovered, why the Atherton Scrolls after all these years mean something! You tell me why this all adds together!"

"Agent Banner" snapped Bingham, "Enough... As it stands we have no more leads. Until we have the translation of the scroll there is nothing for us"

I thundered back into the chair and saw the guffaw erupting in people's heads. They were all laughing at me. At McCloud and me, both of us the only ones to know and nobody will believe me! "I am sorry Agent Banner but for this part of the briefing I must ask you to leave. This is for department heads only" said Bingham whose face pleaded an apology. Without a word I got up and left understanding the anger that McCloud carries around with him every day.

The next day brought with it a heavy hangover and the stale smell of cold pizza all illuminated by the lancing sun stretching from the open blinds to my bed. Over a dozen cans were sprawled across the floor followed by another six bottles of the same stuff. Carling Black Label, so addictive it could kill you. There were also several cigar ends and my old Bob Marley vinyl and soon training school came back with a stark reminder. I had tried in vain to focus my eyes on anything in the room but everything was just a messy blur. I thought back trying to recap the events that led to this and remembered leaving the offices in a huff, fuming and boiling I remember driving home and talking to Carter trying to calm down but she was snowed under with work and I decided to let her be.

Then I remembered trying the pubs of Morley. It all came back in a swift aggressive swing of the reapers scythe. I was sat in a pub called The Queen Hotel, knocking back the lagers with alarming ease, struggling by the end of the night to remember what it was I actually did, talking to random strangers and a man called Stuart about the Knights Templar... then coming home to drown my embarrassment. My alarm buzzed, I slammed it down hard as it bounced off down on to the floor but the noise failed to cease and it soon became apparent it was my phone. "Get down here Banner", it was Bingham on the other line, "Charlie's cracked the scroll"

There was a buzz of electricity as Charlie stood over a desk with Bingham rapt to attention as she seethed through sheets and sheets of paper. "There are four parts to it...." she said turning and smiling as I walked in. Bingham saw straight away the beer in my eyes, "How much you have last night?"

"Don't ask"

"I don't really wanna know. Its hard being in that room I know, but try not to let it get to you. If it's any comfort I did the same, and so did McCloud"

"It's not any comfort.... but I appreciate the effort"

She held the translation up with pride. Charlie may not be top of my list of people to admire but there was no doubt about it, she knew what she was doing and she had put in all the effort I didn't expect after we kidnapped her from the Vatican and stuffed her in a boot. Funny how people react to different situations. "What does it say?" I asked, "Does it tell us where Alpha is going?"

"It's a story" said Charlie, "It was in four parts. It's a bit of a loose translation but it mentions ten conditions that the world must be under, and then it speaks of something called the Key of Kings, a Tongue of Salem and for some reason repeats the Atherton Scrolls"

"What? So what does it all say?"
"It's split into four and it says:

1)   Go down, charge the people, lest they break through unto the LORD to
gaze, and many of them perish. And let the priests also, that come near to the LORD,
sanctify themselves, lest the LORD break forth upon them.'
And Moses said unto the LORD: 'The people cannot come up to mount Sinai; for
thou didst charge us, saying: Set bounds about the mount, and sanctify it.'
And the LORD said unto him: 'Go, get thee down and thou shalt come up, thou, and
Aaron with thee; but let not the priests and the people break through to come up unto
the LORD, lest He break forth upon them.'
So Moses went down unto the people, and told them.

2)   If thou commandments fall /
Seek the King of the Garden /
For if thou mans flame should stall /
Thou Babylon's stalks tall /
The door is blocked but can be changed /
The Key of Kings is thoust only answer.

3)   And so the LORD spoketh with the tongue of Salem /
With thoust hellish breath and sharpening of teeth /
Then clay listened and obeyed the cries of the LORD /
Delivering the curse that set clay free.

4)   Just as the weeds are collected and burned up with fire, so will it be at the
end of the age. The Son of Man will send his angels, and they will collect out of his
kingdom all causes of sin and all evildoers, and they will throw them into the furnace of
fire, where there will be weeping and gnashing of teeth. Then the righteous will shine
like the sun in the kingdom of their Father. Let anyone with ears listen!

Bingham and I steadfast for a moment to let the years of information roam free in our heads and although I had wanted to say it since she began, it was Bingham who managed to shake some sense into his voice. "So what does that mean?"
"I don't know. I think it leads us to something. It is a direct reference to the Ten Commandments in the first part and then it talks of something called the Key of Kings, which has something to do with

Babylon. Then a Tongue of Salem and I have no idea what that is and finally that same quote"

"Is it me?" I said hastily before anyone else got the chance to speak, "Or does it all seem like a list of conditions?"

"What do you mean?" asked Bingham quickly

"Well... its mentions the Ten Commandments Charlie says, then gives us two riddles that will lead to the '*weeping and gnashing of teeth*' and the appearance of Gods Angels... you don't supposed this is a way to God?"

"Are you seriously suggesting that this scroll tells us the directions to Heaven?" said Bingham almost mockingly until he saw Charlie's face. Through everything she had been quiet stood rapt to thick attention at the theories being thrown around the room.

After she realised we had been looking at her Charlie drifted toward the window and stared at the cloud cover attempting to smother the Leeds skyline. Her skin glowed a soft honey colour from beneath a pair of new and expensive looking leather trousers. They certainly showed her... figure. "I think you may be right" she said, "And what scares me most is if someone out there finds there way to heaven... someone like this Alpha..."

"You think it might be some kind of weapon?" said Bingham

"I don't know what it is" she snapped back quickly, "I just know that if proof of Gods existence was true. Think what it would do to the world, it might not affect us but what about the Middle East. What about the other religions, Muslim, Buddhism, Islam... all of them would be dust"

"And that means war" said Bingham, "Which means if this thing is true we need to act fast. That means we are going to Babylon... which is near Iran is it?" asked Bingham in the direction of Charlie.

"Iraq" she said sharply.

"Just what we need" he said, "Searching for mythological treasures in a war zone. God sure did like to make it easy didn't he?"

We had been prepped for the jump into Iraq nearly an hour ago and hooked up to a series of gas masks all releasing a dose of pure oxygen. It was a strange light headed feeling, as if we had been forced to down a bottle of Jägermeister and then drugged at the same time. When we stood on the precipice of the open cargo door I looked at Bingham and saw the same dazed look in his eyes. The whole process was supposed to stop hypoxia, to flush the nitrogen out of your body and prepare the system for the HALO jump that was to follow.

As Bingham and I stood side by side fitted with our library of accoutrements that included polypropylene garments, we looked like robots ready to be hurled off the back of a plane. It was a risky move; Iraq has been a strict no fly zone for the SES for the past six years and after the public militaries became involved there was too much chance of getting caught but we didn't have much of a choice.

I could tell the wind was cold. Not because I could feel it through the thick polypropylene clothes, but because frost was forming on my visor and my oxygen mask. The drop off was in the ancient Mesopotamia region now known as the Babil Province due fifty five miles south of Baghdad. The report clearly said to get to the sight of ancient Babylon and find out exactly what the Key of Babylon is, and when we find it we will be dropped a vehicle by HAHO so we can reach a suitable location for pickup.

The red light to the right of the cargo plane door flashed off and then green signalling we needed to go. Bingham turned to me, but I could only see the sunlight in his shaded visor and then with a burst of speed he was gone and off the edge of the plane. Tightening my fists and taking a heavy dose of oxygen I ran and feeling the wind pushing against me jumped into the early morning sky.

Baghdad was not the friendliest place to be in the world right now. With rival militia groups and PMC's stalking the badlands surrounding the Iraqi capital, we expected a lot of attention as we stood on the precipice of the tore. Hiding under what must have been decades of rubble and dust we found a petroglyph flush to the jutting stone and knew then that we were in the right place. Hidden by the war zone of Baghdad and the tyranny of Saddam for decades was potentially the most religious site that the modern world could possibly see.

I could see the heat haze rising above the sands making the distant Baghdad look like it was baking in the heat. From here, it all looked so peaceful...

Bingham began to tap away around the corners of the huge tore while I stood and basked in the hot sun like a lizard sat on a rock. The petroglyph glared at me; running my hand along it my fingers I noticed that it was almost perfectly flush, but not completely, and with an extra bastion of grit I pushed hard against it sending it into the rock itself.

At first there was nothing but noise from underneath as if an old squeaky wheel was being forced to work for the first time in centuries and then a creak of stone followed at last by a hiss of smoke as the millennium of built up hydraulic steam shot from the cracks forming around the opening floor. Bingham gave me a sharp look, "I really hate you"

"Such animosity" I said, "I have a knack for this sort of thing"

After a few moments picking through our rucksacks we found a pair of torches and shone the light down what looked like an ancient set of wooden stairs each one more crumbled than the last. Again Bingham ransacked his bag pulling some rope and a grip and setting up a crude but solid abseiling position, and with a firm tug deemed it usable. He looked at me and I looked at him. "After you" he said

"Oh no. I wouldn't dream of taking this discovery from you. After you..."

Pulling one last time on the rope he swallowed a lot harder than normal and took the plunge. "Ha!" he screamed, "Never had any doubts!"

"What's it like in there?"

"Dark"

"Anything I didn't know"

"Well... it's a bit... smelly"

I held my rope firm tugging three then four times hard hoping that it would give way so I didn't have to go down there. It held firm. Gripping two torches I said, "Right behind you"

Actually stepping off the rock into the hole was a rush all of its own and when the snap of the rope held firm and I hung there floating next to Bingham my heart literally exploded. The dust shone in the torchlight as we followed the stark circle of light across the eroded staircase that must have been built thousands of years ago. It was strange, it was as if we were abseiling into a castle that had been encased underground and lost through time. I stepped down first, not to be disrespectful toward Bingham but simply because I didn't know anything of his skills out in the field. I'd always looked upon him as a pencil pusher, someone good with numbers and not with a gun but as he pushed on ahead of me with his luminous green strip I could tell my theory was completely wrong. The walls lit up around us in a green haze, the dregs of ancient roots sprouted from the ceiling and a smell that was all too familiar surrounded us like tear gas. "Its gunpowder" said Bingham holding the light up to the walls, "The walls are lined with it"

"Some ancient self destruct mechanism?" I questioned

"I have no idea"

McCloud would have known. The shadows of the stalagmites bounced off the glistening wet walls and the faint distant sound of creaking masonry soon became reality as we stood on the precipice of a staggering wide open space. Circular in shape, the space was like the inside of the Roman coliseum with arches on several different rows and columns leading south into the earth's core with no end in sight. Bingham lit a new strip of light and threw the old one down into the abyss and we lost it not more than twenty feet in front of us. To our left there was an ancient staircase groaning with age and pitted with rusty nails. A constant moan from the wood told us that the way down was not going to be this way. Then I saw something to our right on the wall covered in old dead vines, occasionally shining in the luminous green. As the vine pulled away with ease, a brass plaque with writing in what looked like Aramaic was fixed teasingly to the wall. "Bingham, come see this"

He made his way over, the sounds of emptiness providing a haunting ambience as he brought out a small notebook phone and took a picture. The flash of light temporarily lit up the arch to the side of us, and I swore I saw a figure. I pushed it from my mind and focussed on the phone, "What are you doing?"

"When we built the programme that managed to change the distorted Aramaic symbols into true Aramaic, we built the programme into our phones. This will read the Aramaic and give us a 98% accurate translation of the text"

As he said, the phone whizzed through the information in the photo and began spitting out the numbers before forming the words: 'THE HANGING GARDENS OF BABYLON'.

"Well we are in the right place at least" I said, "But this doesn't look like a city"

"I agree. Something is not right here"

I looked out into the open air ahead of us. The size was huge, maybe a mile in diameter but so tall that countless rows ran round and round to the bottom, each individually being at least forty feet tall. The old stone had weathered well down here and reminded me of the pictures of the acropolis' stone, as if it would have been white centuries ago but age had taken its greying toll. "Pass me a light" I said as he handed me a strip. I banged it against the wall and then tightening my teeth around it reached out clinging to the wall and started to squeeze around into the arch to my right. "Just be careful Banner. We don't know how far it goes down"

I managed to gain some sort of purchase on the next arch when I felt a rope like vine come away from the decaying stone. I gave it a firm tug and feeling that it may take my weight used it to swing my whole body around in a single sweeping motion. I hit the floor with a bang knocking something that was swinging above me. As I lifted the glow stick high above the full horror at what was in front came into scarily focussed green, the swinging corpse of a hanged man looking like he was floating in the arch, his body fully decomposed leaving only the loincloth rag behind. "Banner!" shouted Bingham. I heard his clambering around the arch and his fingertips scraping against the stone. "It's okay Bingham, I'm fine"

"Jesus Christ Banner" I heard in a mumbled breath, "Is there anything there?"

"Just a hanging body. Looks like it has been here for centuries"

It was then that with the aid of the green light source I could make out similar figures in each arch. This was not a garden, this was a tomb. "Bingham... I've got a really bad feeling about this place"

"You don't suppose Banner that this place is really a...."

"...death garden?"

We heard the voice but couldn't figure out its location. In the panic I reached into my pocket and whipped out my silenced pistol but held it up to nothing but black. The voice was an echo, shuddering around the walls and reverberating in the arches bashing against our ears. "The hanging gardens of Babylon are one of mythologies greatest triumphs. Hiding the truth behind a pack of lies that conveniently held true"

"Where are you?" shouted Bingham and that was when I heard the crash of falling body. "Bingham?" I shouted but to no response.

"Your partner is on the ground with a gun against his head" said the voice, "Now you have already translated the scroll it seems or else you wouldn't be here now" the voice was American, "And it seems you are all very resourceful men, bringing down Miss Wood's private helicopter was quite a feat but I can no longer tolerate your interference. Your intrusion into the Vatican brought my plan under threat from the Church and that is an ally I cannot afford to lose"

I was no good at talking or negotiating. If McCloud was here he would have known what to do, he would have talked him round into telling us the evil master plan and we would have been home by Christmas. Who was I kidding? The world is never that simple, I had to talk to him but I had never been one to talk my way out of problems. "What is this place?" I said. It was the only thing I could think of.

"This place?" he said with a cocky streak of American northwest. "These are the Hanging Gardens. Gardens because down below there was a magnificent garden filled with the most exotic trees and wild flowers you could ever imagine, all of which surrounding a deep lagoon which ran from a pipe built from the Tigris River nearby. Yet the reason it is known as the 'Hanging' Garden, well, look around. It was the garden in which the King of Babylon admired the death of his enemies surrounded by the beauty of nature and with many virgins. History is cruel; myth keeps the romance alive at the sacrifice of the truth. But alas..."

"Freeze!"

The air went dead for a moment. I heard a chamber slide and the click of the hammer being pulled back into place, in the gloom I could make out another figure that hadn't been there before and the tiniest shine off what must have been a highly polished gun. "Who the hell are you?" snapped the American voice

"I said 'Freeze'. Nobody in here moves until I let you"

The voice was strangely familiar like that of a cousin you don't see for years and then they ring you up and start talking to you and all the while you are not quite sure who it is. "I demand to know who you are!"

"You are in no position to make demands" said the voice, "I have a gun to your head"

"Hahaha"

The laughter haunted my very soul, like that of an over the top theatrical laugh, or one from an Iron Maiden song, and as I stared up into the open mouth of the corpse above me just for a moment it felt like the dead were laughing with him. "You fool" he said, "There is one of you. You have your gun against one of my guards, not me. And the several other guards surrounding this courtyard of death will soon add you to its list of casualties. Kill them"

I dropped down to the floor. The muzzle flash of more than seven automatic machine guns lit up the hall like a mad paparazzi at a press conference. I could see as my eyes adjusted to the darkness the guise of Agent Saunders diving to the ground alongside Bingham. We had seconds, maybe not even that, and only one chance of escape. "Jump!" I screamed, "There is a lagoon down there! Jump!"

It occurred to me only moments later that over the centuries the chances of their being a lagoon there at all were very slim indeed. Thankfully I hit the water feet first, straightening myself up like a pencil, and was quickly swallowed by the thick rancid waters. I felt the other two hit the water and before I knew it Bingham had his gun, dripping with thick sludge, aimed directly at the barely visible head of Saunders. "Who the hell are you and what the hell are you doing here?" said Bingham as he stared through reddened eyes.

Saunders went to hold his arms up but his head sank lower, "I'm from MI: 5.... was from MI: 5. I was disavowed yesterday morning"

"So why the hell are you here now? Speak!"

"I got a phone call about twenty hours ago, giving me the co-ordinates to this location from an anonymous voice. It told me I could find out the truth and find Banner"

"Why were you disavowed?" I asked. I padded my pockets as he answered back looking for any kind of weapon but I must have lost everything I had in the fall. "I was asked to come off the case. After the death of ex-agent Mayweather I became a little obsessed with finding out what happened. The deeper I dug, the more came out until I was stumbling upon classified files from the fifties and information on a group called the SES"

"The SES?" mumbled Bingham, "We need to get out of here"

"There!" I pointed in the direction of a small tunnel barely the size of a small dog that looked like it had taken a beating over the years. "The guy up there said it led to the Tigris River"

Bingham just seemed to float in thought for a few seconds but his eyes were moving all the time as if following something in the gloom. Then swimming closer to the tunnel he beckoned me and Saunders forward to him, "Remember the gunpowder? It leads all the way down here"

"So?" I asked desperate to reach the outside world once more.

"So... let's light the thing and send those fuckers back to hell!"

As we waded through what felt more like treacle than water, Bingham resourcefully took some dry dead vine roots and used them as kindling against the gunpowder and then using two stones, grinded them together to make a harsh round spark. The gunpowder erupted in a bright green flash, which then weaved in and around the stone walls as if dancing to a ferocious beat. As we watched in awe at the trail of green light we felt the whole cavern shudder, and realised this was the time we had to leave.

With force, the three of us tugged at the damp but weak flotilla of moss and plant uncovering the tunnel leading to the river, it was only wide enough for us to leave one at a time. Bingham shouldered his way through the hanging leaves and thick vegetation but found that only on his front pulling himself along could he make progress. "The tunnel is too narrow!" he screamed, "I can barely get through!"

"Push on Bingham!" I said looking above me, masonry and what was left of the creaking staircase was beginning to hammer into the water. "We don't have a choice anymore!"

As Saunders feet disappeared at last behind Bingham, I managed to squash myself into the narrow gap, my fingernails tearing and pulling apart as I forced myself on, water dripped in my ears and I felt a thousand years worth of thick slime splatter in my face, but we were safe. The tunnel finally began to widen, air began to seep in through holes in the pipe above us. I managed to turn myself around with my gained few feet of leeway, and bending my legs back kicked at the rusted iron above me. It buckled and so I did it again, and again and again until eventually the iron collapsed on me, sand following it until my body was just about covered and then through the grains and the pipe work the sun shone down harsh and strong but as hopeful as ever the sun had been.

After a bit of light digging and upper body work we all managed to sit down on the open plains of Iraq staring at the vast horizon of heat haze and sand. The odd blip on the panorama saw a militia tower or part of Baghdad but it was so far north it was impossible to make out through the haze. Bingham and I ragged off the hot clothes that had allowed us such an easy HALO jump and were soon down to our tank tops and burning in the sun. I felt like I should be in a modern day war film.

"I want to know everything" said Bingham in the direction of Saunders, sweat glistening in the sun. "Who called you? What was his voice like? Why you?"

"I don't know. He was English, and gruff, we couldn't track back the call either. It was encoded so whenever we tried to find a match it told us a different location every ten seconds"

We didn't say anything but the way that Bingham looked at me made me sure that it was McCloud who had rang him. A whole range of emotions clambered for position in my head, why? Why send an ex-MI: 5 agent? And who the hell was the yank? "We need a pickup" said

Bingham reaching into his recently removed jacket and removing the phone that was also a translator. After a few presses he got an answer, "Yeah Rich, hey man. Pickup please, somewhere south of Baghdad.... yeah.... three of us.... nice one, see you soon"

"How the hell did the phone survive the water?"

"Water proof technology" I said, "You gotta love those Japs"

Compared to the angry sunshine in Iraq, Leeds town centre gave us a more sombre affair with a faint drizzle outside the 'Slug and Lettuce' bar. The bar had cool and class rolled into one but unfortunately one of the worst names I had ever come across, it was something that seemed to afflict a lot of the bars here up north. Sitting in the corner booth staring out onto Bank Street felt like a world apart from what I was doing only two days ago. Bingham sat down with four pints, one for himself, one for me and one for Saunders who had that unease about him that suggested he was watching every door for danger. The fourth pint was for McCloud who was coming in on crutches and therefore had to wait for public transportation.

When he did come in hopping along on crutches, he didn't say much until he had had half a pint of the strong bitter, then finally said "I sodding hate busses"

As he sat the pint down on the table again he turned to all of us and said "I've read Richard's report. Seems like you three have had quite a journey"

"McCloud, did you contact Saunders?" I asked instantly before anybody else had a chance to speak.

"Yes I did" his voice more gravelled and torn than normal, "He has become disavowed and I have told him this would lead him to his true urge. To understand what we have been up to. I think he can help us"

"How the hell can he help us? He doesn't know anything about what we are doing!"

"I know that you are searching for the answer to the scrolls that you found"

"How do you know that" said Bingham

"MI: 5 are not stupid despite what everybody thinks. Yes they leave information in stupid places and lose laptops containing material not for the outside world but they still know what is happening, they know you are looking for the answers"

"The MI: 5 know a lot" said McCloud, "But not about us. They just know something is going on, the fact they have dropped the case shows we have not shown enough suspicion to warrant our pursuit. Saunders disagreement has led to him being sent out into the wilderness if you will, and I have picked him up"

We all had a drink at the same time as if we were waiting for someone else to say something, I managed a quick glance in the direction of Saunders and knew that there was something about him I didn't trust, I just didn't know what it was. "So what did you all find out in Iraq? I haven't seen *your* reports yet"

"Because we haven't done any yet sir" said Bingham and I noticed instantly that he didn't say McCloud. There was no doubt as I glared into Bingham's eyes as he focussed on McCloud that he did not approve of the current situation. "I felt it was necessary for the lads to unwind with a pint after what we had just gone through. I didn't fancy re-living traipsing through that pipe again any time soon"

"Was it bad kid?" he asked me

"Yes sir"

"We found the Hanging Gardens of Babylon, lost deep within the ground nearly a mile from the only above surface remnants. We were confronted by what seemed to be an American unit, who then opened fire on us telling us we could not interfere anymore. Thanks to some quick thinking by Banner and some daredevil stunts we managed to get away"

"And blow up the remains of the Gardens"

"Excuse me sir?"

McCloud turned to the side and pulling a lone mans attention said, "Could you please hand me that paper on the table"

The man did so to McCloud's thanks and then placed the paper open on the fourth and fifth pages. A grim headline, 'BABYLON ON FIRE'. "So any explanation of why the hell it was blown up? And four people dead? What the hell?" he said

"I can answer that one sir" I said with dread, "I had decided that it was our only means of getting away from the enemy. We would have had only minutes to escape but this cut us off from the above threat"

I could sense Bingham's stare. Taking the rap for what he had suggested in the heat of the moment was not something he was used to, you could tell. I just prayed that Saunders had the sense to keep his mouth shut.

"Hmm. This doesn't seem like something you would do"

"Strange things happen when you are being shot at"

"True. I suppose you needed to do it, just don't let it happen again y'hear me?"

"Yes sir"

"And finally, there was no sign of the Key of Kings?"

"It could have been anywhere sir" said Bingham, "But if it was there we certainly didn't see it"

After what McCloud had called a 'casual' briefing he let all of us go home and do what ever it was we all did to calm ourselves down. I had taken it upon myself to go alone to a squash court, racket in hand, and hit the ball as hard as I could relieving as much of that pent up aggression as I could. That bastard Saunders can't just muscle in like this, who the hell does he think he is? At least I hadn't been disavowed from the MI: 5, the bastard! What a bastard! I swung again, feeling my shoulder wrench slightly before the ball was back at me and I swung again and again and again.

The ball eventually slowed to a trickle and I heard a knock at the glass behind me. I turned into the eyesight of McCloud who started to make his way down, hobbling along as if even disability was not going to stop him. The last of my sweat had been absorbed by my red headband when McCloud pushed through the doors, "How's it going kid?"

"Fine"

"No its not" he said flatly, "I may be a lot of things kid but I ain't stupid"

"I don't trust Saunders sir" I said, "I think he is undercover"

"I don't trust him either" he said to my amazement. He moved to lean against the wall and padded his pocket for a smoke before realizing where he was. "I think he is a sneak"

"So why let him in to the operation?"

"You guys needed help down there kid and you know it. This mission is completely off the record. Thanks to that arsehole Jordan in your lasses department he has stopped any excess funding for me, which means I couldn't send in the cavalry"

"So you found a disavowed agent? C'mon McCloud give me some credit"

I got the impression that he wasn't going to let me get away with calling him McCloud again in these circumstances. Amazing the difference a couple of days make. "No Banner" he said, "I got you the only bloke stupid enough to fling himself head first into a war zone. You might have saved his life but not before he saved yours"

"Fine"

"Spit your dummy out kid. This is war! Sometimes you got to get your enemies as close as you can before shoving your foot up there arse. Sometimes you even have to let them be licking your boot when you aim it between there arse cheeks"

"That's fine sir but I just don't want there to be a time when I have his gun pointing at my skull"

"If that happens kid, I will personally blow his bollocks off. Is that good enough for you?"

I couldn't help but raise a crooked and black smile. "Yes sir"

"One thing before I carry on. Why did you cover Bingham?"

"What do you mean?"

"Now you give me some credit kid. I know it was Bingham who lit those explosives; you wouldn't be stupid enough to do it. Why cover him?"

"Because I didn't want to jeopardise his position sir"

"You wouldn't have done kid. I need to tell you that there are no secrets in this group other than we are a secret. If you had blown it up I would have expected you to have told me"

"I will from now on sir, forgive me but how did you know?"

"Bingham just phoned and told me"

"Oh"

"Come on, let's go for a smoke"

As I picked up my things McCloud adjusted himself so that he was able to walk, we clambered slowly but positively out of the leisure centre. The Morley afternoon was fairly redundant in the dim sun and ever present drizzle but there was the slightest hint of blue sky on the horizon. All the time I could tell McCloud wanted to say something, it was unlike him in every way, he was almost anxious. He finally managed to muster some words when we got to the car. "I want you and Bingham back in action... tomorrow"

"Tomorrow?" I said in disbelief

"I want you in Jerusalem to find this Tongue. Whatever it is I think it is part of this whole scheme Alpha has. You as point man and Bingham on communications"

"We don't know anything about it though sir!"

"Charlie is as we speak trying to figure out what the Key of Kings could have been. She seems to think that whoever was there before you, be it Alpha or not, took it when you arrived. If that's the case we are level with them in the race"

"In the race for what?"

"I don't know yet kid. Whatever that white throne is, hopefully Charlie will give us more later"

"Do you really think Charlie is doing her best for us?"

"You're a suspicious one kid aren't you?"

"I just don't feel as if we are getting anywhere. We seem to keep hitting brick walls, as if we are missing something"

"It's all part of the game kid, all part of the game"

CHAPTER 9
THE TONGUE OF SALEM

I'd only seen Carter for all of an hour but I instantly felt happier, I didn't know what it was but she had changed me in a way I didn't think I could be changed. I didn't have that same desire to run around skirts in the bars and I had genuinely begun thinking about family. The sheer notion of something along those lines was completely forbidden in my head only two years ago, now since being in the SES, life has become somewhat clearer and more... fulfilling?

Jerusalem was a five to six hour flight filled with nothing to see but sand below as we crossed the deserts of the Middle East. I had acquainted myself with a newspaper back in Manchester Airport and after reading it several times read the article again about the underground bombing of the Gardens of Babylon. Some history professor from Cambridge had been to have a look and had said the myth of how we always saw the gardens were obviously deranged and wrong. It wasn't a romantic ideal that we all love to think of but a torture house, apparently some of the still composed corpses showed signs of leg and arm breaks and one even missing all his teeth as well as several broken fingers. History has a fantastic way of lying to the world, he said in his article; don't be surprised if the Colossus of Rhodes turned out to be a fantastically ornate jail.

I had always been a fan of history but only like a son has no choice but to follow football if his father is a footballer. I had been subjected to all kinds of historical nonsense over the years and had a passing fascination with everything Roman, I guess I had grown out of it but the knowledge happily remained and it came in very useful at pub quizzes.

As I flashed through the article I did notice that there was mention of sacrifice. Not ancient ones however but modern ones performed within the last few days, and then what McCloud had said in the Slug and Lettuce, that four were named dead in the gardens. It was then that Bingham sat down next to me passing me a folder. "Ey up Banner" he said, "It's the de-briefing on Jerusalem and apparently it was called Salem before Jerusalem so we are going there. Who knew eh? There isn't a lot; I had to do it myself last night because we are doing this whole mission rogue. Nobody knows about it except us few"

"What about Saunders?" I asked

"I think McCloud wants to keep him out of the loop. I don't think he trusts him too much"

"I wouldn't either. It all seems too much of a coincidence"

The Israeli capital was something to behold as I managed to push through the busy streets meeting stare after stare from the curious civilians. I had dropped off my accoutrements at the hotel and was now out on the prowl, so to speak. Quick looks around made me think back fondly to my short time back in Egypt, about how biblical the whole area looked. How with every step you feel like you are making a footprint in the history of this great city.

The old city was on the horizon with the great sights being gazed at by a flood of American and Japanese tourists all of them living up to the stereotype of the most ignorant of travellers. It was however where I knew I had to be and although I only had my phone fancied the chance of seeing the Old City on my own as a tourist and not as an SES agent. I flicked the phone out of my pocket and rang Bingham, "I am going into the Old City now"

"What about tonight? Are you not going to try an infiltration?"

"I don't think I need to" as I approached the Old City, "It all seems pretty lax and I am only having a look around"

"Just remember that I installed the translator on your phone. You should be able to read any Arab text, whether it be Aramaic, Hebrew or anything else"

"Cheers Bingham"

It made me sad to see but there was something distinctly decrepit about the state. I had never been to Israel before but was under the impression that my every move was being watched, much like the British did to everybody with a beard and a certain coloured skin after the 7/7 bombings back in 2005. I wasn't one of them, and suddenly it felt horrible being on the other foot. I walked past an open meat stall, slabs of cow's leg thrown onto a bloodied wooden table allowing the flies a treat.

It was not much later that I found myself passing through the Zion Gate into Old Jerusalem and everything changed. Danger lurked in every corner, a woman with two children passed me by with an uzi clutched to her chest and the look of fear in her eyes. A male hooker sat watching me, the glint in his eyes a completely different one to that of the woman's.

There were several sign posts through the Armenian Quarter through into the Christian Quarter where I thought I would begin my search and after managing to somehow navigate my way through the narrow streets and crumbling masonry, I made it to an exit called the Jaffa Gate. The sun was beating down strong and the midday temperatures, although not humid, were too strong without water and so I found the nearest restaurant and standing for what seemed like hours finally got the attention of a young waitress who without knowing it, had somehow managed to look achingly beautiful in her own way, a talent not known to many Western women.

After a smile and a bottle of water I found myself on the tourist trail for the Church of the Holy Sepulchre and it was here that the mass of Americans were starting to swell and multiply like a virus. The ancient building ahead of me didn't need to gloat or show off; because the thousand year old church was as awe inspiring as anything I had ever seen before. A radiation of mystique grew out of the classical brick, a miasma of religious prestige and godliness oozed freely across everyone who stood beholding it. "Wow" was all I could muster.

My jaw was then picked up by a friendly looking American. He stood no more than five and a half feet, and had a belly like he had swallowed an old fashioned medicine ball but, as the sun melted his face an unhealthy red, he managed a smile. "Impressive ain't it?"

"It sure is" I said staring quite helplessly at his stomach. His chest was flat, and then a ball of fat ballooned out of him. He was resting his arms on it. His thin grey hair was shaped naturally into what was a deceiving Mohican, "I've been here four times now and I never get tired of the sight of it"

"I can understand why. Are you a religious man?"

"Hell no. What makes you say that?"

"Just with you saying you come here often. I wondered if you meant for pilgrimage or something"

"Nah son. Me and the missus just like taking separate vacations that's all. She likes to go on vacation to burn herself the same colour as our sofa and I like to see some culture"

I had the nagging sensation to tell him it was a holiday but it quickly passed. It was strange though because all the time I was talking to him I could see something to the side of the Church wall. It was well hidden, but compared to the rest of the building and infrastructure looked completely out of place. It was like back in Egypt when they had begun restoring the old hieroglyphic walls; brand new sandstone with permanent marker outlines had been set in place. "You seem distracted son" said the American

"I'm sorry. I came here to see something but don't know what it was"

"You mean…" he leaned closer; his face was only now flush with his stomach. "… you were called here?"

"No… don't be silly"

"Sounds to me…"

There was something there but the Americans nosy and obtrusive belly was getting in the way. "Excuse me" I said calmly even though the blood was boiling. "I just need to take a look at this"

Moving closer my neck craned forward in anticipation I noticed that in an attempt to break it away someone had chiselled at the inscription. With a bit of light brushing with the tips of my fingers I managed to remove the dust and using my phone took a picture hoping for a translation. It simply read 'Salem'.

I was on the right lines in terms of location but there was so much to the Old City that it would be impossible to search unless you knew what you were looking for. The smell of male deodorant sat on my head as I turned into the American, "Hey look at that. Looks like its been chipped away"

"I know. It says…"

"…Salem"

For a moment I wondered if I had said the word in my head but the American was stood with a fixed grin of pure satisfaction. "You know this language?"

"I should do, its Hebrew. I read about it for my dissertation back in the States"

"You don't know what the Tongue of Salem is then do you?"

"Its Hebrew son"

"What? Wait, what do you mean?"

"Well, the language in which the Salem citizens spoke was Hebrew. Some people say it was Aramaic or something else like that but Hebrew was the only true language, around which all others were based"

The 'tongue' of Salem. It wasn't literally a tongue but the language spoken by Salem, which meant that according to the scrolls, Alpha would need to use the Key of Kings and speak in Hebrew to bring forth the gnashing teeth. There was a swelling in my throat and yet, as close as I was it just didn't feel right, there was still something missing in the middle of the puzzle. It was all starting to come together in my mind as to what the whole scroll could mean. There are ten conditions, the Ten Commandments are the conditions by which life needs to be lived and if the conditions of life are not adhered to, then we are to find the Key of Kings and using the language of Salem, which is Hebrew, we will be able to unleash the fury of gnashing teeth. The only thing I didn't understand now was what on earth the gnashing teeth were or is. It could simply by a statue or maybe a work of ancient art or even something religious in a way that reminds people of what being true to the Ten Commandments was.

"Do you want to get something to eat son? I'd gladly pay for you"

I woke up, dazed and confused by my latest trip into conscious reverie. "Yeah, that is probably a good idea"

As we traversed through the narrow streets back from the Sepulchre we talked at some length about the ways of the world down here. I told him of seeing the young mother with the firearm and his lack of surprise told me everything about the district. It all seemed so fairytale from a distance, all the fantastic images we see of this religious capital and yet deep down there is an underlying hatred which is as far from religion as you can get. Israel was beginning to remind me of all those American sitcoms, the ones that show people in low paid jobs living in mansions supporting hordes of kids with white picket fences and beautiful gardens which is not possible in any country in the world unless you have money erupting from your ears.

We sat down in a cosy restaurant with very little detail but a classy overall style with golden painted pillars and hanging red fabrics between them. The tables were rocky and the staff looked like they were coming to the end of their shift and although the American had sworn by the place on our walk here, my impression was dampened by the sticky floor. The menus were slapped onto the table and two glasses followed that looked dull in the light.

The American whose name I still wasn't aware of said something in Hebrew to the waiter and he trundled off swinging his off white towel over his shoulder. "'Y' know son I've been coming here for food for the past ten years, and I still don't know its name. I said to Ange, 'Ange next time I go to Israel I am gunna find out the name of that place that makes me that nice sauce' and y'know..." he said laughing, "... its strange but you must have been called here"

"Why?"

"This place is called the Tongue of Salem"

My heart hit the floor and was suddenly beating like never before. A lump the size of the moon burst out of my throat, I checked the exits and the options around me for any kind of weaponry and I suddenly felt in grave danger. "It's on the menu as well" said the American cheerfully; the whole situation seemed to be amusing him. "It says here that the Tongue of Salem is based around the local myth of a golden sheep's tongue that can speak to the angels"

"A golden sheep's tongue?"

"That's what it says here. Seems I was wrong earlier about it being the language, I'm sorry son"

"Its okay sir" I said quickly. A sheep's tongue made of gold that allowed you to speak to the angels sounds interesting but a lot more solid than the idea of it being a language. "You don't happen to know the whereabouts of the tongue do you?"

"I only found out about it just now son. I'll ask the waiter"

As the waiter trundled back barely under his own influence the American took that aggressive nature of speaking Hebrew into overload. Though when the words came out it seemed to fill the young waiter with anger. Even spoken in Hebrew, the vehemence was there in full. "Wow son" said the American as the waiter walked off, "Seems we hit a nerve there. He said that the tongue of Salem has long been lost but belongs to the people of the Old City. He knew that the tongue was being held underneath the church and many people had died for it"

"The Church?" I said almost greedily wanting the information fed to me like a pig in a troth.

The American shouted over to the young waiter who replied with a few hardened words. "He says the Church of Sepulchre of course"

"Excellent. Thank you, you have been great but I really need to go"

"But you haven't eaten yet"

"I know but I have to go save the world"

I jumped up almost knocking the chair back behind me and dashed out the door. I pulled my phone out and got a secure line to Bingham, "It's a sheep's tongue! A golden one that lets them speak with the angels!"

"What? Banner, are you crazy?"

"No! It's a local myth and it's hidden underneath the Church of Sepulchre!"

"Underneath a church in Jerusalem! That would be impossible Banner; we can't even begin to try that!"

"We got into the Vatican!"

"The Vatican would be like breaking into a biscuit jar compared to this!"

"We need that tongue Bingham! I'm going in tonight!"

"Not without me your not, get back here and will get ready together!"

We'd hooked up our headsets and synchronised our watches before we set out into the humid night of old Salem. The grounds surrounding the Church were lightly guarded and with a couple of neat sidesteps through the gloom, it was easy enough to navigate my way to the main gate. The quick double flash of Bingham's sniper rifle on the gate itself told me he had visual. It was the only way he could support me on this, once I was inside I was alone, once more grave robbing God.

After the red flashes I started to work. Thankfully on the gate there was a small inner door. I used to remember as a kid back in England how we all used to joke it was the door the little people used. We had picked up an electric handheld saw and a LED light that was brighter than I could imagine and using these set to work on the lock.

God had not however made me a very good lock pick and after nearly five solid minutes of trying I was still finding the resistance too tough. A fizz of static came through the headset and a smug sounding Bingham came over pretending to yawn and saying, "You not done that door yet? I know its radio silence but I can't sit here all night"

"Shut up Bingham, I'm almost through!"

After a few nervous mute seconds he said, "Quiet. Go flat against the gate a minute"

I did as he asked turning off the LED light as I did so and tried with hope beyond hope to slow down my racing heartbeat. I could see movement out of the corner of my eye and knew I had been heard, I could feel my heart lurching out of my chest, the blood ferociously pumping around my system. Then, silenced by a muffle I saw a brief and powerful flash from Bingham's position and then the sound of a body crumpling as it hit the floor. "Go! Get him out of view"

I dashed over and lifted the heavy set guard onto my back throwing him into a wild growth of bushes not more than twenty feet away. "Tranquilizer darts. He will be out a few hours now get that door open!"

Holding the saw with more purpose I thrust the saw blade into the lock and began grinding away with amateurish enthusiasm and with a deep squeak from the bowels of the mechanism the lock clicked and pushed open allowing me access to the grounds and the opening courtyard. I shut the door behind me and looked in front, my spine flush against the gates back. It was a stunning place to be even in the dark. The courtyard was iconic and beautiful with the Church' main entrance dead ahead, "Banner. You have got to find a man made pond or fountain, rumours are that when this place was built they put in a tunnel that led underneath the temple and into some underground caverns that they had constructed to keep things sacred"

"Yeah, I'll bet. Also used for keeping dead bodies in too"

"And worse"

"I don't want to even think about it yet"

"Just remember Banner. I can't help you anymore from here until you get back out of that gate, just give me lots of warning so I can clear the area for you"

"Will do. I'll keep you posted"

There were a few questions now that were buzzing through my head with enough electricity to power London for a few years and they were starting to irritate and most of them were to do with religion. I had tried my best to conquer this army of questions back at the Vatican but as I stood in Jerusalem at the Church of the Sepulchre it was a damn sight harder to hold on to. What were we doing? What would we do in the same situation as the people trying to get hold of whatever was out there? I mean if we beat them to it, what are we going to do with the same power? Keep it? Use it? It nagged me, biting at the back of my neck like a spider unnoticed and I knew very soon that I would have an answer; I just hoped I liked it.

I moved forward, my feet making little noise in the sandy concrete, and neared the main double doors for the Church when I had to turn quickly and silently on the spot like a vinyl on a turntable and stand fast against the wall. Two hooded figures calmly walked forward, hands in prayer and then parted at the bottom of the courtyard. I took the opportunity to sneak in.

As I breached the ancient Church's threshold the full extent of this great religious locale was finally put into perspective. I had the strangest feeling as I looked around myself in splendour; I almost felt I was trespassing in God's back garden. It was incredible to see the extent of the belief that was possessed back then, when the world was still young and the passion boiled over at the mere mention of another religion. This was what religion could give the world; this was the kind of architecture it had given us… shame about the wars.

Ahead of me was a wide open space dominated by tall pillars flourishing at their zeniths into balls of what looked from here like solid gold. Each pillar marked with crosses and religious iconography that I didn't recognise rising into a smooth wooden arched ceiling featuring wondrous frescoes of clouds and God sat with his angels. Even so, despite the dominance, despite row upon row of pew and despite the distant stained glass window, the Church felt empty. There was no one to be seen as I stepped down the long red carpet toward the nave leading to the marble altar draped in deep purple cloth.

Cream linen rested on each side, overhanging and displaying another symbol I didn't recognise but seemed to be of some importance. The altar itself was surprisingly barren with only a solid looking golden cross in the middle, above where I assumed the altar stone would be, ordained with jewels and shining after what must have been hours of polishing.

However, it was behind the altar in the sanctuary that interested me now as beneath a startling stained glass picture of the burning Jacques de Molay was an ornamental baptism font perched on its own biblical stone stand. Age had attacked the old stone and yet some of its ancient design was still visible around the chips and mottled weathering. I couldn't make it out but it appeared to be a kind of lettering and so quickly took out my phone and snapped the weather text hoping to find some kind of translation. No such luck.

What had seemed suspicious was the position of the font itself. Usually within a Church the font is located near the entrance to symbolic of you entering the community.

"Bingham…" I whispered into my com unit. "The only source of water is a baptism font"

"A baptism font? You mean where people are baptised?"

"Yes Bingham. Like I said; a baptism font"

"There's nothing else? A mini fountain, water feature?"

"It's a Church Bingham, not a fucking garden centre!"

"Alright, alright. That must be it then"

"But… It must be hundreds of years old"

"Even more reason to…"

"No wait Bingham I don't think you understand. This thing is ancient! It's probably worth more than everything else in here!"

"Banner, we are not thinking of material wealth here"

"I know but…"

"Do it Banner!"

I turned to the font. Standing about four feet tall it managed to hold as much gravitas as the pillars that lined the pews. There was even an intricately detailed bird perched on the edge of it surrounded by leaves. I started to try move it, pushing from each side and even attempted lifting it but it was no use. That font was going nowhere fast until I looked behind me and had a truly blasphemous idea. Picking up the solid and surprisingly heavy golden cross from the altar I turned to the font and then looked into the eyes of the judgemental God. There was no doubt about it, I was going to Hell! '...*Forgive those who trespass against us...*'

With that I swung the golden cross into the stone smashing the bowl to pieces leaving the base and its stalk behind. As the Holy Water hit the floor, I almost expected it to burn through the floor... it didn't.

I knew I wouldn't have much time making as much noise as I did so I swung again and saw the rest of the base fly away hitting the altar and scraping along the floor. As the dust rose and the empty air filled I could see the remnant of the Holy Water start to run across the marble sanctuary floor around the font's base and sink into the smallest hole my eyes could have made out. With one final blow at the base, this time straight down into the ground, I crashed a giant hole in the stonework sending the desecrated remains of the baptism font down into a narrow human size chute. "I don't believe it"

I dropped down into a small puddle no more than a few inches deep with a filtered tube placed just a centimetre in. This presumably would suck up the water to the fountain above and then come back down through another pipe and keep the whole thing going in a continuous cycle. As my eyes adjusted and focussed in the dim green shadows the brickwork began to shine through the grime. It was like an old European sewer with pathways at either side surrounded by high spiked fences stopping anyone and anything big enough from falling into the sewage below. I tried to think of ways to describe the smell and many phrases involving faeces, striking, shit and toilet bowl all sprang to mind but nothing would do the stench justice. It had been down here rotting for thousands of years, possibly undisturbed so the odour was nothing short of pungent to the highest degree.

"Banner. Banner can you hear me?"

"Loud and clear Steve"

"Did you make a lot of noise in there?"

I thought back to the way I dismembered that baptism font, the way the whole thing exploded in noise. "I might have made a little, why?"

"Cos' you got security bombing through the doors of the Church. In other words you have company"

"Great, can't you distract them or something?"

"Are you kidding me? There must be twenty of em' all heading for you right now!"

My mind rushed into overdrive and the long winding tunnel ahead of me suddenly felt a hell of a lot longer than before. I followed the grimy old sewer around until I reached a dead end, a large circular railing blocking my exit and pitched firmly into the ground. I could hear the echo of foreign voices behind me, looking round there was nothing at all to help me. I put my back against the railing, took a deep breath, removed my pistol and aiming dead ahead... saw a brick in the stonework to the side of me that was duller than the rest. I knocked on it and an echo came back, a secret room!

I pulled the brick which slide easily against the slimy walls and then quicker and quicker scurrying at the wall with eager anticipation pulled more and more stone until I was face to face with the Virgin Mary. Dignified and angelic she stood with a proud heir until a bullet whizzed past and broke her nose. I looked into her eyes and pushed... another bullet flew by... her body fell backward with her hand raised in the same stance as George Washington at the Federal Hall in America. The sound of scraping masonry echoed throughout and looking at the space vacated by Mary a slab that must have weighed several tons had began to descend. I looked back, saw the approaching guards and dived into the darkness beyond.

The slab thundered with vehemence sending a wave of dust and ancient spider webs spiralling into the gloom that was ahead of me. I coughed, it seemed like the only thing to do and then turned on my LED light and the darkness turned red. Ahead of me was an altar, behind it, a crucifix the likes of which I had never seen before. It must have been life sized, if not that then maybe a few inches smaller but the image was that of visceral horrificness. The forlorn head of Jesus Christ wrapped with thorns, his wild eyes glaring at me, the wounds on his hands and feet looked as if they were still bleeding and the lashes on his back were as shiny and new as the day they were given. I felt a cold shiver down my spine. I stood in front of an altar that no man had stood in front of for hundreds of years and for a moment I didn't dare move. To each side of the crucifix hung two heavy looking drapes, bright red in colour, and featured a proud Templar cross at their bases with a picture of two knights sharing a horse and a small inscription.... 'Jacque de Molay'.... the last Grand Master of the Knights Templar.

I hadn't noticed at first but behind the drapes were two arches into other rooms. As I moved the light away from the crucifix I could still feel his eyes move, flashing the light onto his face I swore I could see his face turn to me... the darkness was playing tricks... to the right drape there was nothing but a storage room with many barrels and crates all of which had been ransacked at one point in time. I came out from behind the drape into the blackness and felt the shiver down my spine again... I didn't dare to look... what was in here! What *devilry* was in here! I flashed the light up to Jesus; his mouth was wide open and his eyes as black as the night... he was staring at me! I turned off the light. Even in the dark I could see his eyes, they were pure blackness so dark that the darkness itself shone off it.

I fell to the floor into a ball.

Then the sound came...

It had lasted no more than a minute. I managed to grip enough courage to repel fear for a moment and turned my light on and very slowly worked my way to the crucifix. It was the same as when I first entered, detailed and saddened by the course of action he had taken in his journey. I pulled myself up, strengthened my resolve and with the last bastion of power I had managed to pull myself past the left drape into another room.

This was more like it, boxes and boxes stacked on top of each other but not like the storage room. These boxes looked expensive and well made, then I looked at the wall to my right, directly behind the crucifix' wall in the next room and there was a map. It was a map I didn't recognise, with the mouth of a river at the north and a long winding streak of water. Markings were inscribed onto the wall in an ancient Hebrew. I used the camera on my phone to take a full scale picture and in the flash I could see through the faint and eroding fabric. There was a block or a dark patch behind it, and pulling aside the old parchment map it tore off in my hands to reveal a dark square buried inside the ancient brickwork. I reached inside, and pushing aside the spider webs and moss rested my hand on the odd shape of a tongue. There it was, in my palm as I released my hand from the darkness... the Tongue of Salem. Garnished and scratched from the centuries of abandonment, but still reclaiming some of its former beauty. The tongue was curved so that it stood with the base of the tongue facing up; it slumped downward and then flicked up at the tip, and on its tip was a small star. It was no bigger than the surface of a pinhead, but was just visible in the poor light. Enough of that, I needed to get out of here now and with no visible exit it was not going to be easy. "Bingham. Steve?"

No answer. I was alone down here, even though I didn't feel it. I moved back to the crucifix room and positioning my LED light at the base of where I got in, looked around the room far more closely than before. Part of the Virgin Mary's head had rolled by the altar, her eyes gazing into the lowered head of Jesus. Following the path of Mary's eyes I noticed something shine against the illuminating glare of the LED torch. I didn't like the idea of doing this, but jumping onto the basic wooden altar I stared into Jesus' eyes as I lifted him from his perch from underneath his arms. I couldn't help but stare, pupil to pupil, as I held him aloft before putting him down facing away from me. I turned my attention to the silver wheel that was protruding from the wall and putting my hands on it felt a raw surge of untapped power, it felt almost alive. I rested my ear against the wall and felt the oddest sensation of swelling, as if something was pulsating right behind it. As much as I was hesitant to turn the wheel I knew that this was going to be my only means of escape.

I turned the wheel slowly, feeling the ancient steel breaking free from its rusted shell. A long harrowing shriek brought with it more and more pulsing sensations rifling through the wheel itself. I'd felt this before.... it was pressure! Just as I let go of the wheel the wall cracked and splintered and as if it was made of sponge began to grow toward me. A stone flashed past my ear as a stream of water shot into me. Another hole blew forward, then another and another until several where firing randomly in all directions. A deep venomous growl roared from behind the stone. I took a few steps back, bumped into the altar and then thinking in microseconds vaulted the altar and landed on the other side just as the water burst through the rubble sending wave upon wave of crashing foaming water past me. Stones the size of heads thundered into the wooden altar splintering the ancient mahogany. The room began to fill quickly and I realized this was my chance to get out, through the doorway that the water had created. The water had almost come to my shoulders as I started to swim against the rushing current, stones and rocks thrashing through the water toward me. I splashed and fought the waves for purchase to try and fight through but realised that I had to wait, and then when the waters were deeper, swim and hope I reached any kind of air before I passed out.

I could feel my heart splutter into overdrive, the lump in my throat now the size of a small planet, and then taking in one last gasp of air the water reached the cavern roof and I was submerged. For a hanging minute everything seemed to slow, a tranquil heir surrounded the floating crucifix of Jesus and below me; Mary looked as if she was smiling. Feeling the Tongue of Salem in my pocket I pushed with all the might left in my legs, trying to break through the stubborn current of the rushing water. I had no idea where it led but as I sifted through the oncoming debris weaving like a car through traffic my eyes had began to sting as if it was salt water. I carried on; pushing onward and onward until the water calmed, a school of fish swam by and above me I could see a giant orb floating. I swam toward it, my lungs fighting for the last remnants of air left in my blood and with an almighty splash burst from the water sucking in the air as fast and as controlled as I could. I could feel the coastline wind bash against my wet head and within minutes I had frost in my dark hair. I managed to look around and find the direction of the shore as my eyes blinked wildly to rid the salt from my eyes and swam toward it trying my best to stay afloat and most of all, keep breathing.

I struggled but eventually managed to gain some sort of grip over a rock that was next to the shoreline but out of sight from anyone and anything. I could just about see the wall by which the Jaffa Gate stood and fishing through my waterlogged pockets found my phone which had survived quite well. "Bingham"

"Banner. Where the hell are you? I lost signal with you an hour ago"

"Yeah I had to go through an old escape route. It must have been built for Christians as a last chance to get the hell out of there. It's brought me out by the Jaffa Gate shoreline; can we get a pick up?"

"No can do Banner. We got no funding, no support, just me and you mate"

"Great" I said thinking how much a wanker that guy Ian Jordan is right now, "Meet me at the Jaffa Gate in fifteen minutes and if you can, bring me something dry or a change of clothes or something. I'm gunna freeze to death out here"

"Good thinking. Anything else?"

"Not yet. Oh and Bingham...."

"Yeah"

"I got the Tongue"

"It's real?"

"Yeah. I don't know what to think either"

"We will have to run some tests on it when we get back. I just hope we get back soon"

Before I forgot to do anything I found the picture of the map I had photographed inside the cavern. Looking at it with an extra resolution and zoom, I noticed small symbols that looked like Pyramids... I didn't toy with it any longer and sent it to HQ, at least if I lost it now I would have done my job.

After the clumsiest climb in the history of mountaineering, I managed at last to poke my head out over the cliff face and watch as a frenzied group of guards patrolled the nearby area. The climb had calmed my nerves and now I was thinking clearly again without the rushing adrenaline fuelling and dilating my judgement. As I looked around I could see in that moment why this was such a hotbed of religious belief. All those years ago, this must have looked stunning with its landscape made of stars and the blanket of night almost swallowing the land with a superb crescent moon arched, just like the Turkish flag. Suddenly, I realised just how mesmerising the whole thing was and just how important it must be to these people that something created by some insane but very clever person thousands of years ago formed a set of laws that still run our day to day lives.

A dog bark snapped me out of my moment of epiphany and my eyes readjusted and saw that not far from me now the guards had started to secure a form of perimeter. I had no cover but the cliff face, and the longer I hung on the more slippery and crumbling the cliff became. This was not a good situation to be in. The guards were getting closer now, the old greying Mastiff sniffing the ground with anger, his drooping eyes moving up and down and I swore the dog saw me. I dropped slightly, my arms beginning to pull, my fingernails starting to chip away and bleed, my throat started to dry up and all the while the dogs sniffing got closer and louder and more intense right to the point where his nose was almost on top of my head. The Mastiff barked wildly and as I was just about to jump up with a tightened bloody fist the dog ran away barking in the other direction. I felt my whole body relax and sag as I struggled to pull myself up onto the ledge and run in the opposite direction.

"Bingham! Bingham, where are you?"

"I've just saved your arse by whistling that dog! Now I need your help!"

"Where are you?"

"'Bout five minutes from the gate due east"

"I'll find you as soon as I can!"

I ran with purpose toward the city remembering that there was nothing much in the line of vehicles other than a few battered old cars and the odd low cc motorbike. Leaping a small brick wall and bursting into the Old City itself there were more than a few odd glances in my direction and eventually, after near five minutes of searching I found a group of young Israeli kids huddled around a running stunt bike, battered with age and pitted with rust. I tried to tell myself I didn't enjoy grabbing a fifteen year old and throwing him off his bike in front of his posse of mates but I would be lying to myself if I said it. The bike easily outran the teens who gave chase but as it hit the off-road and the rough terrain it started to splutter and struggle. It had to do though and as it bounced up and down the rocky land across from the Jaffa Gate.

I could see Bingham running away from the guards ducking for cover and rolling as the bullets whizzed by him. Ahead of the guards were the heavy Mastiff's giving chase and gaining with every step so I floored the dirt bike as the back tire squealed and screeched sending wave upon wave of flying soil behind me. The leader of the Mastiff's was barely an inch from Bingham's heel as I shot past some of the guards who had stopped and turned hearing the noise of the bike. The dogs however persevered and carried on pushing, drool flapping from their wrinkled faces as they pushed harder, on and on. I stopped about ten foot ahead of Bingham with a shower of dirt arched in a circle and said, "Jump on quick!"

Bingham leapt onto the bikes back and with a swift but hard kick floored the chasing Mastiff leader just in time for us to rev up and start going again. We screamed away into the nightlife, the sound of our engine roaring above that of anything else. My heart was slow, my body relaxed and for the first time I felt I was part of this. I felt I was here to save and here to help.

"You like to leave it in the nick of time don't you?"

"I've learnt from McCloud, what do you expect?"

The bike didn't agree too much with having the both of us on the back with Bingham's sniper rifle to boot, it groaned and spluttered with as much grace as a swan falling over into a lake. "We need to find something a bit better than this hunk of junk" said Bingham as we navigated our ways through the narrow Old City streets bouncing along the cobbles and over mini ramps created by carts parked along the road. Along the barren streets I turned the bike into a half open garage and killed the engine to hear only the silence of the night. The only sound, the twinkling of an ancient spider web hovering above boxes of what looked like junk. "Do you think they will still be chasing us?"

"I dunno. It depends how important they think this tongue is?" I said calmly, "But we still need to get back to our hotel. We have to catch a normal plane at a normal airport and get stuck in customs for hours"

Then we heard a dog bark, aggressively in the distance hounding down our scent. Bingham dashed over to the garage door and pulled it down hard straight onto the foot of an attack dog who yelped away. "Shit how they caught us so fast!"

"I don't think it's the police"

I readied my pistol and Bingham removed the silencer and scope from his snipers rifle to turn it into as much a standard rifle as possible. Pinned into the garage with nowhere to go, a last stand, it was now I started to think back to all the last stands throughout history and realized they were called last stands for a reason. We both heard the cocking of guns outside the garage door, the snap of the safeties and the sliding of hammers resting in place ready to fire.

Steady... keep calm and remember to count your shots. The last thing you want is to run out of bullets just as you need them. They can only attack you from one place, I thought, which is the garage door. As soon as they open that we have an aim..... "Bingham! Grab some of those boxes. We can bottle neck them in!"

"What? Are you mad!"

"Think about it! They can only come in that one way, let's bottleneck 'em and let rip!"

Before he had time to answer I'd darted for the boxes and pulled them away from the wall with a hard metallic thud. Even better, they were made of steel! With the help of Bingham we managed to pull them across the garage door and leave a gap just big enough for one man in the middle, all the while the cacophony of barking and shouting was playing outside. Crouched down and covered by two more boxes we made our stand, odds seeming much more in our favour now, and prepared for the onslaught. Then a thought occurred to me and it was one I had very little time to contemplate, I was just about to pray. In a dirty garage in the middle of Old Salem I was going to pray that I was going to be okay, I was going to pray after storming the Vatican, breaking a baptism fountain that had probably been there since John the Baptist and now stolen a religious artefact from the oldest Church in the world.... God did not answer my prayer.

A small disc the size of an ice-hockey puck rolled and then flattened onto the floor in front of us. "What's that?" I said

"Ah shit... it's a flashban...."

It was an intense bright white light that for a splinter of a second lit up the whole garage with radiant flare. I felt my retina burn; my head swim with the brightness and then knock me to my knees....

I woke up expecting very little but got even less. It was simply a room and nothing more, not even a crack on the wall or a scrawled list of numbers indicating how long someone had been in here for. This was as basic a room as could be, four walls and a light bulb. There were no windows, no obvious door and no sense of escape. There didn't even seem to be a floor, just an extension of the wall that just happened to be laying flat at the time. As I felt about my person my pockets had been plundered and my belongings pilfered including the Tongue of Salem. I was literally sat in a sack.

It was then that I heard the faintest of cracks and as I turned realised very shortly that inside the wall was a door just opening to an outside of pure white light. It was as if a flash bang had been permanently ignited behind it.

The shape of two figures walked in and behind them two more carrying chairs, they placed them down and the foremost sat down crossing their legs and backs up straight. For some strange reason my eyes wouldn't adjust to their faces as if they had a blurring effect on them. "Now then Mister Banner" said the first man with a stress in his tone. "You are going to tell us all about Donald McCloud"

"What?"

"You're leader, the one who you take your orders from?" said the next man. They worked in harmony; almost Shakespearean in sound, as if they were on a great stage and the entire world were players. "I don't know what you are talking about"

"I thought not"

After a few moments the doors opened again behind them and another chair was brought in and I was thrust into it with my arms, hands, legs and feet bound. "To say we have ways of making you talk would be so clichéd don't you think? Even so I must admit we *do* have some very painful ways of making you talk. And don't worry, your friend is fine"

A volcanic strike crashed into the inside of my rib cage, up from the stomach. If I could describe the pain that shot through my body in that instant I would be known as the greatest living author known to man. "There we go, that was just a taster"

I could see the ape sized man lurch forward again and as he swung I managed to rock my chair to the floor to avoid it. I hit the floor hard, hearing one of the seated men say "He has far more spirit than his friend doesn't he? The other one didn't even put up a fight, just let us beat him out cold"

"Can I do the same to this one boss?" asked the ape. His American accent was as thick as syrup, lucid and swirling like a toilet bowl in flush. "No Prince" said the second man, "You will not. We need the information out of him"

The gorilla known as Prince pulled me back up and this time pushed the chair right up against the far wall so I could fling myself backward or dodge anymore blows. I could feel my insides swell after the first blow, my stomach felt like it had ruptured, and I was not feeling well at all. "Let me explain" said the first seated man, "I want to tell you a story.... would you like a cigarette?"

I looked him up and down, his face still distorted by something; it must have been the light from behind. I shook my head and said, "I only smoke cigars"

"Ah well forgive my attempt at politeness. I want to tell you this story so that you know of my plight to this moment. I was eleven years old when my mother told me of my destiny and of my past, my descendant's journey across barren lands with the Knights of the Temple. Of how the knowledge passed on to me was that of great responsibility. My mother told me that when the Ten Commandments were failed and the two pieces of divine will left on this earth were collected we could bring forth God once more to rid this earth of the evil of men.

You must have seen it too! To what levels man has stooped. Crashing planes into buildings, the violent robberies and the teenagers who have no desire but to destroy, I have had enough and so has God, he has spoken to the Calivari, told us that this day was coming and now we stand on the precipice of the end and you and your fucking Commander dare to stand in my way!"

"We don't think its right for you to pass judgement on this world!"

"God will pass judgement! Not I!"

"What, so all the Catholics live and all the Muslims die, is that it?"

He had gone from pure irate anger to almost satirical the next. His voice weighed in with laughter after which he said, "You don't know of it yet do you? You prod and poke and try to interfere without knowing what you are handling here?"

"Sounds like a very American thing to do"

"There is not many gods as you would have believed. There are no religions. There is no plural. There is One God, and One message. Throughout every religion and teaching there is this one message that we are bringing forth. In the Kabbalah it is known as the ten Sephirots, codes and virtues to live your life by. We know them as the Ten Commandments, every religion has them and they believe them to be the rules of life. They are right of course but what people fail to realise is these laws have punishments for disobeying. In life we go to geol, in religion there is simply God and we will bring him forth for his Final Judgement"

"So what was it?" I said now wishing that I had taken him up on his offer for a cigarette, "What was it that made you think its time to bring forth God?"

"Look around you Banner" he said and it was then that the light behind him faded. It looked like a studio or a television centre behind and for the first time I could see the two men's face. Both of them clothed in US Air force Uniform and bearing as many decorations as any war hero, grinning inanely from ear to ear and enjoying every minute of this. The one to my left and the first man to sit down held a cigarette to his side and with legs crossed looked incredibly feminine were it not for the aged stubble. "It was the people who chose this will. Those people who bomb our cities, invade our land, kill our wives and children. It is them that deserve this"

"And what about the people who don't? Will they be killed? According to the Ten Commandments everyone is a sinner!"

"It is for the Lord God to decide"

"What if he chooses to kill you?"

"If he deems me surplus to this world than so be it. It would be better dying in this old world of evil, than to have a sinner in Gods new world"

There was quiet for a while as I contemplated his thoughts. I could see his wide dark eyes staring deep into my soul, watching for any sign of life he could grasp hold of. They were genuinely trying to cleanse the world of all evil and all sin, to kill everything that was bad. There would be no need for war, no need for revenge and none of the satanic devilry that lurks in alleyways and dark passages would exist anymore. No more would an unlucky man walk home to discover his wife and family have been raped and murdered; no more will people like McCloud have to have his parents taken from him at such an early age...

"Tell us about McCloud" said the second man

I didn't know what to say anymore. My mind was swimming with thoughts and emotions too rare and deep to be known, this was far rawer than anything I had ever felt or ever seen before. The chance to save the world by destroying it...

"Tell us about McCloud Mister Banner"

For a brief moment, I had visions of telling him everything. Telling him about the HQ in Leeds, about the cover of Hellz Records, about everything that McCloud had done, his real name, which regiment he was in... Then it all fell down around me, smashed by the sledgehammer of sense. This was a war against these men and women who wanted to destroy the world; they were making the decision to destroy us, not the people themselves. Free speech is a word bounded around a lot these days, but being given the freedom to live your life how you want it is something worth fighting for. "Fuck you!"

"Excuse me" said the first seated man seemingly genuinely taken aback.

"I said fuck you! Fuck your organisation; fuck your right to send us all to God! *Fuck You!*"

There was silence for a moment, then "Jonathan, Jonathan, Jonathan. We had such high hopes for you, and so did your Professor. He told us about you three years ago..." The Professor? "He knew of your talents then and instead of us you picked *them*. Those dirty mercenaries that call themselves the SES.... instead...." he sighed from deep within, "I shall tell Alpha and Bravo personally"

"Alpha? Bravo?"

"Of course, we are all named under the phonetic alphabet. But to your everlasting end, you shall never be one. Prince... Kill him"

I had given myself up as a martyr. Dying in what I believe but unlike every other martyr who has lived, I won't be remembered. I won't be seen as a man who stood in front of the tank that was this beast of an organisation. The gun was directed at my forehead, resting inside the wrinkling caused by my looking at the barrel. It brought back memories of Egypt, remembering how my teeth ached from pain, and at the hard intensity that came with the danger of having a gun at my head.

This time there was no such fear, no thoughts running through my mind, it was as if my brain was telling me that I could get out of this, that it was so confident of my escape it didn't need to fuel the panic into my bloodstream. I must have had the most casual eyes of any person that this man Prince had killed for in that moment. I did not care what happened. I was at peace with my own body and then with pure and perfect accuracy a thought enlarged onto the forefront of my brain shrouded with pride and joy. It was the professors face staring at me back in class two years ago slamming my lack of morals and now here I was, tied to a chair willing to sacrifice myself for the morals I had attained... funny old world.

It was while thinking through all this that I managed somehow to loosen the grip around my ankles and sneak one foot clear. I gazed into his eyes and saw him ready to fire; I flung myself down onto the ground to the side as the bullet pushed through the wall. I swung my leg around dropping the big ape from his knees and as he dropped, managed to put my foot square against his jaw knocking it completely out of place. The blood muffled screams were enough to ignite my adrenaline again and with an almighty pull managed to pull apart the chair holding me back. The two back supports of the chair were still strapped to my arm, the legs still tied to my shins; it was like having a suit of armour made from wood. "Get him!"

The two uniformed men pulled long machete looking knives from their side sheaths and stared with a glimmer of insanity in their eyes. "We have you now Mister Banner!"

The two swung their knives at the same time from different angles and with a twist managed to catch them onto my new wooden limbs. With a swift push I managed to force the blade back at them knocking them both on the head and sending them to the floor, I felt unstoppable, unbeatable, I wanted to scream with anger and delight all rolled into one raw animalistic ball. I turned; the hole that the bullet had made was enormous and revealed that behind this wall was a huge open space. Without a thought I lunged at it head first and burst through with a roll and a stumble and into a gigantic hanger. To my right I saw another room just like mine; I ran straight for it and collided with the hard plasterboard falling through like a dodgy entrance onto a kids show. Bingham was on the floor unconscious and then the rest was like a blur... picking him up on my shoulder... looking everywhere I could for the Tongue but failing and then fighting off a horde of mechanics who all seemed a little puzzled by my being here. Especially dressed in a sack and carrying another man over my shoulder. In the distance I could see a small helicopter, or what looked like the frame of a helicopter and someone had stuck a cab on it. I aimed for it dodging spanners and wrenches thrown by the many engineers and slung Bingham into the tiny passenger seat. A single brave worker grabbed hold of the rising chopper but found himself falling from a good thirty feet and gaining nothing but his shins through his shoulders.

Completely transfixed I somehow managed to make a journey out of it, banking from side to side, swaying as the sand whipped up a storm below. I felt in a dream land, I knew what I needed and that was to reach an airport and then contact McCloud and... Everything would be fine.

"So let me get this straight" started McCloud who was perched on the edge of his desk, "You had the Tongue, lost it to a band of American speaking uniformed men, broke out by having strips of wood tied to your arms and legs, then somehow managed to fly a helicopter to your airport and fly home?"

"That's the gist of it yeah" I said nursing my arms which had taken a swift beating from the machete wielding attackers back at the hanger. "It's all in the report"

"You were supposed to keep this quiet Banner" he said and then turned to Bingham, "And I would have thought you would have known better"

Just for that moment I had images of me and Bingham sat in front of the headmaster of school being shouted at for messing around in the playground. McCloud couldn't but help smirk; it hindered matters that Bingham kept touching a wound on the side of his head just below his temple as if it was in pain. McCloud shook his head and dropped down from the desk, "I've got Charlie and Carter working on that image you sent us Banner. Hopefully it will lead us to them"

"Carter?"

"Oh yes. After I had a few stern words with Ian Jordan I managed to sort us out a new member of staff. Your lady friend, Miss Carter"

The door flew open and Charlie stepped in, a sheet of paper in her hand, hair flailing as if she had been running. "It's Egypt! I knew I recognised it"

"The location?" asked McCloud

"Yes! Me and Carter were working on it all night, it all points to Egypt! To Karnak Temple!"

"The library?"

"They must be having some sort of congregation. Bringing everything back together, the Key of Kings and the Tongue of Salem all in one place! There must be something in there!"

"How long do you think we have?" asked McCloud

"Maybe a few days sir," said Carter walking in behind Charlie. I wanted to take her there, standing in the doorway, caressed by the soft lights, she was beautiful. "I think I might have found something in the Atherton Scrolls that we might have missed sir,"

"Oh?" queried McCloud, "What?"

"Well after giving it to Charlie to translate, it reads..."

"By Thebes' shining light whilst cometh thy fiercest fright/

Thou Niles time by waxing moon/

For the Rapture will come soon" said Charlie jumping in, giddy like a schoolgirl and after giving her a closer inspection also looking like one. She looked like she had made an effort to make sure all her make-up was faultless, not one eyebrow hair out of place, not one tiny smudge of flawed foundation, it was perfect and rather off putting.

"How did you miss that?" I asked confused at how such an important part of the puzzle could be missing.

"I dunno" she said dumbly, "But I think it means three days after the Nile floods"

"Which is when?"

"Three days" motioned Carter looking at me and winking.

It had come down it seemed to the last corner, the last twist, the final curtain. I tried to make it as exciting as I could but as I felt now, I couldn't bring myself to do it. All the adventures I had been in since turning into this profession, all the near death experiences had made me redundant to the feelings of adventure. The maelstrom of emotion that normally flooded the body just wasn't present anymore. The thrill, the romance, the Hollywood... it all disappeared into the mist of an explosion. I looked up at McCloud; saw the scars on his face and hands, the bandage that was barely visible underneath his shirt, the obvious sight of knee braces supporting his legs... I didn't want that. This was my last stand, this was my last mission.

"Right kid" said McCloud, eyes fixed with that permanent pent up rage just waiting to explode, "Me and you are taking point. Bingham, you and Saunders get on the perimeter keeping in touch. Carter, Charlie... you two are to stay half a mile away from the sight but keep in constant radio contact with any information. Got it?"

"Yes sir" we all said in muttered appreciation. Fatigue had set in, the past few weeks had not done any of us well, we all felt like shit. As if someone had scraped us from the bottom of the barrel and spread us along the road for the cars and lorries to run us over. "All of you" said McCloud, "This is it. This is the final piece of the puzzle, the time when we can finally end this and get some time off. When we can go home to our families, to our wives, girlfriends, children... *I ask... one... last... push!*"

CHAPTER 10
THE RAPTURE

Two days later...

Karnak Temple. It's where it all began and now it seemed where it was all going to finish. The media hubbub had died down since the explosion that Mayweather had delivered to its fragile walls and now nothing but a yellow tape surrounded its gaping entrance. The night was surprisingly cold as the Egyptian full moon made the sand shine up a brilliant white and all through the temple grounds nothing but the sound of the wind whistling through the pillars could be heard. It was eerie.

"Bingham, you read me mate?" said McCloud

"Loud and clear sir. Me and Saunders are by the gate. Nothing so far"

"What about you Carter?"

"Read you sir. Charlie is here with me too sir but when you go deeper into the temple I think our lines may be cut"

"Okay Carter. If that happens just record the time we went in and get as much information about our position as you can"

"Roger that sir"

Backs against the Karnak wall we both turned into the devils mouth and began our descent to the forgotten library again. The stalagmites and stalactites prodded and poked again and the memories of adrenaline flooded back when I saw the green strip lights I had used to see before were on the floor in front of me every few feet. I could see in the old footsteps how much panic was in me, how scared of what I would see. This time was different, I could see it in McCloud's eyes, the fear of seeing the torches lit all the way down the passageway, the fact that someone had been through here not long ago and lit them all. "How are the legs?" I asked switching off communication with everyone else.

"I am only here because of the painkillers kid" he said doing the same, "I'm glad your here with me though"

"Really sir?" I said amazed

"Yeah kid. Bingham isn't up to this sort of thing, he isn't like *us*" he said, "And I wanted to talk to you about something"

"I wanted to talk to you too"

"Just lemme see what your answer is to this kid first. I need to tell you that I am leaving after this assignment"

"What?"

"I also need to tell you the reason..." he said backing up against the wall, I followed suit. "... I've been diagnosed with Cancer. That's why I have been away a lot at different GP's, medical appointments and such. And my rheumatism is now at a stage my muscle is deteriorating so rapidly I might not be able to lift my arm in a few weeks time"

"...sir?"

"I want you to head the unit. I want you to do what I can't do and look after England for me. Look after the old girl, treat her right and make sure you save her arse when she needs it"

"I... I don't know what to say"

We slammed our backs against the wall as we neared the overhang with the white throne painted on it. The stars on the ceiling painted some centuries ago looked all the more dazzling tonight and as we both peered into the flame lit ante-chamber we knew we had picked the right night.

Inside the heart of the building the flames that Mayweather had lit still spiralled around giving away the acrid aroma of hot oil but the library looked so mystical because of it. The pillars glowed healthy sandstone orange and the intricately carved statues of the Lord God beamed under their supernova flare. From our position just outside the main chamber we could see the direct line of sight that led to the White Throne and below it a great bowl that held the fire that Mayweather had lit, I hadn't realised in the dim light before just how large the library was and now with at least twenty people ordaining each side of the aisle leading to the throne it came into stark reality.

In front of the pan was an altar, large and ornate drooping with long burning candles and red drapes. The Tongue of Salem was sat on a small cushion and next to it was a triangle of what looked from here like solid gold that must have been the Key. Breaking away from the crowd was a hooded individual and as he neared the altar a mass of other people started to flood in from side chambers in between the rows of bookshelves toward the pulpit. A chant began to build; incense swung from gold canters, a deep disturbing miasma of religious fanaticism began to rise.

I looked at McCloud who looked back. His eyes as confused as mine, he had readied his pistol out in front of him, barrel to the ground in preparation. I could see through his black sneaking suit he was ready to take a breath, I removed my pistol and we both turned into the chamber, guns ready, chamber poised and with a crescendo of a furious heartbeat we both lunged out screaming "Freeze!"

As the air hung dead for a moment we realised the desired effect was not quite what we had in mind. The chanting momentarily stopped, the incense cleared for all of a few seconds and the precession slowed like a dying train. Then as if loosening the spanner from the works the march carried on. McCloud looked at me square then shouted, "I said..."

"Put down the gun Mister McCloud. You will not slow this ceremony down any longer"

We turned around and found two guards both with pistols aimed at our heads and McCloud reacted like a wild animal swatting the gun out of the guards hand as quick as he was back in Egypt, swept the guards leg and aimed his own pistol at the mans face before another batch of guards charged from the tunnel in front. With four machine guns aimed at his chest now McCloud finally calmed but the anger was there, building up behind the façade of calm, he was ready to pounce if there was ever an opportunity, like a tightly coiled spring. Then from the gloomy cavern walked Laura Wood, her dress swaying from side to side like a vampire from an old b-movie and wore the same expression as we had seen back in Scotland. "So Mister McCloud, you made it to our ceremony?"

"Certainly looks that way"

"I'm glad you made it in time to see. To meet our great friends"

"So which part of the phonetic alphabet are you then?" I asked watching her eyebrow raise in surprise. McCloud turned to me temporarily losing his anger in intrigue.

"I am Delta Mister Banner. You are very well informed of our methods I must say; now if you will excuse me I have to take my part in the ceremony. I am sure Foxtrot here will keep you company"

Passing the person known as Foxtrot on her way down the cavern she whispered something in his ear but in the light it was impossible to make out there face. The guards surrounding McCloud were obviously on edge, knowing the capabilities of McCloud was enough to do that to you but the appearance of Foxtrot had done something else, it had added another dimension of fear. It was unclear as to what it was Foxtrot was actually doing but in the gloom I am sure he was fiddling with his pockets before I saw two small shafts and a flash of silver that had caught in the torchlight. Foxtrot raised them to its mouth and the shining silver object flared up a flame and lit two cigars inside his mouth.

For a moment I am sure I saw a face I knew behind the light before the cigar smoke blocked the view. He motioned two guards towards him who did so fighting the raw instinct to run and gave them the two cigars that they dutifully passed on to McCloud and me. It was a strange position to be in, but smoking the cigar now felt very much a natural state of affairs. It was McCloud though who overcame the calming effect of the nicotine. "So you have proven yourself a good host. Now let's see the face"

Foxtrot took a step forward, his shoes catching the torchlight and gleaming like a soldiers boot. A pair of black trousers held up with a belt hemmed with a cross, a tight well fitting silk suit pinned together holding back a crimson tie and then the face....

"Saunders! Saunders, you're... you're Foxtrot?"

"Surprised?"

"You bastard!"

"Take heart McCloud" he said and then turned to me, "The best is yet to come"

He opened his arms taking in the surprise, soaking up the anger like a sponge, like a Superman villain fuelled on some otherworldly substance. "Where is Bingham you son of a bitch!" shouted McCloud, the bile almost following his words.

"He is down there somewhere" said Saunders, "With a few more special guests. We have quite a line-up tonight"

McCloud had already turned when Saunders was mid-sentence and his eyes casting over the incense fuelled cavern we both saw Bingham at the same time, bound by his hands and feet just a few feet from the altar. He wasn't alone, sat next to him blindfolded and gagged I am sure I saw Carter... it was!

I turned. A red mist had descended fired by a raw rush of personal emotion gushing through my red hot glowing veins, incensed at what my eyes had seen. Saunders became a red dot on my horizon. I would rip him apart! I charged for him with my fists out. A guard attempted to grab me but I pushed him away with a straight arm powered by hate and managed one swing before a gun was jammed into the side of my head and a familiar face stared at me from down the barrel. "Charlie?"

"Yep" she said and then kissed me on the cheek, "Go back and stand with McCloud Jonathan"

"What? What are you...?"

"Give it up kid it's been staring us in the face the whole time"

Charlie... the third word of the phonetic alphabet. I stood back with McCloud as she asked, a fuming anger still coursing through my veins hot as lava. "So the whole time... it's just been a lie?"

"No not a lie" she said through her childish but achingly beautiful expression, "You got more truth than anyone. My father is the pope, but what I didn't tell you is my father is also the Alpha Calivari"

"The pope?" McCloud and I looked surprised, "I thought the President was Alpha?"

"My word no" she laughed as if we were the dumbest people on earth, "President Andrews is only a rather pitiful X-Ray, easily manipulated by the people who really run the planet. We pull the strings Jonathan, not the US government"

"So you're father, the pontiff, is Alpha?" said McCloud

"Yes" she said looking over his shoulder into the procession, "In fact he is right on time. Guards, bring them down here with me and Foxtrot. And watch that one" she said pointing at McCloud with the gun.

They marched us down into the main hall where a series of faces I recognised were partly concealed underneath their monk like hoods. TV presenters, football superstars, tennis players, actors, politicians and more, all of them here for the revival of mother earth. The incense had made the air thick and aromatic while at the same time sweaty and moist, droplets of smelling water falling occasionally from the stalagmites above. The heat as we got near the pan was incredible, sweat began pouring out rather than blotting causing my throat to dry up within minutes.

The guards sat us down with Carter and Bingham and before they did anything to me I removed her gag and blindfold. I fell into her starry eyes, tears welling ready to burst, I loved this woman. The orange light around us dimmed and through the central aisle leading toward the altar three selected monks, their robes as red as blood and tied with a golden rope, began to walk with their hands clasped towards us.

As they neared the nave they split, one walking to the left of the altar and picking up the Key of Kings turned to their buying public holding it aloft to a rapt reception. Another did the same but turning to the right and picking up the Tongue of Salem. Seeing the slightest glimpse of their face, I realised it was Wood. I twisted myself so I could catch the light of the first to take to the altar. It wasn't a good light but I could make out the face of a saddened looking President Andrews. Finally through the middle of the two came the last, his head bowed and clutching a golden cross in his tightened hands.

He didn't turn; instead his gaze was lifted directly into the eyes of the carved Lord God bursting from the wall. Powerfully pushing the cross downward onto the altar it stood, shining in front of the great fire roaring away in the pan, the incense was starting to spread again powering out like a fog machine. The middle monk raised his hands and gently moved back his hood revealing an old man, his little hair withered and faded to a snow white, liver spots trailing paths along his head and features attacked by age and wrinkles. It was the pope, it was Alpha. He started to mumble before breaking into what sounded like pure Aramaic, a clear and purpose filled response came from the crowd.

Then there was silence.

They say silence is deadly. The silence I was witnessing here was just that, it was so loud that it was smothering the sound of anything that dared to make a noise. The once ferocious fire that roared in the pan was soundless and quant, even the random coughs and splutters from the monks was toned down and surrounded in a silent darkness.

Then the largest grin I had ever seen began to stretch across Alpha's face. He saw me looking at him, his eyes wild and glaring, inside his head something had gone click and broken down. "It is here!" he shouted, "It is the Rapture!"

In front of him on the altar fizzled an ancient image blurring for a few moments and then coming crystal clear, it was like an old television broadcast, flickering and distorting but incredibly it was there! "Am I hallucinating?" said McCloud looking at me, "Do you see that?"

It was six foot tall now. Standing on the altar was a long haired man with a scraggly beard untouched it looked for centuries all in grainy black and white. It buzzed and then from everywhere came a voice hidden in the previous silence that had embodied the cavern, I didn't understand it and I don't think anybody else did either but following the sentences the pope translated... "Through thost most hollowed cavern must the wise man see" he started as the Aramaic carried on behind us, "And a cocooned devil must the rapturous see. Thou white chariot is called from heavens unreached. Stare into the devils eyes and take thy prize" the Aramaic stopped, "And fear the home of the devil"

The image faded and as quickly as it had come the image was once more banned into the cells of hallucination. "I don't believe I just saw that" said Carter

"I don't think it has gone too well" said McCloud in my ear. A smattering of disconcerted grumbles began to build around the cavern until everyone at one time heard an almighty crash. Everyone's eyes turned up and saw the beginning of a cave-in starting to swell, a stream of dust began to descend, bits of stray rock, smooth sandstone and the noise of grating stone erupted around us. Alpha turned on the crowd and shouted, "Run!"

There was instant panic as a boulder the size of a car dropped into the pan of fire spraying a stream of liquid flame rolling along the ceiling and dropping like rain. Capes set ablaze as they pushed and pulled each other away and to safety through the cavern entrance. "Come on kid!" shouted McCloud as he untied Bingham and pulled him to his feet. "Grab Carter and let's go!"

He was up and running for the exit with Bingham and Carter but I had waited for a few moments. I don't know what it was that made me stay or why I felt no need to panic amongst the rubble collapsing but I was busy staring past the altar into the eyes of God. "Stare into the devils eyes and take thy prize" I muttered to myself and within a second of me saying it the eyes of God glowed red and then set as black as night. The same as the crucifix back in Jerusalem, the Lord Gods mouth opened and inside I could see a parchment no bigger than a hardback book and as delicate as tissue paper. I reached out for it, "Stare into the devils eyes and take thy prize!"

"Kid! C'mon!" screamed McCloud as I pocketed the parchment. "We need to get the fuck out of here!"

He grabbed me by the arm and tugged me along the altar as another rock crashed down straight through the marble table sending the golden cross flaying across the cavern. Dodging and weaving in and out of the crumbling rocks we reached the exit, the white throne blazoned across the roof as the painted stars on the ceiling began to shudder behind us. "Not so fast!" shouted Saunders as he jumped out from the shadows, gun at the ready. "We may not have succeeded here but by the Lord I will rid this earth of one parasite it will never need!"

Before I had time to blink McCloud had reached out and pulled the chamber clean from the handle of the old gun. Saunders stared at it as a fist the size of melon crashed into his nose splattering blood into the air in front of us. McCloud grabbed him by the chest, the pent up anger that he had kept away exploding out of him, and lifted Saunders high off the floor. "You're right"

Without a blink he threw him behind us into the crumbling cavern just as the last of the rocks began to fall through and seal off the exit. "C'mon kid, we still got a bit to go, Carter and Bingham are up ahead"

"Where has everybody gone?"

"There all making there selves scarce. The noise must have been heard in Luxor!"

When we hit the night air we heard the sirens on the horizon bellowing with integrity and purpose and in front of us were thirty or so monks running for the hills or in most case, their helicopters. "I'd have loved to have caught Alpha"

"It's alright kid..." he said as Bingham and Carter stood alongside us, "... I get the feeling things are going to be okay"

He dashed ahead of us, a smile starting to break along his face with the sense of satisfaction surrounding him like an aura. An old monk was struggling to keep up to the running crowds who were running as fast as they could in the opposite direction to the incoming police cruisers and pulling on the old monks hood stopped him in his tracks. I managed to catch up a moment later where McCloud was happily sat with the old monk clutching a lit cigar and enjoying the Egyptian night, "Hey kid" he said, "I want you to meet... what was your name again?"

The pontiff turned away in disgust. No bodyguards were here to help him, no protection and no hidden weapon to try and dissolve the situation. He would have been protected by the numbers of the Calivari and now they had run for their lives it was every man for himself. McCloud sat there smug, looked up at me and through the cigar smoke said, "You guys better get out of here. Bingham, you know the escape plan, take the usual extraction"

"Yes sir"

Seven days later...

'The inquest into the Pope's participation in the collapse of Karnak Temple is still trying to be found as the hunt for the rest of a mysterious group known as the Calivari continues. Rumours are that the sect were trying to bring forth a religious ceremony called the 'Rapture' which in modern times has been adapted to be a glorious phrase...'

I switched the TV off as the reporter babbled on about what the whole time had meant and the implications of his arrest. The truth is we will never truly know what happened, about what went wrong, about why the rapture didn't come after all the build up and murder. One thing I was sure of though as I stepped out onto the beach from our ocean view hotel here in Grenada was that with me was the woman I loved.

Carter had almost married the deck chair and was toasting her skin a rather unhealthy brown as we enjoyed privacy in our SES retreat building out on the beach of the capital S.T George. Crashing down next to her she lifted her sunglasses and leaned out for a kiss then returned to slouching and enjoying the sun. "I could get used to this" she said turning over to start the cooking process again but this time on her back. "Three whole weeks"

"Not bad is it. Must be a perk of the job"

Not a single cloud broke the blue skyline ahead of us. The palm trees swayed, the waves gently caressed our feet and civilisation was four miles away, she was right, I could get used to this. There was something that was beginning to burn away at me though and it was sat underneath my deck chair tucked into my flip flops. I hadn't dared to look at the parchment that I had taken from the devils mouth for fear of unleashing something to do with the rapture but curiosity was beginning to gain the upper hand. I pulled it out and gently holding it in my arms began to tear the decaying ribbon that held it together, "What is that?"

"I found it in the forgotten library. Hidden in the Devils Mouth"

She suddenly sat up; sunglasses ripped from her face and turned to face me and the parchment that sat in my lap. "You mean what the pope was babbling on about?"

"Yeah"

"What does it say?"

"I don't know... I haven't dared open it"

She looked into my eyes. The sweat from the heat running down her forehead, her hair tied back and shining, she was definitely the one for me. I unravelled the parchment with sweat pouring from my skin, the lump in my throat was no longer the size of an acorn but the size of a small planet, and I could feel the centuries dropping from the old paper as the dust pealed away. An ancient text looked at us and without thinking I picked up my phone and took a picture for the translation...

... We sat and looked at each other for a moment. "What do we do?" she said, "I mean this proves the existence of God!"

"It proves the existence of a God. Not God as we know it"

"But, all religion would be solved! No more war, no more terrorism!"

"No... It would bring even more. Muslims claiming it was a fake, Islamic separatist's doing the same... it would all implode on itself..."

"Then what should we do?"

"I think we should burn it"

"But its proof that someone or thing exists as a God doesn't it? You can't!"

I looked into her eyes and we made our decision together.

Three weeks later...

"Right have you got everything packed babes?" I said as I scrubbed myself down in the shower, the last time I would before returning to England as head of the Unit. McCloud had denied help for his condition and had disappeared shortly after turning in the pontiff back in Egypt. As much as we all wanted him to return, we also knew if he wanted to disappear there was no way we were ever going to find him.

"Yeah just need a few more things but should be done soon" she answered back.

It's a funny old world that nearly three years ago now I was sat on an assault charge back in MI: 5 training and thinking morals were for losers... now I had a set of morals and although they were based on those of McCloud's, who doesn't have someone they adapt their morals from? We all create father figures or mother figures in our heads, who to aspire and look up to. McCloud was the father I never had, the training I needed which I never received up until now... he was my hero.

I made my way out of the shower wrapped in my bright yellow towel dripping water along the bedroom floor and seeing that most of the packing had been done went outside to see Carter. She turned to me and smiled, a smile so filled with beauty and happiness that it made my heart melt every time I saw it.

I saw it in her eyes first. It was the way that her pupils widened and her sparkling diamond eyes nullifying. Then the blood exploded from her chest toward me drenching me in a shower of crimson. Her wingspan stretched out wide, her head tilted to one side silhouetting the sun that roared behind her. The birds in the trees howled and flew away. The waves crashed along the shoreline. Right in front of me my love fell to the ground crestfallen.

My eyes welled. I stared down at my blood drenched body and looked back at the crater the size of an apple in her back glistening red. I didn't know what to do say or feel but along the line of sight I glared into the tree tops and heard the guffaw of a speedboat powering away in the distance before I saw a small box land by my feet.

I picked it up, eyes ready to burst, heart ready to stop; the heartstrings had been torn in half. A tiny red button sat on the black boxes top and pressing it I heard a loud beep before...

"Hello Jonathan. The past few months have been great, I have really enjoyed being by your side and showing you the way to your next objectives. It seems you came to trust me too soon. I told you many truths and many false but it seems we couldn't achieve our goal. There was a safety feature in place in the cavern meaning as soon as someone calls forth the rapture only the truly worthy people can collect the instructions of how to initiate it. It seems no one was worthy of this prize.

I have instead decided to live by my God and conclude that as is said in the bible, an eye for an eye. You have taken my father from me, so I will take your love from you. I am not a monster... I have given you time to enjoy yourselves...

Love from Charlie..."

There was only one thing I could think of doing...

"Bingham..." I said down the phone, "... Carter is dead. Charlie has shot her, we need to find her"

"Shit man, you okay? I mean, you want us to send out for you?"

"No" I said solid and emotionless, "I will make my own way home"

The beach held nothing more. I walked into the ocean, it reached my chest now and only then did I cry. "... Good bye Carter"

And as the rain clouds descended on this once tropical paradise, nothing but the ocean could hide the tears I cried. Wrapped up in a bubble of hatred filled with my own sense of self pride I thought about the rapture and how it was people like this that made you want to end it all.

Not today though... not today.

THE END

Lightning Source UK Ltd.
Milton Keynes UK
27 November 2009

146769UK00001B/145/P